PRIVATE DECEPTIONS

by roy glenn

PRIVATE DECEPTIONS

by roy glenn

Brittney Press Publishing

On the Web @ http://www.brittneypress.com/

E-mail: privatedeceptions@brittneypress.com

© Copyright 2001 roy glenn enterprises
ISBN: 1-893196-07-0

Jacket design: Keith Saunders & roy glenn
Back jacket photo: Hank Gary

Table of Contents

In Your Arms

a little something
by roy glenn

In Your Arms

a little something from roy glenn

In Your Arms

Phase 1

It was just after ten o'clock when Marcus Douglas arrived at the Marriott Residence Inn. That afternoon he had his secretary, Janice, got a room for him in her name, in case my wife Randa was looking for him. He walked down the long hall to his room and stuck the key card in the lock. He entered in the room, dropped the key card on top of the television, and turned it on. While Peter Jennings reported the days World news, Marcus wandered around aimlessly. This was his home now.

Marcus loosened his tie and took off his jacket. He reached in the pocket and pulled out a pack of cigarettes. It had been five years since he smoked his last Kool. He sat down on the couch and lit a cigarette. He took a long drag, then blew out the smoke. It hurt his chest and he coughed a little, but he hit it again. Today had been the worst day of his life.

If this was going to be his home for awhile, there were a few things he'd need. "Soap, tooth brush and tooth paste. Deodorant would be a good thing. And I need to shave in the morning." He got up and started for the door. Realizing all he had were the clothes on his back. He would buy some clothes in the morning. "This is going to get expensive." Marcus drove his 735i BMW down the street and turned into Krogers parking lot. It had been years since he had to shop for himself. Randa did all that for him.

He picked up a basket and headed for the pharmacy aisles. The store was quiet and empty for the most part. Marcus had picked up just about all the items he'd come for when the quiet was interrupted by the sound of high heels, clicking against the tile. His eyes were immediately drawn to the sound. There was a sense of urgency in her walk. Marcus glanced at her as she moved closer to him and had to take a closer look as she passed. She stopped and tried on a pair of sunglasses and kept on walking. "I know her." He followed as she proceeded down the next aisle. When she stopped to pick up a box of hair color, she turned and looked at him. Now he was sure. Even though she turned away quickly, Marcus was sure that he knew her. "Yvonne Haggler." It had been nine years since he'd seen her. She looked good, even better than she did nine years ago. "If that's possible." He remembered the day that she came to his office.

"Marcus."

"Yes, Janice."

"Your two o'clock is here."

"Give me five minutes then send her in."

Five minutes later Yvonne Haggler was seated before him. She was an attractive young woman, barely twenty-one years old. She was simply, but tastefully dressed. She didn't wear any makeup and her hair was pulled back in a ponytail. "Mrs. Haggler, tell me what I can do for you?"

"Mr. Douglas, I need your help. My husband, Richard, died two month ago."

"I'm sorry to hear that."

"Thank you, Mr. Douglas." Yvonne spoke with the deep Mississippi accent that she hadn't managed to lose in the five years she'd been in Atlanta. Yvonne was born and raised in Cold Water Mississippi. Her father died three years earlier and her mother was having problems making it by herself with nine children. The oldest of nine children, Yvonne was an average student in her junior year in High School. She met Richard Haggler when she was sixteen years old. Richard was twenty-eight. Richard was born in Cold Water as well, but his family moved away when he was ten. He came back to town to settle some personal matters for his recently deceased mother. When he met Yvonne he fell deeply in love with the pretty young girl. Two weeks later he asked Yvonne's mother permission to marry Yvonne and take her back to Atlanta with him. Yvonne's mother had known Richard's family when they lived in Cold Water and he seemed nice enough, polite, and respectful, and Yvonne did seem to like him. Richard had a good job and promised that he could make a better life for Yvonne in Atlanta. Cold Water was a small town and her mother didn't have any money to send her daughter to college and began to see that as an opportunity for her daughter to get away from there. Richard also promised he would be able to send her some money every week to help out with the family. After very long and deep consideration, her mother consented for her daughter to be married.

They were married in a simple wedding a week later. Leaving for Atlanta the same night. They moved into Richard's mother's old house in Clarkston a suburb of Atlanta. Richard was an old fashioned man and insisted that Yvonne not work. He told her she didn't have to finish high school if she didn't want to, but Yvonne felt it was important that she be the first in her family to graduate from high school. Other than going to school, she lived a quiet, somewhat sheltered life as a housewife. She had a few girlfriends that she met in school, but Richard thought it was inappropriate for a married woman to be going to nightclubs and things like that, so Yvonne made a very happy life for her and her husband. She was totally dependent upon Richard for everything. She didn't mind, even though they didn't have much money, Richard was a good husband, and he treated her like a queen.

"Richard left a ten thousand dollar insurance policy and I gave it to the funeral people to pay for his funeral. Well, my husband was a simple man and I thought he'd want to go out that way. The whole thing came to a little less than seven thousand dollars. They told me that they would take care of things with the insurance company and I'd get what ever is left over," Yvonne explained.

"That's pretty standard."

"But I still haven't got the money."

"Was there some problem with the policy?" Marcus asked as he took notes.

"I don't know, they wasn't tellin' me nothing. Everytime I called to find out what was going on, they told me it would just be a few more days. Until two days ago." Yvonne reached in her purse and pulled out an envelope. She took out the letter and handed it to Marcus. "I got this in the mail. They said I could get my money after I signed it."

Marcus read over the letter while Yvonne continued talking. He glanced up at her and smiled. There was an innocence about her. She spoke without making eye contact. He thought that her accent was adorable.

"I showed that letter to my girl friend Tyisha. Her mama died last year and she said she didn't have to sign nothing like this. She told me I should show it to a lawyer."

"Well, Mrs. Haggler, even though it doesn't come right out and say so, this letter is worded to give the funeral director power of attorney to settle your husbands estate."

"Estate? What estate, Mr. Douglas? Like I said we're simple people, we got the house his mama left us. The house is paid for, but other than that, we ain't got nothing."

"It does seem a bit unusual to need power of attorney to settle an insurance policy. Have you spoken with the insurance company?"

"No, I just came to see you. Do you think I should sign it, Mr. Douglas?"

"No, Mrs. Haggler. I don't recommend you sign anything until you get some more information about why this is necessary. Would you like me to look into this for you, Mrs. Haggler?"

"Would you please, Mr. Douglas. Richard used to handle all the business for us. I'm not very good at talkin' to people like that."

"I would be happy to, Mrs. Haggler."

"Don't have much money. I just got a job at Kmart and I'm not making that much."

Marcus smiled at her as he got up and showed her to the door. "Don't worry about that now, Mrs. Haggler. For now all you need to do is see Janice before you leave. She has some paper work for you to fill out. I'll look into it and get back with you in a few days."

Marcus was glad for something different to do. He had opened his own practice a year ago and dealt with the usual stuff. Accident cases, divorce, DUI's, but it would be nice for a change to actually help somebody. He would do it pro bono if he had to. Marcus checked with the insurance company and, as he suspected, they informed him that they were waiting to receive power of attorney from her representative in order to settle Mrs. Hagglers claim. As it turned out, even though Yvonne and Richard lived a simple life, in their simple, paid for home in Clarkston, it wasn't because they didn't have any money. Richard not only left her a ten thousand-dollar policy, there was also one for two hundred and fifty thousand. And that was just the tip of the iceberg. In addition to the insurance policies, there was a trust fund he had set up for her to receive once she turned thirty, worth another three hundred thousand.

7

He also owned a number of properties in Georgia, Alabama, and Mississippi. Marcus estimated his estate to be worth well over a million dollars.

A week later, Marcus called Yvonne and asked her to drop by his office that day to discuss her case. She told him she was working that day and asked if he would mind staying late until she got off. "It's my first job and I don't want to lose it." He started to tell her that she could quit if wanted to. But he didn't want to tell her over the phone that she might stand to inherit quite a bit of money. Yvonne arrived at the office a little after seven thirty. "Thank you for waiting for me Mr. Douglas. Did you find out something for me?"

"As a matter of fact Mrs. Haggler, I have some very good news for you. Your late husband does have an estate to settle and at this point, and mind you I've only made some preliminary inquires, but I estimate your husbands estate to be worth over a million dollars."

"Whaaat? You're kidding, right? That's not possible. Richard didn't have that kind of money. Where'd he get it?"

"I don't know at this time, but we'll find out." It was obvious to Marcus that Yvonne was taken completely by surprise by the revelation that she might be rich. "Do you know if your husband had a Will?"

"Don't think so," Yvonne said as her smile widened.

"Have you gone through his things?"

"No, I haven't. I just didn't have the heart to. I was kinda waiting to settle this business first. It just didn't seem right to start going through his stuff until he was resting peacefully."

"Do you know where your late husband worked, what he did for a living?"

"He worked as a property manager for Imperial

Properties."

"That makes sense, he owns quite a bit of property. He might even own the company. Mrs. Haggler, what I want you to do is go home and go through your husbands things. See if you can find a Will or any other legal documents. Have you been to his office to clean out his desk? Or had any contact with them at all?"

"No," Yvonne said with a shy type of smile. "I never even called them to say he was dead. They didn't call tryin' to find out why he didn't come to work. I just figured they didn't care."

Marcus smiled and let out a little laugh. "Call me in the morning and we'll make arrangements to go to Imperial Properties. But I don't want you to go there by yourself."

Yvonne went home and spent the rest of the night going through Richard's things. By two in the morning she had looked at every piece of paper, in every file in Richard's office and had found nothing. However, if there was any doubt in her mind that Richard was much more financially well off then she was led to believe, none remained now. She was going to be rich. Yvonne left the office and headed for the closet in their bedroom. She stopped in front of the bed, realizing that this was the first time she had been in there since she found Richard dead of a heart attack. Suddenly she felt tired, she'd gotten up early and had been on her feet all day running the register. Yvonne took a deep breath and resumed her search. Still nothing. "Where else?" She wandered around the house searching and by four o'clock she was exhausted. She sat down in the living room and looked at their picture on wall by the front door. That's when she saw it. "The hall closet." In a box on the shelf, Yvonne found a small metal box packed under a pile of old newspapers. The metal box was locked and for the next half an hour she tried to pick the lock with a hairpin. Finally she went out to the garage and returned with a sledgehammer. The box surrendered its contents after her third swing. Yvonne picked up the papers and went through them. She found an envelope marked "Last Will and Testament." She stood there awhile looking at the envelope but she was afraid to open it. She put the envelope down on the coffee table, lay down on the couch, and went to sleep.

Once Marcus reviewed the Will, the rest was simple. In addition to the insurance policies, the trust fund and the property, as expected Richard was majority owner Imperial Properties and held stock in several companies. There was a provision in his Will that in the event of his death, his partners would arrange financing to buy out his share of the company and the proceeds from that sale be given to his chosen heir, Yvonne Haggler.

When it was all said and done Richard's estate was worth 2.2 million dollars. Yvonne had Marcus liquidate his entire holding. Marcus was able to convince her to keep the stocks and make some investments that would provide her with an income from dividends. After all the transactions were completed Yvonne moved to Los Angeles. He received a letter five years ago from a lawyer named Tom Mack, informing him that he had been retained to handle her financial interests and that his services were no longer required. Marcus never saw or heard from her again. Until now.

Marcus moved closer to her as Yvonne read the label on the box of hair coloring she was holding. There was a certain sophistication about her now. No longer the innocent young girl he had turned into a millionaire.

"Yvonne? Yvonne Haggler?" he said. She jumped when he spoke and she started to back away from him. Yvonne stopped and looked at Marcus. Then she smiled.

"Marcus Douglas. How have you been?"

"I'm doing okay," Marcus replied, knowing he was lying. Other than seeing her, he felt terrible. "How about you? You look great."

"Thank you, Marcus. Are you still practicing?"

She was even prettier than he remembered. She had lost her Mississippi accent in the last nine years. "Yes, I am. The practice is doing quite well. I've added a few new associates since I last saw you. Why?" Marcus smiled. "Do you need a lawyer?"

"No Marcus, I don't think a lawyer is what I need right now." Yvonne replied as she walked to the registers. Once she paid for her hair color she turned to Marcus. "It was great seeing you Marcus. Maybe I'll see you again while I'm in town."

Marcus took out his wallet and gave Yvonne his card. "Give me a call and maybe we can have a drink or something."

"I'd like that," Yvonne said, but she knew she wouldn't be around long enough to take him up on it. Nine years ago she had what she called a schoolgirl crush on Marcus. She tucked his card in her purse. "Good night, Marcus." While the cashier scanned his items, Marcus watched Yvonne as she walked out of the store.

Yvonne started walking through the parking lot when she noticed two men standing by her car. She stopped dead in her tracks and looked around the parking lot. There was nobody in sight. She looked around again. When she saw Marcus coming out of the store, she walked toward him quickly. Just as he reached his car. "Marcus!"

"Hello again," Marcus said, his smile growing.

"I was wondering about your offer for that drink. If maybe I could take you up on it?"

"Sure. You've got my card, just give me a call and we'll get together anytime you're free."

Yvonne looked back at the two men standing by her car. "Actually, I was talking about now. That is if you're not busy."

Marcus looked at Yvonne curiously. "No," he said slowly. "I'm not doing anything right now."

"Good," Yvonne said and walked around to the passenger side of the car.

"What about your car?"

"Ahh, it's not - - - it will be all right here for awhile." She got in quickly. Marcus closed her door, shrugged his shoulders, and got in the driver side. He started the car and started out of the parking lot. As they passed her car, Yvonne dropped her purse and busied herself picking up the contents until they were well on their way. She looked out the back window, and there didn't appear to be anyone following. Although she couldn't be sure. She looked at Marcus and smiled as he drove. Continuing to look behind her.

"Is everything all right, Mrs. Haggler?"

"Huh? Oh, everything is fine. Where are we going?"

"There's a Bennigens not too far from here."

"Bennigens. Isn't there someplace a little more quiet. So we can talk and get reacquainted."

"I'm staying at a Residence Inn not too far from here. I think they have a bar."

"Sounds good to me. Mind if I ask why you're staying at a Residence Inn?"

"It's a long story, Mrs. Haggler."

"Yvonne. You can call me Yvonne."

"Okay, *Yvonne*, but it's still a long story."

"Okay, okay, I won't push it. You don't have to cop an attitude."

"I'm sorry, I didn't mean to snap at you." Marcus turned into the parking lot. "Maybe I do need a drink. Maybe two or three."

The hotel did have a bar but it was closed. "That's okay, Marcus. We can talk in your room," Yvonne said and led Marcus away by the arm.

"My room?" Marcus asked sheepishly.

"Don't worry. I promise I won't bite you. I haven't bitten anybody in years."

"Make yourself comfortable," Marcus said as they entered his room. Yvonne immediately walked from room to room and opened every door. "A little paranoid, are we?"

"Just a habit. I like to know where I am." Yvonne answered as she peeked out the window. She wasn't sure if she liked the fact that the room was on the first floor. She sat down. "Don't just stand there, sit down. This is your room."

Marcus sat down in a chair across from Yvonne. She made him feel nervous and uncomfortable. He tried not to show it, but it was too late.

"Am I making you feel uncomfortable, Marcus?"

"No, no, of course not. It just that - - - well, - - -you see - - -"

"Marcus."

"Huh."

"Just relax and say what you're trying to say."

"Well, Yvonne, I ahh, I left my wife today."

"Oh, Marcus, that's too bad," Yvonne said. Her accent had suddenly returned, only now it sounded phony. "Or maybe it isn't."

"What do you mean by that?"

"You could be happy you left your wife."

"No, Yvonne, I'm not happy about it," Marcus said quietly and slumped down deeper in his chair.

"You wanna tell me how you feel about it?" Yvonne asked, kicking off her heels and curling up on the couch.

"I don't - - - wait a minute, I'm the one who is supposed to be on the couch."

"Oh, you mean like a shrink. I been in therapy before."

"You're not crazy, are you?" Marcus said with a smile.

"No, I was just depressed about some things. Therapy helped me deal with them. But you gotta really get into it. You know what I mean? Dig deep down and get in touch with the source. I know it sounds kinda dippy, but it worked for me."

"So what were you so depressed about?"

"Some things were happening to me, but that was just at the surface. What was really happening was I had never really dealt with what my mother did to me."

"What did she do?"

"Marcus, I was a sixteen year old virgin when I met Richard. I liked him but I barely knew him. He arranged the whole marriage thing with my mother. They came to me after they had worked it all out and she told me that I was going to marry Richard. That it was the best thing for all of us. She said that she couldn't afford to do anything for our family and Richard said he would send her money every week. She sold me to him. "

"I didn't know that. I'm sorry."

"It all turned out all right. Richard was so sweet. He treated me good and I learned to love him with time. But she sold me, like I was a slave or something. Suppose Richard wasn't a good man, she didn't know him from a can of paint. Anything could have happened to me. She didn't care. I was just another mouth to feed. So I had to go. She did the same thing to my sisters when they got old enough. Found some old man, and sold them too. Beverly's husband wasn't bad. He just worked her like a slave, but so did my mother, so she was use to it. But Virginia, she wasn't that lucky. Denny was an animal. He stayed drunk most of the time. He treated her like dirt, beat her, and raped her when he felt like it. Forced her to have sex with his friends."

"My God. Is she still with him?"

"No."

"How did she get away from him?"

"The hard way. He hit her in the face with an iron because she wouldn't have sex with him. She ran out the house screaming and just by chance, the police were driving by. They took him to jail. We had to beg her to press charges, she was so afraid of him. They gave him ten years and I moved her out to LA with me."

"That's good."

"Not really, Marcus. She was pretty shot out when she got out there. Fell in with the wrong people, started smokin' crack. Let some nigga turn her out. He made her turn tricks to support their habit."

"Where is she now? Is she all right?"

"I don't know. I haven't seen her is years. I hope she's all right. I use to go looking for her when I hadn't heard from her in awhile. The last time she disappeared I never did find her."

"I'm sorry, Yvonne. I never knew."

"Don't sweat it, Marcus. I've come to grips with all that. But we're supposed to be talking about you, not my dysfunctional family. Tell me about your wife."

"My wife." Marcus stood up and walked around the

room. He picked up his jacket. "You mind if I smoke?" he asked, pulling the pack of Kool's from the pocket.

"I am so glad you said that." Yvonne replied, digging in her purse for her pack of Benson and Hedges 100's. "I've been dying for a cigarette all night." They both lit up, inhaled deeply and exhaled, like a common sigh of relief. "Now I need a drink."

"Are you sure that you don't want to go somewhere and have a drink?"

"No!" Yvonne said quickly and firmly. "I'm sorry, Marcus." She laughed. "Now tell me about your wife."

"My wife, Randa, what can I say about my wife Randa." Marcus returned to the chair and sat down. "She was a wonderful woman. She was beautiful, intelligent and she had so much energy. She was always doing something for somebody. She volunteered at a retirement home a couple days a week. She had a teenage girl she was mentoring. We were very happy together. She was my best friend. We had so much in common and we would spend hours together just talking. That's the hardest part of dealing with this. I loved her sure, but we were so close. I feel like I lost the best part of myself. We did just about everything together. People called us the poster children for the perfect relationship."

"Sounds like you guys had a good thing going. I mean, you do make her sound like she was just the perfect little woman." Yvonne rolled her eyes and took a drag.

"And like a fool, I bought into it. Hook, line, and sinker. But she wasn't right. I was such a fool. I was so blind. How could I have been so blind?" Marcus leaned forward quickly in his chair. "I saw so much in her, but I guess I saw what I wanted to see. I put her on that pedestal, she was bound to fall off."

"What happened, Marcus?"

"What happened? You really want to know what happened to make this the worst day of my life?"

"I'll try not to take that personally."

"Please don't. Seeing you has been the only high point in an otherwise fucked up day. Excuse my language."

"That's all right, Marcus, I'm a big girl now. All grown up. I've heard people curse before. I've been known to say a curse word or two myself. But you stop trying to change the subject. Tell me what happened."

"The day started out like any other. The alarm went off, we made love to each other, just like we did every morning."

Yvonne smiled. "I like it in the morning too. Makes the day go so much better." She said, seeming to purr like a kitten as she stretched. "I'm sorry, Marcus, go on."

"We showered together and she cooked breakfast while I got ready to go to the office. Randa mentioned that she might go shopping with her girlfriend, Deloris. I asked her to pick me up a new tie."

"What color?"

"Black. Anyway we ate breakfast and I left for the office, just like we do every morning. I had been working at home the night before. Getting ready for a meeting with a client that I had this afternoon and I left the papers at home. I called Randa to see if she could bring me the papers and we could have lunch together. But there was no answer. I needed those papers, so I went home to get them. When I got home her Benz was in the driveway. I figured that Deloris came and picked her up, and she had gone shopping. I went inside and called her name a few times, she didn't answer. I went in the den and I couldn't find the papers. So I turned on the computer so I could print them. I had just picked up the papers off the printer when I thought I heard a noise. I stood still for a second, but I didn't hear anything. So I turned off the computer and headed for the door. I was out the house Yvonne, and I was just about to close the door when I heard the noise again. I turned around and walked up the steps straight to the bedroom and opened the door. There she was. My wife Randa. Pullin' her hair out ridin' some mans dick. I stood there. I couldn't move. I stood there, - - - I guess it couldn't have been too long before I went back downstairs. I just walked outside and I sat down on the steps. I don't know how long I'd been sitting there when I heard the door open and close and open again. When I looked up, Randa was standing in front me." Marcus lit another cigarette from the one he was smoking.

"What did you say to her? Better yet, what did she say to you?"

"She asked me if I had been in the house. I just looked at her. I guess she got tired of me staring at her not saying anything and she went back in the house. The two of them came out, got in the Benz I pay for, and left."

"Damn the least she could have done was make the brother go home in a cab. Show you some respect. She needed to stay there and handle her business."

"I thought so too. But remember, I'm a fool. What makes it worse is after she leaves, the neighbor woman walks up to me."

"The neighbor woman?"

"The neighbor woman, that's what we call her."

"Okay."

"The neighbor woman says, 'I'm glad you finally woke up. And don't let her tell you that this was the first time.' Then she walked away. Now I felt embarrassed on top of feeling stupid. If the neighbor woman knew, the rest of the block did too. Maybe even the whole subdivision."

"I don't know what to say, Marcus." Yvonne stretched

and repositioned herself on the couch. "Did Randa come back?"

"Yeah, she came back. While she was gone I thought about all the things I would say to her. How could you? Who is he? How long has this been going on?"

"Maybe you should have asked the neighbor woman." Marcus cut his eyes at Yvonne. "Sorry, dagg, it was a joke."

"When she came back I couldn't say anything. She tried to explain, telling me that this was the first time. But the neighbor woman cleared that up. Told me how sorry she was. And she promised me if I forgave her it would never happen again. I couldn't say anything. I thought of a hundred things to say, but I was so mad, the words just wouldn't come out. After awhile I just got up and left."

"I'm so sorry, Marcus. I know that must have hurt." She yawned.

"Of course it hurt. You know what's funny about this whole thing?"

"What's that, Marcus?"

"I met her the day after you moved to LA. I remember thinking that maybe I'd get lucky and find a woman as beautiful and as sweet as you."

"Oh, Marcus."

"I love her, Yvonne." Marcus stood up and began to wander around the room and continued talking while he paced back and forth. "But she betrayed all that. Not just me, but us. Everything about us, everything we meant to each other. She betrayed everything that we were. Everything we talked about. All of our plans. Our hopes. She betrayed our future. That's what hurt. We used to talk about growing old together. Sitting on the porch watching our grandchildren run around. Grandchildren. We had been talking about having a baby. We had even gone out and started buying stuff we knew that we'd need for the baby. She betrayed all that. While I was building a future for us, she was tearing it down. I don't know what I'm gonna do without her."

Marcus stopped talking. "No comment from the peanut gallery?" He walked to the couch. "Yvonne? Yvonne?" She had fallen asleep. "Stop me if I bore you." Marcus went and got the spread off the bed. He laid the spread over Yvonne and kissed her on the cheek. "Good night, Yvonne."

Phase 2

When Yvonne woke up the next morning, Marcus was already gone. He left a note on the television that said, "Gone shopping. Be back around noon. Please wait for me." Yvonne smiled when she read it. Then she picked up the box of hair color and went into the bedroom. When she came out she no longer had long black hair. Yvonne now had short auburn hair. She gathered her things and called for a cab to pick her up. When they asked what her destination would be she hung up the phone. She put on her sunglasses and left the room through the sliding balcony door and went into the lobby. She asked the desk clerk to get her a cab and said she would be waiting in the bar as she walked away.

Once the cab arrived she offered the driver a fifty-dollar bill to take her where she wanted to go if he wouldn't call it in. The driver quickly promised and they were on their way. Yvonne told him to drop her off at the Indian Creek MARTA station. She would walk from there.

Yvonne walked down Redan Road and up South Hairston to the Main Street subdivision to the home of Tyisha, whom she had gone to high school with.

"Yvonne, I wasn't expecting you for a couple of days." Tyisha said, giving Yvonne a big hug. "Come on in out that heat girl. It must be ninety-five degrees out there. You're drenched, what did you walk here from California?"

"No girl, just from the MARTA station."

"Where's your car?"

"Don't ask. Did you get that package I sent you?"

"It came yesterday."

"Good." Tyisha got the package and handed it to Yvonne.

"What's in there? You ain't in no trouble are you,

21

Yvonne?"

"Better if you don't know. I need one more favor from you. Then I gotta go and I want you to forget about this package and that you ever saw me."

"Whatever girl."

"No, Ty. You never saw me or this box. Now you promise me, Ty."

"Okay, okay, I promise. Now what you need?"

"I need some clothes and I could use a shower."

"No problem." Tyisha got Yvonne some clothes and Yvonne disappeared into the bathroom. Taking the package with her. She turned on the shower and began to get undressed. She sat down on the toilet and lit a cigarette. Yvonne opened the box and removed its contents. The box contained a bag intended for a laptop. She opened the bag and took out a nine millimeter automatic and laid it down on the vanity. She looked in the bag at the legal-size envelope and the money. She shook her head and wondered how could things have gone so wrong. Yvonne opened the envelope, took out the papers and stared at them wishing she knew what it said or what language it was. She returned the papers to the envelope and put it and the gun back in the bag. She finished undressing and got in the shower.

While she was in the shower, she thought about Marcus and Randa. She felt badly for him. And as much as she hated to involve him in all this, she needed an ally and Tyisha wasn't the one. Marcus wasn't exactly James Bond, but he was all she had. Now he was the only one she could trust.

Yvonne asked Tyisha to call a cab for her, but she insisted that she could take her anywhere she needed to go. "All right, Ty, take me to the New China Buffet."

"Are you hungry, Yvonne?" Tyisha asked on the way to open the door. "I could have made you something to eat."

"That's okay, Ty, I'm just meeting someone there." She hated having to lie to Tyisha, she was her best friend before Yvonne moved to LA. They managed to stay friends, real friends, in spite of the money. Once the word got around that Yvonne was to receive a large sum of money, most of her friends changed. But not Tyisha. She always kept it real, which was exactly why Yvonne wanted her to have no part in this. When they arrived at the restaurant they got out and Yvonne said good-bye to Tyisha. "Thanks for everything, Ty. You take care of yourself and remember, you never saw me."

Tyisha hugged her friend, "Girl, you too much," and returned to her car. Yvonne stood at the door and watched Tyisha drive away. When she was out of sight, Yvonne came out and started walking down Memorial Drive heading for the post office. On the way, she made a mental note of the name of an apartment complex and kept walking.

Yvonne was hot and tired when she reached the post office. She went to the counter and asked the clerk for a box big enough to send a laptop and some tape. Yvonne looked around the post office for a secluded spot and proceeded to pack the box. She took the gun out of the bag and taped it to the bottom of the box, then placed the bag with the papers and money on top of it. She sealed the box and then she retrieved Marcus's card from her purse. Yvonne addressed the box to herself in care of Marcus and marked it for next day delivery.

With that taken care of, Yvonne went to the pay phone and made arrangements to get a new fake ID and passport. Then she called a cab. She had the cab meet her at the apartment complex and take her back to the Residence Inn. When she arrived she didn't see Marcus's car, so she let herself in through the sliding door. She turned on the television, laid down on the couch, and went to sleep.

Yvonne was awakened by a knock at the door. She had started to open the door, but she paused for a minute. *"It might be his wife looking for him,"* she thought. The peep hole revealed nothing, so Yvonne reluctantly said, "Who is it?"

"It's me Yvonne. I forgot my key." Yvonne opened the door and was shocked to see the two men that were waiting by her car in the parking lot the night before.

"Good to see you again, Yvonne," the first man said as he slapped her. Yvonne fell to the floor and tried to crawl away.

The second man snatched her up from the floor, "Love what you've done to your hair," he said, then slapped her too. He picked her up and threw her on the bed. "Where is it Yvonne?" The first man said pointing his gun at her.

"Where is what? I don't know what you're talking about." Her heart pounded. Tears rolled down her cheeks.

"Check the room. But don't make a mess." The other man searched the room and found nothing. "I'm not going to ask you again, Yvonne. Where is it?"

"I don't know what you're talking about!" she screamed. The man grabbed Yvonne by her hair and punched her in the eye. He drew back and was about to punch her again. "It's not here!" Yvonne yelled.

"Where is it?"

"I can't get it until tomorrow."

"I guess we'll just have to keep you company until then." He grabbed Yvonne by the hair again and pulled her to the door. "Now we're going to walk through that lobby. If you scream or try to run, I'll kill you. It don't matter to me, I'll still get paid."

At nine o'clock, Marcus returned to his room, armed with a new wardrobe and a bottle of Hennessy. "Yvonne. You here?" He put down his packages and looked around. He had thoughts all day about Yvonne and hoped that she would be there when got there, but she was gone. He sat down on the couch, he could smell the scent of Yvonne's perfume. It made him smile. Throughout the day, Marcus allowed himself to slip into the fantasy of Yvonne standing by and supporting him through his divorce from Randa and then they would get married. "Maybe she'll be back." He poured himself a glass of Henny. He stayed up waiting for Yvonne to come back until he fell asleep after two in the morning. The following morning, Marcus woke up and slowly came to the realization that he would never see Yvonne again. He tried to shrug it off as if it didn't matter. But it did. The truth of the matter was that he had fallen in love with Yvonne nine years ago. He thought that her coming back into his life on the very day that he left his wife was some kind of sign. He put his dream down and prepared to go to the office.

He arrived at his office after one o'clock to see his first client. After they left Janice told him that he had received, "This package addressed to Yvonne Haggler. I was wondering why you seemed so happy today."

Marcus took the package from Janice and took it in his office, closing the door behind him. He was overjoyed. He jumped up and down and danced around like a kid on Christmas morning. This meant he would see Yvonne again. He put the package in his desk and locked it. At four o'clock, Yvonne called.

"Hello, Yvonne. How - - -"

Yvonne had no time for pleasantries. "Did the package come for me?"

"It came about an hour ago."

"Marcus, I need you to bring it to me right now."

"What's wrong, Yvonne? Are you in trouble? Should I call the police?"

"Marcus, everything is fine. I just need that box as soon as you can," Yvonne said trying to sound as calm as she could with someone listening on the other line and a gun pointed at her head. "I'm in the West End on Peters and Whitehall. There's a warehouse on the corner. Just come inside, I'll be waiting there for you. When do you think you can get here?"

Marcus looked at his watch. "I should be there in about an hour."

"Good, I'll see you then."

"Yvonne."

"Yes, Marcus."

"Maybe when you get finished with your business we can have dinner."

"Marcus," she said franticly. Then she calmed down. "I'd like that."

"Then it's a date. I'll see you in an hour." Marcus hung up the phone and called Janice. He told her to clear his calendar for the rest of the day. "For the rest of the week, Janice. I need some time off. Maybe I'll take a trip."

"Marcus, I know you're hurt. I know you want to get back at Randa for what she did. But give yourself a chance to heal."

"Thanks, Janice. Sometimes I don't know what I would do without you."

Marcus finished up his paper work as quick as he could in anticipation of seeing Yvonne. He drove downtown, stopping on the exit ramp to buy a red rose for Yvonne, wondering if she would like to go to Aruba with him. He arrived at the warehouse and went inside. When he came through the door, Yvonne came to meet him. Marcus saw her swollen eye. "Yvonne, are you all right?"

"Thanks for bringing this to me, Marcus," Yvonne said loud enough for her new friends to hear. She took the box from Marcus and whispered, "Wait for me outside, have the car running." She looked over her shoulder. "Sorry I can't do dinner, but call me tomorrow and we'll do lunch." She took the rose and kissed him. "Please, Marcus, just go." She whispered and turned away.

Yvonne looked back as Marcus walked quickly to the door. Once Marcus made it safely out the building she tried to hand the men the box. "Open it."

They watched closely as Yvonne put the box down on the table and opened it. She handed the bag to them. The bag was opened. While one busied himself with the papers, the other smiled at the money and Yvonne removed the nine from the box. She fired two shots, returned the papers to the envelope, put them back in the bag, picked up her rose and headed for the door.

When Marcus heard the shots coming from the warehouse, it only served to increase his already heightened sense of anxiety, to say the least. He got out of the car and had just reached the door when Yvonne came out. "What happened in there?"

"Not now, Marcus, we gotta get outta here. Get in the car and lets go." Yvonne shouted as she walked quickly behind Marcus.

Marcus got in the car and drove away quickly. "What happened? Are you all right?" he asked to Yvonne as he looked in the rear view mirror.

"I'm fine, Marcus, just drive."

"Where to?"

"I don't know. I'm making this up as I go. Just drive."

"Okay, we'll go back to my hotel."

"No, they know about that. That's where they found me."

"Who is they? What are you involved in?"

"Not now, Marcus, please I need to think. Go to a hotel near the airport."

"Did you kill those men?"

"Yes, Marcus I killed them. Now please let just think for a minute."

"Why, Yvonne? Why did you kill them?"

"They would have killed me and you too!" Yvonne yelled. "Is that a good enough reason for you?"

"It has something to do with that box, doesn't it? What have you got me mixed up in?"

"I don't know, Marcus. I really just don't know what this is all about." Yvonne took a deep breath. "Please, Marcus, I'll tell you everything as soon as we get settled."

Marcus looked in the rear view mirror again. "Well, it doesn't look like the police or anybody is following us," he said, not really sure if he said it to reassure Yvonne or himself.

"This isn't a movie, Marcus, the police aren't on our tail." He looked at the bag at Yvonne's feet. She had just killed two men over that bag. Marcus said nothing else as he drove to the Hilton near the airport. As they entered the hotel Yvonne stopped.

"What's wrong?" Marcus asked.

"Do you have cash?"

"No. I was going to put it on my credit card."

"No. Let's go to an ATM."

"There's one," Marcus said pointing at the ATM in the lobby.

"No. They can track your credit card transactions. Go to a bank, and not one close to here either," Yvonne said, as they left the Hilton and got back in the car.

"Won't they can still trace the transaction at the ATM?" Marcus asked.

"Yes, but at least they won't know exactly where we are."

Marcus drove past five bank ATM machines before stopping at a First Union. With cash in hand they returned to the Hilton. Once they got in the room, Marcus went straight to the mini bar. He poured a drink and downed it. He poured another drink. "I'd like one too. If its not too much trouble." Yvonne laid down on the bed and Marcus brought her a drink. "Thank you, Marcus. And thank you for my rose. It was sweet of you."

Marcus lit a cigarette and sat down on the bed. "You're welcome. It's not every day I give a woman a rose right before she kills somebody." Marcus smiled. Yvonne let out a little laugh. "What's going on, Yvonne?"

"Give me a drag of you're cigarette."

Marcus handed Yvonne his cigarette and she inhaled deeply and blew out the smoke.

"I'm a courier, Marcus. Those men were assassins sent to kill me and recover the contents of that bag. There's a hundred thousand dollars and some papers in there. I don't know what's on the papers. It's in some language, I don't know which. I think that just about covers it."

"A courier?"

"I travel to different places and pick up things from one person and deliver them to another."

"I know what a courier is, Yvonne. Why do you do it? Is it excitement?"

"No, I do it for money."

"Money?"

"Yes, Marcus, for money. Isn't that why most people do things."

"I know that. But you've got money."

"I'm broke, Marcus."

"Broke? What do you mean, broke. The way I had you set up, you should have been able to live comfortably."

"It's a long story, Marcus."

"We seem to have plenty of time. We're not going anywhere."

Yvonne and Marcus lay on the bed quietly for the next two hours, sharing cigarettes, drinking and thinking. Marcus thought about how the events of the day would affect him. He was now an accessory to murder. Not only was he going to jail, but also he would be disbarred. In two days he had lost his wife, his career, and his freedom. He looked at Yvonne, eyes closed smoking the cigarette he had just handed her. She opened her eyes and noticed him starring at her. She handed him the cigarette and closed her eyes. Marcus desperately wanted to know what was going on. Not only to satisfy his curiosity, but also to begin planning their defense. If those men were actually trying to kill her, then their deaths were in reality, self-defense. But Yvonne had shut down.

Yvonne, for her part had just a bit more on her plate. Things were pretty cut and dry for Marcus. But her world was much more complicated. She felt badly for involving Marcus in her mess, but what's done is done. There was no turning back now, but he was entitled to an explanation. "When I left here, Marcus, I was set. I was twenty-one, rollin' a Benz, nice little condo in Northridge, and more money than I ever dreamed possible. And thanks to you, it just képt rollin' in. I was getting checks just about every week from people and places I'd never heard of. I just knew it would never run out. I was spending money buying whatever I thought I wanted, clothes mostly. Brought a house for Mama and sent my whole family money. And traveling, I loved to travel. I had never been anywhere, never seen anything. My eyes had opened up to a whole new world and it was mine to command. I went everywhere, did everything I wanted. Even took my newfound fake friends on a cruise. All expenses paid by me, of course. I was a fool, a foolish young girl with money. I remember my papa tellin' me that a fool and his money are soon parted. Well, that's exactly what happened to me. I remember going to New York one day with this guy I met the night before. We had dinner at a French restaurant, after we left, we caught a cab to go back to the hotel, and we were talking about how the food wasn't that good and how the service was poor. He said, 'too bad we can't have dinner in France.' I told the cab driver to take us to the airport. Next day we were in France having late supper with a view of the tower."

"You were out the box, Yvonne."

"A fool. A damn fool. After awhile, I found that I was running out of money. The checks were still coming but that wasn't enough."

"You could have changed your lifestyle."

"Marcus, that would have been too much like right. I had met this guy named Paris. He's the type who's into everything, knows everybody, you know the type. Anyway, we were hangin' out and I was tellin' him about my money problems and he asked me if I would do some work for him as a courier. I told him no. So he introduced me to Tom Mack."

"The lawyer you gave power of attorney to."

"The same. He told me that if I let him make some investments for me that I would be set for life. I would be able to quadruple my money in less then a month. So, I gave him fifty thousand dollars. Three weeks later he wrote me out a check for two hundred thousand dollars."

"You want me to tell you happened next?"

"Okay, go ahead."

"Old Tom Mack tells you that you could have the check or you could reinvest it, and since the market conditions are right, you could make half a million dollars."

"Yeah, how did you know?"

Marcus smiled. "Old scam."

"Yeah, well the fool fell for it. Two weeks later he called me and said that we were close to flippin' that money, but he was on to something else that had the potential to be far more lucrative. I told him that I was just about broke and that fifty I gave him was really all I had to invest."

"Well, Yvonne, in another week you'll have half a million dollars. But I hate for you to miss out on this," he said.

"I do too, Tom, but there's nothing I can do until I get some more money."

"Well maybe there is."

"What's that?" Yvonne asked greedily.

"Paris mentioned to me that I had some investments that were providing you with a nice dividend income."

"Go on."

"If I had control of those investments I might be able to leverage those gains on this new deal and make it happen."

"What would you need?"

"Who controls those accounts for you?"

"My lawyer, Marcus Douglas, in Atlanta."

"I would need you to fire him and give me power of attorney."

"I don't know Tom, that money is all I'm living off

now."

"I understand, Yvonne. Maybe it will come around again, but I doubt it. Anyway, I'll call you when I have some news for you."

"Wait a minute, Tom."

"Yes, Yvonne."

"Go ahead and draw up whatever you need. I'll be there in an hour."

"Three weeks later I got a call from Tom, letting me know that the market dropped and I'd lost everything. With nowhere to go I went to Paris once again for help. He put me to work the next day as a courier. My life style was saved and for the next five years I've made the occasional trip, picking up and delivering whatever Paris asked me to. My plan was to only do it until I turned thirty and then I could collect on my trust fund."

"What went wrong, Yvonne?" Marcus asked.

"I don't know, Marcus."

"Well what happened?"

"Paris sent me to Singapore. Everything was going fine. I picked up that bag and went back to my room. Then this man shows up at my door. He said that Paris sent him. That there was a change in plans and Paris wanted me to give him the bag and to meet him back in LA in a week. I told him that I needed to call Paris to confirm. Paris always said that if there was a change in plans I would hear it from him. If it ever happened I should kill whoever told me any different before they killed me. He stopped me from calling. Said that things were going on that I had no knowledge of and my calling would put too many people at risk. I said I was calling Paris anyway. He grabbed me, we wrestled around for awhile, I'm pretty strong for a Mississippi country girl. Anyway, I broke away from him and ran into the bedroom. I got to my gun and I shot him."

"You ever kill anyone before?"

"No. That was the first time I ever had to use it. Since I had to carry a gun, Paris made me learn how to use it. I was great on the range but I never thought that I'd have to use it."

"What happened then, Yvonne?"

"I freaked out and I grabbed the bag and got out of there. I went straight to the airport and caught a plane to Hawaii and went to the drop off point, but nobody showed up. I was really scared by then, so I called Paris. But I didn't mention anything about the man I shot. He said he didn't know what was going on and told me to come home and bring the bag to him. When I got back to my condo, there was somebody waiting for me."

"Did you shoot them too?"

"No, I jumped off the balcony and ran to my car and took Interstate 10 out of town. I just kept driving until I was too tired to drive any further. I stopped for few hours in Picacho, Arizona to get some sleep and I was gone again. I drove to El Paso, Texas. I was going to cross into Ciudad Juarez in Mexico, but I didn't want to use the fake ID & passport I had gotten for Paris and I was in too much of a hurry when I left to get mine. So I went to FedEx and sent that box to Tyisha. And then I drove here."

"How did I get involved in this?"

"Those two men were waiting for me in the parking lot the night we met in the store. I didn't mean to get you involved but they were at my car, you were the only way I could get away from there. I made arrangements for a new passport to get out of the country. Then I sent that package to you. I figured that it was kind of an insurance policy. I was set, but I didn't want to leave without saying good-bye to you."

Marcus got up from the bed and paced back and forth thinking of a way out of their predicament. "Paris."

"I was thinking about Africa," Yvonne said.

"No, Paris is the key to it all. We'll go to LA and I'll return the bag. They shouldn't bother you after that."

"Are you crazy? For all I know Paris may kill me on sight and take the bag off my dead body."

"True, but we got to convince him that it's in his best interest to leave you alone."

"How you gonna do that?"

"Yvonne, I'm a lawyer, I'm a very good negotiator." Marcus and Yvonne argued about what to do well into evening. Marcus was convinced that talking to Paris and returning the bag was the only way. Yvonne, on the other hand, hated that plan, she just wanted to get away. "I say we see the passport guy and go to Africa." She felt like she was talking into a brick wall.

Then it hit her. "You're right. Going back to LA is the only way out of this." Yvonne opened a new pack of Bensons and walked to the window.

"Good, I'm glad you finally see that." Marcus reached for the bottle on the nightstand and poured a drink. He took a sip. "We'll catch a flight and be in LA first thing tomorrow morning.

Yvonne sat on the bed and took the drink from Marcus in exchange for her cigarette. "We'll do it your way Marcus." Yvonne yawned and laid down on the bed. Marcus gave back her cigarette. "We'll never be safe until we settle things with Paris." She curled into the fetal position. "And then it will be over."

Phase 3

The next morning, Marcus, and Yvonne set out for California. Yvonne insisted they fly into San Francisco, catch a flight to Santa Barbara, and drive down the 101 into LA. They checked into the Wyndham Hotel at the Airport. As soon as they got to the room, Yvonne called and left a message for Paris to call her message service. "Paris this is Yvonne. I want to meet you somewhere tomorrow to return those items to you. And hopefully this will end our relationship without any further need for outside intervention." She checked every half-hour to see if he returned her call. Hours dragged on. With nothing to do they occupied themselves ordering room service and watching movies until it was almost two. Marcus had fallen asleep hours earlier, but Yvonne kept up her thirty-minute vigil. At two-thirty, Yvonne called again. *"Yvonne, it's good to hear your voice again. It's late and I'm tired. Be at my house in El Segundo at eleven."*

"I don't think so." Yvonne called him back and left a message that Marcus would meet him at Bruce's Place on West Grand at eleven and he would give him the bag. "One more thing, Paris. Come alone." She started to wake up Marcus, but he looked so peaceful she didn't want to bother him. Yvonne turned off the lights and laid down next to Marcus. He stretched and put his arm around Yvonne. She smiled and went to sleep.

At ten the next morning they left the Wyndham to meet Paris. As Yvonne drove she gave Marcus a description of Paris. "You can't miss him." She dropped him off on Main Street and West Grand, about a block from Bruce's Place. Marcus got out. "Wish me luck."

"Good luck, Marcus. I'll pick you up here when it's

over." Marcus started to walk away, Yvonne got out of the car. "Marcus!" He turned around and walked back. "You know you've slept with me for the last three nights?"

"Yeah, and I haven't even kissed you," Marcus said as he leaned against the car.

"No, you haven't." she kissed him on the cheek and then gently on the lips.

"I love you, Yvonne."

"I love you too, Marcus. When all this is over I'll show you just how much."

"See you, Yvonne."

"See ya, Marcus."

Marcus walked down the street and entered Bruce's Place. He went into the bathroom and took the garbage bag out of the trash can. He placed the bag in it and replaced the garbage bag. Then he took a seat in the back so he could see the door. He checked his watch. It was eleven o'clock. He tapped anxiously on the table. His tapping reminded him of the sound of Yvonne's heels clicking against the tile that first night at the store. He looked up and Paris stood before him. Yvonne's description of Paris was dead on target. Dressed in a dull gray suit, white shirt, opened at the collar, black raybands and wet look hair.

"Marcus, I'll take it. Yvonne used to speak of you all time. You wouldn't mind standing up and opening your coat, would you."

"I'm unarmed," Marcus said as he did as he was asked and sat down.

"May I sit?" Paris asked.

"By all means. Let's get this over with."

"Yes this has been a very big misunderstanding. I never intended for any of this to happen. I don't know how much Yvonne told you, but ---," Marcus cut him off.

"I'm just the delivery boy."

"When she didn't come see me, I simply had to take steps to recover the items."

"Right."

"May I see the items?"

"Excuse me for a minute." Marcus went into the bathroom and returned with the bag. He handed it to Paris. "Here you go." Marcus stood over Paris and watched as he opened the bag and looked over its contents. Once he had satisfied himself that the items were intact, Paris got up and walked toward the door.

"Please tell Yvonne that I meant her no harm."

"She'll find that very comforting."

As soon as they were outside, Yvonne drove up quickly and to Marcus's surprise, she fired one shot to Paris' head. Paris fell to the ground. Marcus started to pick up the bag. "Leave the bag!" Yvonne yelled.

Marcus ran to the car. Once he was in, Yvonne drove away. "Why did you kill him? It was over. All he wanted was his shit back."

"How naïve are you, Marcus. As long as Paris was alive it would never be over. Can't you see that? He would just keep sending people to kill us."

"Why'd we leave the bag?"

"I'm glad to be rid of it. Let the cops worry about what those papers mean." Yvonne and Marcus drove back to Santa Barbara. They caught a flight back to San Francisco and brought tickets to Seattle. Yvonne knew someone there who could get them new passports. And would help them get out of the country. They sat at the gate waiting for their plane to begin boarding. "You know it was the right thing to do, Marcus."

"I know. But you could have told me what you were going to do."

"If I told you, would you have gone along with it?"

"No."

"That's why I didn't tell you," Yvonne said with a smile. "Tomorrow we'll be safely out of the country. And I'll spend the rest of my life in your arms."

"You still could have told me." Marcus kissed Yvonne on the cheek. "I'm going to get some water." Marcus walked away, Yvonne watched him walk until a lady walked up and stood before her. "Is anybody sitting there?"

"No, have a seat."

The lady sat down, slowly removing a thirty-eight with a silencer from her purse. Yvonne looked at her and the lady shot her five times. The lady got up and walked away as Marcus returned. Yvonne struggled to her feet.

"Marcus." He caught her as she fell.

She died in his arms.

PRIVATE DECEPTIONS

*a
story
by
roy glenn*

PRIVATE DECEPTIONS
a story by roy glenn

Brittney Press Publishing

On the Web @ http://www.brittneypress.com

e-mail: privatedeceptions@brittneypress.com

The characters Nick Simmons, Wanda Moore,
Freeze, Jamaica, Bobby Ray, Camille Augustus,
Cassandra "Shy" Sims & Mike "Vicious" Black,
Originally appear in
"Is It A Crime"
a different type of love story by roy glenn

The characters Marcus Douglas & Yvonne Haggler
Originally appear in the short story,
"In Your Arms"
a little something by roy glenn

Special Thanks to:
Arvita Roberts, Sonia Powell,
Tanesha Hendricks, Tina Smith
&
Magdalene Breaux, Author of Imaginary Playmate

Dedicated
2 U

Chapter One

"Okay, Nick, you're free to go," Detective Kirkland said.

I stood up and looked at my watch. For the last seven hours I had been in the interrogation room with Wanda, answering all of the questions that Detectives Kirkland and Richards had to offer. Kirk opened the door for Wanda and they walked out of the interrogation room together. I followed them.

Thinking.

"It's really not necessary for you to walk me out detective," Wanda said, and looked back at me.

"These halls are filled with dangerous criminals." Kirk always did have a thing for Wanda, so he had to escort her out the building.

Dealing with Kirk was old hat to her. "I've played this game with Kirk before," Wanda said once we were out of the building. "So don't worry, I got this."

I wasn't worried. I've known Wanda Moore since I was eleven. She was a good lawyer, and like she said, she's played this game with Kirk plenty of times during his attempts to make a case against Mike Black. "Thanks for hanging in there with me," I said, as I started to walk away. There were still too many unanswered questions that I had to have answers to. The most pressing of which, is how I got to be the only suspect in four murders.

I needed to think, retrace my steps; do something, anything to get myself out of this. Or maybe I'll just go straight to the airport and catch a plane to the Bahamas to become Black's new permanent houseguest.

"Not so fast, Nick." Wanda grabbed me by the arm. "You're coming with me. You need to tell me everything. Not those covert army, need to know, bullshit answers you just fed Kirk. The whole story."

I looked at Wanda, thinking about giving her some covert army, need to know, bullshit answer, and hailing a cab.

But I knew she was right.

Wanda led me to her car and we drove to her house in the old neighborhood. It had been ten years since I'd driven through these streets. A strange kinda chill came over me that started me thinking about the old days.

"Black know about this?"

"Of course he does. Who do you think put up your bail? You know anybody else with a million dollars? He wouldn't turn his back on you when you need him. Even though you ran out on him when he needed you. First Jamaica, then you."

"Lighten up on me, Wanda. I've been draggin' around that burden for the last ten years."

"I'm sorry, Nick. I didn't mean to go there. I just - - -"

"It's okay, Wanda."

"What happened, Nick?"

"There must be something I missed."

"What is it?"

"I don't know."

"Start at the beginning, Nick. Don't leave anything out. Even if you didn't think it was important at the time."

"It started when Mrs. Gabriel Childers sat down in front of me. No. That's not right, it really began two weeks before when Uncle Felix called and said he had a job that required our talents. 'A simple job,' he called it, and it was."

Until about a year ago, I had been a part of a special operations unit. Things went wrong on our last assignment and only three of the members of our unit got out alive. James "Jett" Bronson, Monika Wynn, and me. We were flown back to Fort Brag where we were promptly debriefed and processed out. Uncle Felix approached us the day after.

He recruited us to do jobs for him that required our skills. Jett's specialty is electronic surveillance, computers, and all that high tech stuff. Monika's specialty is munitions. The girl really gets a rush out of watchin' things blow up. Me, my specialty is weapons, commando tactics.

You know, the killer.

At Felix's request, I convinced Jett and Monika to come with me back to New York. Felix set us up in front business as private investigators. To maintain our cover we actually did some surveillance jobs. Some insurance jobs, a few slip traces. Nothing major, but it paid. Besides, the real money was in doing those little jobs for Uncle Felix.

"Just acquire the target and deliver. A walk in the park. And it was. A simple surveillance to get his pattern down and decide when to snatch him. Jett installed a remote video system. Once it was installed, the system used standard phone lines that provides transmission and monitoring in real time at 28.8 kbps."

"In English, Nick."

"Sorry, Wanda. It operates at high speed, so the transmission provides clear color images at up to fifteen frames per second over a single phone line."

"Thank you, Nick," Wanda said.

"I'll try to keep it simple." Wanda let out a little laugh. "What's so funny?"

"Nothing." She laughed. "I just remember when you could hardly read."

"Yeah, well, things change."

"Go on, Nick."

"It went off just the way it was planned. We picked him up at his house, and then Monika blew it up so there wouldn't be any trace. Then we left him alone, as instructed, in a car on Pier 17 off of Fulton Street. The next afternoon I went by the office to type up my report for

Felix and get out of there. But I was tired, so I sat back in the chair and before I knew it, I was asleep. I had been asleep for at least an hour before I opened my eyes and there she was, standing in the doorway."

Thursday, July 9; 3:47 PM

"I'd like to hire a private investigator." Her voice was deep.

"That would be me. Come in. Please, have a seat."

In my dimly lit office, it took my eyes a minute to focus while I shook off my nod. She walked toward me. From my vantage point, I could make out only that she was very well dressed, tall and slender, but not skinny by any definition I'd ever heard. She had the type of legs that I'd probably enjoy watching when she walked out, but I couldn't tell much more about her. "Tell me what I can do for you, Miss?"

"Mrs.," she said with attitude. "Mrs. Gabriel Childers. And I'd like to hire a you to find my brother."

I started to tell her that I don't handle cases like that.

But I didn't.

With my eyes now focused, I could see her face. I wanted her to stay.

Mrs. Childers, huh?

The way she said it, with so much attitude about it. So I decided to have some fun with it. "How long has he been missing, *Mrs.* Childers?"

"As far as I know, about two weeks."

"Any possibility that he could have just gone out of town? Took a vacation and not told you?"

"It's possible, Mr.?"

"Simmons, Nick Simmons." I liked the sound of her voice. It was soothing. "Please call me Nick."

"Okay, *Nick*. It's possible, but it's not like Jake to be gone like this. Neither me, nor my sister, Chesará, have heard from him. Jake is kind of - - - well, anal. You know, everything in its place, all about details."

"Have you gone to the police, Mrs. Childers?"

"No. I haven't gone to the police."

"Mind if I ask why, Mrs. Childers?"

She looked at me for awhile. She had pretty eyes, but they weren't soft. They were cold and distant. She shifted around in her chair and crossed her legs.

She dug around in her purse and pulled out a pack of cigarettes. "You mind if I smoke?" she asked, almost as an after thought.

"Please, be my guest."

She lit up. "I think my husband might be involved."

"All the more reason to go to the police."

"I don't want to go to the police until I'm sure that he's involved. That's why I want to hire you, to prove that he's involved in it."

"Are you afraid of your husband, Mrs. Childers?"

"Yes," she said quietly and looked away. Her fear came through loud and clear. "My husband is a very dangerous man, Mr. Simmons."

"Nick. Please, call me, Nick. What's your husbands name?"

"Alvin, Alvin Childers."

I laughed to myself, thinking how dangerous could somebody named Alvin be? "What makes him so dangerous?"

"He's involved in drugs. If he even thought I was talking to you about him or his business he'd - - -"

"Has he hurt you before?" I asked, and she dropped her head a little. I had taken notice of the dark circles under her eyes that her makeup didn't quite hide.

"I don't see what that has to do with anything." The fear in her voice quickly gave way to attitude. But it was that attitude that I liked about her.

"Look, Mrs. Childers, you want me to prove that your husband is involved in your brothers disappearance, and prove it to the police at that. You have to tell me everything, Mrs. Childers."

She took a deep breath. "All right. What do you want to know?"

"Answer my question."

"Yes, he's hurt me before."

"Once, twice, daily?"

"More than once, and let's leave it at that," she said quickly, and defiantly.

"All right, Mrs. Childers. Tell me about Jake then. Where he lives, where he works, his girl friends, who he hangs out with?"

"He has an apartment on Bronxwood." She wrote down his address and handed it to me.

"You got a key?"

"No."

"Know of anybody who does?" I asked.

"Jake is too particular about his things for him to let a lot of people have a key."

"He have a girlfriend?"

"Lisa Ellison," Mrs. Childers replied. I could tell by the way she said it that she didn't like her.

"What about her? She got a key?"

"I don't know."

"You know if she's heard from him?"

"I don't know."

"You ask her?"

"No."

"Why not?"

Mrs. Childers rolled her eyes. "I don't like her." At least she was real about it.

"What about friends? Anybody he hangs out with?"

"I don't know. He's got a friend Rocky. He grew up down the block from us in Philly. Him and Jake hang sometimes, but not that often."

"Do you have a picture of Jake?" Mrs. Childers reached in her purse and handed me a picture. "Looks like the bomb party. What's the occasion?"

"Jake's last birthday. We never had birthday parties when we were kids. So we really make a big thing of them now."

"How old is he?"

"Jake's thirty."

"He the oldest?"

"Yes."

"Whose that in the picture with him?"

"That's our sister, Chesará."

"Him and Chesará close?"

"Yes." She sounded offended by the question. "All of us are very close."

"How old is your sister, Mrs. Childers?"

"Chez is twenty-three." Mrs. Childers leaned forward and went cleavage on me. "Are you trying to find out how old I am? - - - Nick."

The way her voice dropped when she said my name. *Nick.* It overcame any objection I still had about taking her case.

Since I was trying to find out how old she was, I asked. "How old are you?"

"I'm twenty-seven."

That sounded good too, but not as good as, *Nick.*

"When was the last time you saw Jake?"

"About two weeks ago, he came by the house. He told

me that Chilly had been looking for him."

"Chilly?"

"My husband."

"Go on. What did your husband want to see him about?"

"He wouldn't tell me. But Chilly wantin' to see Jake was unusual. Jake didn't have much to do with Chilly."

"Is your brother involved with drugs too?"

"No. Jake is a chemist at Frontier Pharmaceuticals."

"Any reason to think that your brother is dead?"

"No!" Mrs. Childers said.

I wasn't sure what to read into the way she answered, but there was something about the look in her eyes that screamed that there was something she wasn't telling me. I knew then that this was something that I didn't want to get involved in. But still, there was an innocence in her eyes that cried out for my help.

"All right, Mrs. Childers, I'll look into it. Give me a day or two and I'll get back to you."

"When you need to contact me, leave me a message on my voice mail and let me know when and where I can meet you. Or call my sister; she'll give me the message. I really don't want to come back here." Mrs. Childers reached in her purse again, this time to retrieve her checkbook. Without asking what my rates were, she wrote out a check and handed it to me. "I hope this will cover your fee, or at least get you started. Money isn't a problem, so if you need more - - - "

I looked at the check. "No, Mrs. Childers, I think ten thousand dollars is enough to get me started." She stood up and I escorted her to the door. "One more question, Mrs. Childers. Why do you think that your husband is involved?"

"Just a feeling. But that *is* why I hired you."

I left my office thinking. Not about the case I had just taken on, but about Mrs. Gabriel Childers. I found her to be a very attractive woman to say the least. Thinking about how any man could do anything to hurt someone as beautiful as her, or any woman for that matter. The way she sat there with confidence and poise. Until she started talking about her husband. Whatever he had done to her had left her with a lasting impression.

Now I had a real missing person's case. We'd done a few slip traces, but this was different. My first thought was to tell Jett and Monika about it, but it made more sense to find out what, and who I had gotten them involved with. Suppose Mrs. Childers was right? Suppose her husband was involved?

This could get hectic with a quickness.

Jett and Monika grew up in the burbs. They came from nice middle class families and knew nothing about the dope game. But not me. I knew the game all too well; being a solider for Vicious Black before joining the army two weeks after André met his untimely demise.

I drove to Jake's apartment to have a look around. I put on my gloves, let myself in, and proceeded with my search. The place was immaculate. Everything in place, just as Mrs. Childers said it would be. I ran my finger across the coffee table. Very little dust. I went into the kitchen and opened the refrigerator. The date on the milk bottle had expired ten days ago. The bathroom was next. Sink and shower were bone dry. The toilet had that blue water in it, so I flushed it. It came back even bluer. I moved on to the bedroom. There was nothing out of place in the closet. Bed was made. It was a safe bet that no one had been there in at least a week.

I went back into the living room and turned on Jake's computer. Once Windows 2000 finally opened, I went into all the items on his desktop. I used an old DOS command to show hidden directories. Then I went into Explorer and ran a search on all documents modified in the last thirty days. There was a directory filled with word document files, and a directory with spreadsheet files. There was one file in each directory whose last modified date was eight days ago. I tried to open them, but they were both password protected. I turned the computer off and decided I would come back tomorrow with Jett.

"Ouch!"

Chapter Two

"How long were you out?" Wanda asked. She had changed into her robe, made a cup of coffee, and had made herself comfortable on the couch.

"Not long. Ten, fifteen minutes maybe."

"Any idea who it was?"

"No."

"What happened then?"

"I could feel the blood running down my neck. That's when I realized that I only had on one glove. The right hand glove was on the floor."

"So we know that somebody wanted your fingerprints. What'd you do then?" Wanda asked questions just like Kirk. Hard and fast.

"I looked around the apartment again and got out."

"Where'd you go when you left?"

I stood up and walked around the room. Deciding how I was going to answer the question. "I drove to the Childers' house."

"Why'd you go there?"

"To get a feel for the layout. Just being thorough, Wanda."

I couldn't bring myself to tell Wanda that I went there to see if I could see her again. But it was the truth; there I was sitting outside her house.

In complete darkness.

I opened the trunk, got my bag out, and took out my camera. This gave me an opportunity to try out my new Predator night vision goggles. Jett says they'll give me high performance in low light.

"These are great, Nick!" Jett said, louder than he needed to, as he handed them to me. "Check them out. They're lightweight, only 550 grams. They are powered by a single

1.5-volt AA alkaline battery. Their design is particularly well suited for helicopter pilots flying night missions. But you should be able to carry out search operations under low light conditions."

Time to see if he was right.

It was a big house. I hopped the fence and walked around the house looking around for any security. "I hope they don't have no dogs out here." Which was a great time to think of it.

I got a few shots of the house. It was surrounded on all sides by trees. The long driveway led to a big garage and more trees behind it. There were six cars in there.

I walked back to the house surprised that there was nobody patrolling the grounds. The alarm system was nothing fancy. I disabled it and was inside in two minutes.

"Nice set up. These drug dealers sure know how to live," I said.

With my night vision goggles on, I walked around the house planting listening devices and taking pictures of the entire house. Timing myself as I moved from room to room, until I reached the master bedroom. I checked the closets. The really big one was hers naturally. I can't really think of a word to describe her wardrobe.

I put a listening device behind a picture of her and Chilly next to the bed. "What did she see in him?"

The curtain was opened so I looked out of the bedroom window at the trees over the garage. I bugged the phones before returning to the car and waited. It was one thirty-four when she drove up in a white Porsche.

I put the goggles back on.

What was I doing?

She stopped to open the gate. I watched as she opened the car door and her leg appeared. First one, then the other. Her outfit matched the car. I wondered if she coordinated her outfits with which car she was going to drive.

After awhile, lights began coming on inside the house. She immediately closed the curtain in the front room. Ten minutes later, the downstairs light went out. I wanted to see her one more time, and then I would go. I got out of the car and went over the fence again, heading for the garage. But I was too slow. The bedroom curtain closed just as I walked up. I turned in time to see headlights stopped at the gate. I ran behind the garage and made my way back to the car. There were now three cars parked in the driveway. A sound check of each room let me know that there were at least ten people in the house other than Mrs. Childers. She was still upstairs alone. I sat there for the next ninety minutes listening and trying to place voices with names. Picking up on Chilly was easy. He was the loudest, and did most of the talking. "I don't think I like him."

Chilly announced that he was going to bed, and awhile after that, most of the people left. I got pictures of each of the players as they came out of the house. The lights stayed on downstairs, but I didn't hear Chilly's mouth. I switched to their bedroom.

"*Gee, you sleep?*"

"*I was. Do you always have to turn on every light in the room?*"

"*I gotta see.*"

"*I know, but why every light? All you need is one.*"

"*Yeah, well, you'll be a'ight.*"

I heard Mrs. Childers mumble something under her breath. But I couldn't make it out.

"*I thought you were coming to the club tonight, Gee?*"

"*I just didn't feel like being bothered with all of those people.*"

"So where you been?"

"I went by Chez."

"What y'all do?"

"Nothing."

"Chesará didn't have nothing to do on a Friday night? That ain't possible. What y'all do, Gee?"

"I told you, we didn't do anything. We just talked."

"She's good at that. 'Bout all she good for is talk."

More mumbling from Mrs. Childers.

"I want you to do something for me tomorrow."

"I have plans for tomorrow."

"Well cancel them. This shit is important."

"And what I have to do isn't?"

"Nope. Just more of your usual bullshit."

"It's your usual shit that's bullshit," she whispered.

"What you say?"

"Nothing, Chilly. What do you want me to do?"

"You just be dressed and ready to go by eleven."

"Yes, your majesty."

"That's right. I'm the King here. Your ass be forgettin' that shit sometimes."

There was a long silence. Then, *"Stop!"*

"You the one that needs to stop."

"Stop it, Chilly. I'm tired."

"Come on, now."

"No, I said I was tired. --- Ouch! --- You're hurting me."

"Stop fightin' me. --- Come on now."

"All right, all right. Go ahead."

It was pity pussy time.

I hate it when that happens.

There was more silence. Followed by a few minutes of Chilly grunting like an animal. Mrs. Childers made no sound. I imagined her lying under him, eyes closed, wishing it were over.   Then, *"The least you could do is move, Gee."*

She didn't answer.

"Ahhh!"

I started my car and went home. I was sure now. I don't like him.

Chapter Three

Friday, July 10; 7:04 AM

I called Jett and told him to meet me at Monika's house so I could tell them about the case. When I got there, I laid it all out for them. I left out the part about me listening while Chilly forced himself on Mrs. Childers. "Come on now, Nick," Monika said. "We ain't no real private investigators. This is just a cover. What you know about finding somebody anyway?"

"It's no different then them slip trace jobs we did," I said, pleading my case.

"Sounds like fun to me," Jett said. "Besides, Monika, what else do we have to do?"

"Shut up, gray boy," Monika said, rolling her eyes at Jett. "You got a weird sense of what's fun." Monika frowned at me. "What are you gonna do now?"

"I wanna go back to Jake's apartment and have another shot at his computer. And I could use some help."

"I'll go with you, Nick," Jett said, enthusiastically. Which saved me the trouble of trying to convince him. "Come on, Monika, it will be a blast. Do something different for a change."

"Let's go, Jett. I want to get finished at Jake's in time to pick up a tail on Chilly around eleven."

As we started out the door, Monika said, "Y'all wait up."

"Thought you weren't interested?" I said, smiling at her.

"I'm not. That don't mean I'm not part of this team," she said grabbing her bag and joining us at the door. "Somebody has to keep you two fools out of trouble."

On the way to Jake's I filled them in on what happened there the night before. "Any idea who hit you or what they hit you with?" Monika asked.

"Don't know who it was, but I'm pretty sure it was the butt of a gun. Heavy caliber, forty five maybe."

"You know what this Chilly guy carries?" Jett asked.

"No, but I can find out. I'll ask Mrs. Childers."

"You got a picture?" Monika asked.

"No."

"You don't have a picture of the guy you're looking for? How do you expect to find him?"

"Oh, him."

I handed Monika the picture of Jake and Chesará at the party. Both Monika and Jett looked at me like I was crazy. I thought they wanted a picture of Mrs. Childers.

"Not bad. That the client, Nick," Jett commented as he dissected the picture with his eyes.

"No, that's the client's sister."

"What does the client look like?" he asked.

"An older version of her."

"What's her name?"

"Chesará."

"Wouldn't mine tailin' her. If you know what I mean."

"See, that's why I'm here," Monika said, as we arrived at Jake's. "Nick already got his nose up ones ass. Now you dyin' to get your head up the sistah's ass."

"Calm down, Monika," I said.

"This is a serious matter. These people are drug dealers, and if they are involved, they're not gonna think twice about killin' you for stickin' your nose in their business."

"I was thinkin' more about stickin' other parts of my anatomy in her," Jett said, still looking at the picture of Chesará.

Once we got to the door, I went to work on the lock. "Don't you have a key?"

"No, Monika. I don't have a key." I replied, as I opened the door and went inside.

"That is breaking and entering. Now we're about to tamper with evidence in what may be a crime scene. How much she payin' us?"

"Ten thousand, to get us started. There's more if we need it. Money is not an issue."

"Still, I don't like the way this is goin' already."

"Tell you what, Monika," Jett said, as he prepared to hack into Jake's files. "If shit gets too thick, we'll let you blow up the building."

"Very funny, Jett." She looked around the apartment. "This place is cleaner than my house."

"Yeah, Mrs. Childers said he's kind of anal like that."

While Jett worked on the computer, Monika and I searched the apartment again. "I'll have it in no time, this is pretty simple stuff. Just hack into this password file and - - - damn! It's encrypted."

"Pretty simple stuff," Monika said.

"Yeah, he'll have it in no time."

Monika looked in the bedroom, while I went through his file cabinets and the mail. Ten minutes or so had gone by when I heard Monika say, "Well now, what do we have here?"

"What you got?"

"Safe."

"Where?" I asked, joining her in the bedroom.

"In the closet under this box. Guess you missed this, huh, Nick." Monika started digging in her bag for something.

"What are you looking for?"

"What do you think I'm lookin' for? Something to get this safe open."

"Jett, come open this safe, before she slaps some C-4 on it."

"Na, C-4 would be too messy for that small a safe," Jett

said, while he wrote a program to decrypt the file.

Monika gave us the customary rolling of her eyes and attached a small device to the safe. "Bet I have this safe open before you get the password."

"You're on," Jett yelled.

"Beat ya. Ha, ha."

"That wasn't fair."

"What you white folks know about fair?" Monika asked.

They were fun to work with. Even though Jett thinks Monika is mean, overbearing at times, and has a tendency to be a pain in the ass. And she holds Jett personally responsible for the sins of the white man; they would do anything for each other. That's why we're alive today. On our final mission, Monika fell on approach to the objective. Her ankle was broken and she couldn't continue. She wanted us to leave her, but Jett refused. While the three of us had a philosophical debate over the need to follow orders and proceed to the objective, the objective blew up. Jett got on the radio and tried in vain to raise any member of our unit. They were all dead. Jett's loyalty to Monika saved our lives.

Monika handed me some papers from the safe to go through while she examined the rest of the contents. She opened a box that had a large envelope in it. It contained pictures and three videotapes. "Hey, Nick."

"Yeah."

"Who's that in the picture?" she asked, pointing at the picture next to the bed.

"Lisa Ellison. That's his girlfriend."

"Then who is this?"

Monika handed me the pictures. "Damn. When Mrs. Childers said he was anal, I didn't think this is what she was talkin' about."

Monika laughed. "Looks pretty anal to me."

All of the pictures were of Jake having sex with the mystery woman. In an interesting variety of positions. "I'm willin' to bet these tapes are more of the same."

"Got it!" Jett yelled.

I took one of the less intense pictures of Jake and the woman, and joined Jett at the computer. "What's in those files, Jett?"

"You did say this guy was a chemist. Formulas, looks like. And each doc. file has a corresponding spreadsheet. I'll make a copy and show it to a guy Monika knows."

"You done, Monika?"

"Just about. I need to take pictures of some of these papers. They look like formulas too. If we can find out what he was working on, maybe we can find out what happened to him."

"Very good. Nancy fuckin' Drew here."

"Fuck you, Jett."

"Two things prevent that," Jett said, as we left the apartment and headed for the car. "Good taste, being one of them."

"What's the other, Jett?" I asked, expecting a snappy come back.

"It would be too much like fuckin' your sister."

It was eleven thirty when we arrived at the Childers residence. We were late, but so were they. We parked the car to the sound of Chilly yelling. *"I ain't gonna call you no more, Gee! Get your ass down here right now so we can go!"*

"Go without me, then!" Mrs. Childers screamed back.

"You just get your ass down here, right now."

"You set this up, Nick?" Jett asked.

I nodded, trying to hear the argument.

"Not bad work. A little staticy, but not bad. You set up cameras too?"

"No, but I got pictures of each room."

"We need to go over those pictures. It will make it easier to complete the set up."

"No time now. I gotta follow them. Find out what was so important that she had to go with him."

"Get your head out her ass, Nick. You go with Jett. I'll follow the happy couple."

I started to insist that I had to go, but she was right. The sooner we could go over the pictures, the sooner we'd have the place covered.

When Mrs. Childers came to open the gate, we got out, and Monika took off behind the Childers. Me and Jett went back to the office to develop the film. "How'd you get in, Nick."

"Simple alarm and cheese ball locks."

For the next hour I went over the set up of the house with Jett. Once he was satisfied with my review of the set up of the house, he prepared to implement his plan to maximize coverage. "Where are you going?"

"To see Lisa Ellison. Then I thought I'd talk to the sister."

"Not without me, you're not."

"Jett, you heard what Monika said, and she was right. I know these people, some of them I probably know personally. They will kill us for involving ourselves in their business."

"Come on, Nick. We can handle them."

"I know you're a tough guy and all, Jett. But we are out-numbered and out-gunned." The way I left Black. "We need to be a step ahead of them all the way," I said, as I armed myself. I did know these people, and when the guns started coming out, I wasn't about to be the last one to pull his. "We need to stay on task. So, I'll go talk to the sister. And you get your head out that woman's ass and set up the surveillance."

Chapter Four

"So you and your partner are strung out on these women," Wanda said.

"I wasn't strung out on her, Wanda. I thought she was a very attractive woman, but I think strung out is a little strong."

"Okay, Nick, whatever you want to call it."

"Wanda, I - - -"

"Anyway, Nick. You left Jett, and you were on your way to talk to Lisa Ellison."

"Yeah, but I was thinkin' that we were gettin' ready to go up against Chilly and his crew. But other than Mrs. Childers' *feeling*, I had no other reason to suspect him. That wasn't good enough. If I was gonna play private investigator, it was time I started investigating, and consider the possibility that Chilly wasn't involved. I still thought covering the house was a good idea, just in case he was."

"That was a good idea. So where did you go after that?"

"To see the sister."

"What's her name?"

"Chesará Rollins."

Chesará lived on Manhattan's, Upper East Side. None of that suburb shit for her. When I arrived at her building, a doorman met me. He announced my arrival and asked Miss Rollins permission to send me up. She consented to see me and I was on my way up.

She opened the door wearing a blue silk robe, "Hello, Mr. Simmons." And as near as I could tell, nothing on under it. "So you're Gee's private detective. I've been expecting you."

"Can I come in?"

"Of course. Please make yourself at home."

"Thank you, Miss Rollins. I'll try not to take up a lot of

your time. I just have a few questions to ask you."

"I'm all yours," she said, locking her arm in mine and leading me into the living room. She led me to the couch and sat next to me. "Tell me what I can do to help." She looked a lot like her sister. Only her look was soft and playful. Not the hard edge her sister had. Jett would be losin' his mind right about now. As a matter of fact, I was having a hard time maintaining my composure, and her hand on my thigh wasn't helping.

"When was the last time you saw your brother, Miss Rollins?"

"The week before last. He was on his way to Gee's house."

"He come by here often?"

"Often enough. Maybe once or twice a week."

"Jake like to travel much?"

"Jake, no. He never went anywhere. Unless you call goin' to Jersey traveling."

"Has he ever been gone this long before without you or your sister hearing from him?"

"No. Like I said, Jake is over here at least once or twice a week, and he calls just about everyday. I think Gee is right, that bastard she calls a husband had something to do with it."

"What makes you say that?"

"If you ever met Chilly, you'd know what I mean. He's an asshole. I wish Gee could get away from him."

"I guess you don't like your brother in-law much."

"That's a good guess. But hate him would be more like the truth of the matter. The way he treats Gee is terrible. I wish he were dead."

"Okay. Other than that, any reason why you think Chilly is involved?"

"When Jake left here he said he was goin' to see Chilly.

Then he disappeared. Chilly is, well, - - -. He's a drug dealer, but I guess you already know all of that."

"Your sister did mention that."

"I'm sure Gee told you alotta stuff. I know I would tell you anything you wanted to know. You married?"

"No." I smiled and she licked her lips. "I've never been married."

She went cleavage on me. "Good for you."

"Do you have any idea what your brother was goin' to see Chilly about?"

"No, Jake never talked to me much about what he was doin'. I always thought that all those computations and calculations was pretty boring stuff. I like things, and men, that are a bit more exciting in my life."

"Just what excites you, Miss Rollins?"

"One day, when you have some free time, I'll have to show you just what excites me." She smiled at me and stood up. The sash of her robe came free. "I'm going to get a drink. Can I get you something?" she inquired, as she took her time retying it.

"Johnnie Walker Black, straight up." I was wrong. She had on a blue bra and panties under the robe, but they were see-through. She turned and walked over to the bar. "You know Jake's girlfriend, Lisa Ellison?"

"Yeah, I know her."

"You talk to her much?"

"We speak when I see her. Which isn't very often."

"Are they close?"

"If you're asking me if she was the only one he was seeing, I couldn't say. Jake keeps his business to himself." She sat down and handed me my drink.

"You know who this is?" I handed her the picture.

"Ooooh, Jake." She looked up at me and smiled. She handed the picture to me back. "No, Nick, I don't know

67

who she is. You show that to Gee yet?"

"No. But I will next time I see her."

"Rocky might know who she is."

"Rocky, that's Jake's friend from Philly. You know him?"

"Sure, I know Rocky. He used to live down the block from us. Him and Jake ran track together. He works for Chilly now."

"What does he do for Chilly, Miss Rollins?"

"Chesará, please, Chesará. Say it with me, Chez - a - ráy." I smiled and laughed a little at her. "He sells dope for him. I hear he's a good earner."

"This is a very nice place you have here."

"Thank you. I decorated it myself."

"You have excellent taste."

"In more ways than you can possibly imagine." Chesará said, and repositioned herself on the couch.

I chose to over look the tone of her remark. "What do you do, Chesará? You a part of the family business?"

"No. I'm not part of the family business. Gee pays for all this. Didn't she tell you?"

"No, she didn't."

"Well, Nick. You mind if I call you, Nick?"

"Not at all."

"Good." She declared, and moved closer to me. "I hate to be so formal. But like I was sayin', I have no desire to be involved in their business."

"Just spend the money," I said with a smile.

"You know what they say, Nick, OPM."

"OPM?"

"Always use other peoples money."

"You something else, girl."

"You talk real nice to me and I just might have to show you just what that something is."

"You talk real nice to me and I just might think about

letting you. But I have work to do first."

"Hmm. Go ahead, keep talking. I like the way you work. But I warn you, I like to talk."

"So I've heard."

"Gee say that about me?"

"No, she didn't."

"Then who?"

"I have ways of finding out things I need to. That is, like, what I do. Find things out about people."

Chesará tipped her head and looked strangely at me. Why don't you just tell her that you have her sister's house bugged and her brother in-law said that about her? I didn't mean to say it, but it was out there now. The telephone rang.

"Hello."

Saved by the bell.

"Hi, Gee."

It was her. I tried to hear what she was sayin', but I couldn't.

"Your private dick is here. You sure know how to pick them."

Whatever Mrs. Childers was sayin' to her, it wiped the seductive smile off her face.

"Bye, Gee." Chesará hung up the phone. She looked at me, the seductive smile returned just as quickly as it left. "That was Gee on the phone."

"Really, what did she say?"

"That I should stop tryin' to flirt with you and cooperate."

I smiled.

"You like my sistah don't you, Nick?"

"What makes you say that, Miss, I mean, Chesará?"

"The funny look you get on your face anytime I mention her."

"How do I look?"

She made a funny face and laughed. "You know, eyes all glazed over. Gee has that effect on men. So do I."

"I noticed."

"Once we have a man, it's hard for him to resist us. Like this guy Gee kicked it with for awhile. He just won't leave her alone."

My back stiffened. "What do you mean?"

"If Gee knew I told you this, she'd freak." Chesará repositioned herself on the couch, which only proved to expose more cleavage. She was flirting even when she wasn't. "While Gee was in St. Martin, she met this guy at the hotel bar. He was there with his wife and kids. Well, he told Gee that he was from Brooklyn. Owned a Used Car lot on Utica Avenue. He gave her his card. So Gee called him and they got together a few times. Now he won't leave her alone."

"Why doesn't she want to see him anymore?"

"'Cause he can't fuck. Gee said that he couldn't keep it up long enough to do anything for her. Gee said she rocked the house two times and he came."

"Don't you hate it when that happens?"

"I'm sayin'."

"Why doesn't she just tell him that? If a woman ever said that to me, I'd stop bothering her."

"But no woman's ever told you anything close to that, have they, Nick?"

"No. They haven't."

"I bet you put on a good show for a sistah." There she goes with her hand on my thigh again. "But I promised Gee I'd stop flirting." She didn't move her hand though. "She did tell him that. Told him to his face that his dick was little and he couldn't satisfy her."

"How'd he take it?"

"Bad. So now he's blackmailing her."

"Blackmail?"

"That same night before she told him that, somebody took a picture of them. But right before the picture gets snapped, this fool kisses her."

"Now he wants money or he'll show it to Chilly," I said.

"And Chilly will kill her."

"What's his name?"

"Ben Josephs."

"Did she pay him?"

"Of course she did. But now he wants more."

"How much?"

"She gave him five thousand dollars the first time, and ten more last night. She just told me that he wants another twenty."

"Where would I find him?"

"I don't know where he lives, but I guess you can find him at the car lot he owns in Brooklyn."

"Why are you telling me all this, Chesará?"

"'Cause if you really like Gee, you'll take this guy off her neck."

"Maybe I'll talk to him."

"If you do, don't say anything about me telling you this to Gee. She would be mad at me."

"It'll be our little secret."

"Something we can share. I like the thought of that."

"Thanks for seeing me, Chesará." I stood up and finished my drink. "And for the drink."

Chesará stood up; her sash came free again. She didn't bother to retie it this time. She locked her arm in mine and walked with me to the door. "You come on back when you have more time. To *talk*."

"I just might."

"You make sure that you do. You'll find me to be a

71

brilliant *conversationalist*. People tell me that I'm *very* oral, when the conversation is stimulating."

"I'd be interested to see."

Wanda shook her head disapprovingly. "I see you still have a way with the women, Nick." She mentioned. "Why didn't she just come right out and say she wanted to fuck you."

"I don't know, Wanda. Why don't you ask her?"

"I don't think so, Nick. I learned a long time ago not to mess with you and your women."

"What's that supposed to mean?" I demanded, but she and I both knew she was talking about Camille. Now why she wanna go and do that?

"Nevermind, Nick. What did you think of the sistah? Other than the obvious, I mean."

"What do you mean?"

"Open up, Nick. I'm not Kirk. This is me, you know, Wanda. I'm only trying to help you. We go too far back for you to be so defensive with me, Nick."

"I'm sorry, Wanda."

"I just wanted to know if you thought she was telling you the truth, that's all."

"I thought so. I didn't think she had any reason to lie about what she told me."

"It seemed like she wasn't all that concerned about her brother being missing. I think she was more concerned with gettin' her freak on with you."

"Whatever gave you that impression?" I smiled.

"Come on, Nick. *Very* oral. If that wasn't an invitation to come back and get some head, I don't know what it was. I'm very oral."

"Like you said, Wanda, I just have that affect on women."

"Yeah. I guess you do."

Chapter Five

The more I thought about it, the more I knew that I needed to know who and what I was up against. I knew where to go, but I wasn't sure if I wanted to go there. Freeze would know, I knew he would. Freeze always knew everything about everybody. If he didn't know, he either knew how to find out or it wasn't worth knowin'. It had been ten years since I'd seen Freeze. Ten years since I had tried to close the door on my past. Maybe it was time to re-open the door.

Besides, I was hungry and I hadn't eaten anything all day. So I drove to Cuisiné. I entered the supper club and looked around for Freeze. I was surprised at what a nice place it was. Nothing like the spots we used to run back in the day. Not seeing Freeze anywhere, I allowed the hostess to seat me at a table.

"Is Freeze here?"

"Who?"

I smiled and continued to look over the menu. "Just tell Freeze that Nick Simmons would like to see him."

The hostess walked away.

It wasn't too long before I looked up and saw Freeze coming toward my table. In a suit no less. "Nick! What's up?"

"You tell me. You're the man. In a suit no less."

"Fuck that suit shit. How the fuck are you, man?" Freeze sat down and motioned for a waitress. Two responded to his motion. "What are you drinkin', Nick?"

"Johnny Black, straight up."

"Bring me the usual. You hungry, Nick?"

"Yeah, I haven't eaten all day."

"You see anything on the menu you want? Never mind, I know you'll eat anything," Freeze said, turning his attention to the waitresses. "Alexia, tell Al to make whatever he's best at for Nick, and you know what to bring me. You, get the drinks."

"Do two waitresses always come when you call? And what's up with the suit?"

"Hey, this is a legitimate, upscale supper club. I gotta look the part. But nevermind all that, Nick. What's up with you?"

"I've been all right, man."

"Damn, it's good to see you, Nick. You should come around more often."

"You know what's up with that."

"That stupid shit between you and Bobby." Freeze shook his head. "You need to let that shit go."

"Has Bobby let it go?"

"Not far as I know. He doesn't talk about it. He gets all quiet and shit when you bring it up."

"Then it's still on."

Freeze laughed. "Yeah, I guess it is. But that shouldn't stop you. You and me been through too much."

Knowing Freeze was right, I let it pass without comment. "How's Black?"

"Doin' good. Island life agrees with him."

"When's the last time you talked to him?"

"Talked to him this morning." Freeze announced, as our drinks arrived. "Black calls me every morning. He likes to keep his hand in. You know how Black is. Shit ain't changed."

"He get up here much?"

"Every once in awhile. He don't like bein' away from Shy for too long."

"I can't believe Black's strung out like that."

"You ain't seen Shy."

"She all that?"

"She's worth the price of admission. You oughta go down there. Ain't like you ain't been invited."

"Black don't wanna see me. I called him a few times when I got back, but we never hooked up. Then he was gone."

"Shit was crazy back then for him and Shy." Alexia returned with our food, Prime Rib. I started eating it like I hadn't eaten in weeks. "You think Black is still mad at you 'cause you left?"

"Ain't he?"

"Hell, no. He wasn't mad at you, not really anyway. He understood why you felt you had to go like that. What Black couldn't understand was why you joined the army to fight for the government when your homies was fightin' a war right here. But he respected your decision. Shit, Black respected you. Said you were the most disciplined man he ever met."

"I was a solider even then. That's why he made me work with you. Your ass was wide-open back then. Wanted to blast everybody."

"Damn near did."

"Black thought you needed discipline. And he was right, but look at you now."

"A lot's changed since you been gone."

"I see this. This is really a step up from The Late Night."

"Damn, The Late Night. I haven't thought about that place in years. We had some good times, - - -" Freeze paused and looked at me. I guess he remembered the last time I was there. "And some bad times." Freeze laughed a little. "Anyway, this ain't that type of place. The Late Night was just that. A late night hang out. We are marketing to a different clientele."

"Listen to you."

"Wanda taught me to say shit like that. When I took

over the spot after Black went to the Bahamas, some of my old road dogs started hangin' out here. They were gettin' to be bad for business. Wanda lost her fuckin' mind, dog. Said they were scaring off the regular clientele. She's a trip, but she was right. She's right about most things. She made us a ton of money over the years. Anyway, I know you didn't come here just to talk about old times. What's poppin'?"

"You know somebody named Alvin Childers?"

"Chilly?"

"Yeah, Chilly."

"I know him and so do you. He used to deal for André back in the day. He's the one who made peace with Black, and they set up the dead zone. Bitch nigga had to make peace, 'cause Black was gonna blast that ass next. Now he runs most of the drugs uptown. What's your interest?"

"Business. His wife is my client."

"Gee. What Gee hire you for?"

"Find her brother."

"Didn't know Gee had a brother."

"Didn't think you would. He's not part of the family business. His name is Jake, he's a chemist."

"Never met him, just her sistah, Chesará."

"I just left her."

"She's a bad mutha fucka."

"So I noticed."

"Wild as hell. Into everything."

"I could see that, yeah."

"Pussy was good though."

"You fucked - - -" Freeze looked at me like I was stupid. "Nevermind. She got anything to do with the family business?"

"No, she's totally on Gee's card. You think Chilly had something to do with it?"

"Mrs. Childers does."

"If Chilly did have somethin' to do with it, your job is easy. All you gotta do is find the body. Chilly likes to make his shit real public. Make a statement, like André used to, you know what I'm sayin'." Freeze laughed. "I know you do, that used to be our thang. Remember?"

I laughed. "Yeah. I remember."

"So let me get this straight. Gee hired you to find her brother. Gee don't think Chilly's involved, Gee knows he's involved. So what does Gee want with you?"

"So I can prove it to the cops."

"Nick. This ain't nothin' you want any parts of."

"I see this. I'll leave it alone."

"You a lyin' mutha fucka, Nick."

I got up from table. "Thanks for dinner, Freeze."

"Nick."

"Yeah."

"If shit gets wild," Freeze stood up. "I'm with you."

"Thanks, Freeze."

I left there thinking about Black.

Whether he respected me or not, the truth of the matter was that I ran out on him when he needed me most. But I wasn't about to let Bobby kill me just to save face with Black. But in spite of all that, Freeze was still for me. It would make my burden just that much heavier. It started me thinking about the old days, the old crew. Black and Bobby. Jamaica and Freeze. I thought about the first time Black told us he was going to kill André. We knew he was planning something big when he called a meeting at The Late Night. Black never had meetings. In spite of that, we were late. Waitin' on Freeze, of course.

"I bet you all are wondering why I got you all over here," Black said, as soon as we came through the door.

"The thought had occurred to me," Bobby said, staring

at me. The way he was looking, I knew then that he knew about Camille and me.

"I'm gonna kill André." Black declared.

There was complete silence in the room.

We all sat there looking at Black and one another, until Bobby started laughing. Everybody did at first, until we noticed Black wasn't laughing.

"You serious, Black?" Freeze asked.

"Deadly." Black flashed a rare smile.

"How you gonna do it?" I asked.

"What you gonna do? Just walk into his office and blast him?" Bobby inquired, but his eyes were still on me. Then he slowly turned to Black.

"No. I have a plan," Black said.

"You plannin' on taking over after he's dead, Black?" I asked.

"The gambling and the houses, yes. But I'm gettin' out of the dope game."

Nobody was really surprised by that. We'd all seen it coming. After Vickie died in his apartment smoking cocaine, Black turned totally against drugs.

"We'd be givin' up a lot of money, Black. I don't think that's good for business." Bobby said.

"Maybe. No. You're right, Bobby, it's not good for business. We'll just have to find different ways of making money. But when I walk around here and I see what it's done to the neighborhood." He looked at Jamaica. "To people. I just can't be involved in that anymore. Anybody who wants to is free to do whatever he wants once this is over. As long as you don't do business around here."

Black looked around the room.

"Bobby, you with me? I can't do this without you."

"You don't even have to ask me, you know I am," Bobby said.

"Even though it's not good for business?" Black asked him.

"Business will just have to suffer."

"Anybody else?" Black asked.

No on said a word.

"All right then. My plan is based on the fact that for every action there is a reaction. If certain things happened, I can get people right where I need them to be. Now, there are enough people who hate André to go around. Cops won't care, and as long as business doesn't suffer, no one else will care either."

"Just as long as everybody continues to get paid, you're right. Nobody will care." Bobby added.

"We have to kill Ricky. Him and André started out together. He'll try to take over. Benny and Dupree are loyal to André, so they gotta die too. And that's it. Now if André dies, Cazzie will try to move on us. So we have to kill him too. Killin' Cazzie will be harder, but not impossible."

"Go on." Bobby said.

"All right now, everybody pay attention. Benny and Dupree are the key to it all. They make the rounds every night to collect the money from all the houses. On Friday nights there's more than a quarter of a million dollars. They start at one o'clock, and by three thirty they'll be coming out of the last house. That's where we'll hit them. Nick, you and Freeze will be waiting for them. As soon as they get to the car, you and Freeze blast them. Nick, you cover while Freeze gets the money."

"Done," I said. Good soldier, you know.

"Now, Benny and Dupree are dead and the money is gone, what's gonna happen next?" Black asked.

"Somebody will call Ricky's punk ass." Freeze said.

"Exactly. Someone in the house will call him to tell him about the robbery. Ricky will be at his after hours spot.

Sitting in that office, just like he does every night. As soon as he gets the call about the robbery, he'll call André and they'll meet at André's office. Bobby, when Ricky comes out of the office and starts to make his way through the crowd, you and Jamaica take him then."

"What about Cazzie?" I asked.

"He's the wildcard in all of this. Problem is, there's no way I can control his movements the way I did everybody else."

"Black," Jamaica said. "Let me take care of Cazzie. I know how to take him."

Black looked at Jamaica for a long time. He knew Jamaica was off the chain with that heroin. We all did. "Okay, I'll leave that all to you, Jamaica."

"What about your boy, André?" Freeze asked.

"When he gets to his office, I'll be there waitin' for him. Now for this to work, everything has to run on schedule." Black gave me, Bobby, and Jamaica a pager.

"What're these for?" Bobby asked. "I already got a pager."

"When you complete your assignment you page the next man. Three sevens if everything goes as planned. If anything goes wrong, you page the next man with all nines. When it's over, we all meet here. Anyone get nines, we abort and meet back here. Any questions?"

It all worked out just like he planned it. Except for Jamaica disappearing, it all went off clean and easy. When he didn't show up afterwards at the Late Night nobody really gave it much thought. We all just figured he was off somewhere getting high. Like I said, we all knew Jamaica was off the chain with the heroin since Vickie died. He and Vickie were real close. Used to get high and hang out all the time. But, shit, hangin' out was all Vickie ever wanted to do anyway. I laughed out loud.

"What's so funny?" Wanda asked.

"Nothing really. Just thinking about Vickie."

"Vickie? What brought that on?"

"Been thinkin' a lot about the old days. You know. How Vickie died and the effect it had on things."

"It affected all of us."

"Yeah, I guess, but not like it did Jamaica. How is he anyway?"

"He says he's all right, but the last time I talked to him, I don't know, there was something funny about the way he was talking. Something about his tone brought me right back to when Vickie died."

"Where is he?"

"He's in the Bahamas. Black says he has gotten himself into a few things down there. I just hope that whatever he's into doesn't involve drugs, is profitable, and doesn't cause any of us any grief."

"You think he's back on?"

"I don't know, Nick. It would be a real shame, because he worked very hard to get himself clean. But Jamaica wasn't the only one who took Vickie's death hard. The one who took it the worst was Mike."

She was definitely right about that. And to be honest, I can't say I would have been any better. After all, she died in his apartment. Overdosed on pure cocaine he had there. Black never did any caine, but those days he would always keep some around 'cause women would do all kinds of shit for it.

But that night we were hangin' out and Black saw Andre' and he gave Black some pure. Black didn't get home until nine the next morning. He said he was getting ready to put a cut on it, but he was blasted and didn't feel like it. So he threw the bag on the coffee table and crashed on the couch. He had been asleep a couple of hours when

Vickie came in. They kicked it for a minute, and then Black passed out again. When he woke up again and decided to get in the bed, the door to his bedroom was locked. Black knocked on the door but Vickie didn't answer. So he kicked the door in and found her laying on the floor naked with the pipe still in her hand.

After that it was like something snapped inside of him. You wouldn't know it to see him or talk to him, but that was when he really earned the name, Vicious Black. The first time I really noticed it he had called me and said, "Come scoop me up, I gotta make a run." Whenever he said that, we knew he was going to either collect some money for André or hurt somebody for not paying. And you hated to see Black coming, 'cause you knew why he was there, and it was all bad. I picked Black up and we were on our way to see an old hustler named Wilson Goode.

"So what's up with good old Mr. Wilson?" I asked.

"He owes André fifty large," Black replied.

"For what? Wilson's a pimp. How'd André get his hooks into him?"

"Says Wilson came to him, wanting to borrow fifty grand. You know at twenty-five cents on the dollar Andre' was more than happy to front it to him. When he couldn't pay, André put that ass to work. But he's been playin' Andre off for a couple of weeks now. Cynt said that Wilson was at her spot late one night and he dropped ten grand playing poker. Said he had some young girl with him."

"Young girl and an old man, cause of trouble since the world began," I said laughing.

"I thought it was a two faced woman and a jealous man."

"Whatever, Black." We both laughed.

"I know the little honey he got himself hooked up with," Black said. "She's a fine ass bitch."

"Can I fuck her?"

"Don't waste your time. She thinks she is too pretty to move. Wasn't even worth the time it took for me to get undressed."

"I hate it when that happens."

When we got to Wilson's apartment I knocked on the door, but nobody answered. "I know he's in there. I hear them talking." Black stepped up to the door and listened for a second or two, then he put both of his hands on the door and pushed it. "Move back." Then he took a step back and kicked it in. Black stepped aside and I ran in with my gun out. Black followed me in calmly with his hands in his coat pockets. There was Wilson and two very pretty young ladies. Both of them were naked, and all Wilson had on was his underwear. On the coffee table was cocaine. Some rock and some powder and two or three pipes.

"What the fuck!" Wilson shouted. "What the fuck you mutha fuckas doing here? And my fuckin' door! Ya'll gonna fix my door."

When Black saw the dope on the table his eyes narrowed.

"Black! You hear me talkin' to you nigga! Black! What the fuck is goin' on here?"

But Black didn't answer. He just stood there staring at the dope.

"Andre' sent us," I finally said. "He wants his money."

"I'm a get him his money, Black. I just need a day or two to make some things happen. You tell him that."

"You two get dressed and get outta here," Black said to the women.

"They ain't gotta go nowhere. Ya'll ain't gotta go nowhere. They were just about to leave."

"I ain't gonna say it again." And with that, both ladies got up and went in the room. "Go with them, Nick." I did so, gladly.

While I was in there watching the ladies get dressed, I could hear Wilson yelling at Black, but Black never said a word. Once I escorted the ladies out, Black took a gun and a silencer out of his pocket. "Search the place, Nick. Find me some money." Black put the silencer on the gun, but the whole time he's staring at the table. I put on my gloves and tossed the place.

By this time, Wilson's whole attitude had changed. Now, with the ladies gone, he was beggin' Black to give him a couple of days to come up with the money.

"I found this under the mattress," I said, handing Black twenty grand.

"Black, I need that money to make this thing happen, for real. Give me 'til tomorrow, Black. I'll make it worth while for both of you."

Black stood up. I started for the door thinking that Black would just take the money and be back on that ass again tomorrow. But not this time. Black raised his gun and fired two shots to Wilson's head.

This is how it went. André would send Black to collect, and Black would kill them. After awhile, André finally sent Black away before he killed everybody that sold for him.

Wanda yawned and got up from the couch. "I'm going to get some coffee, you want some?" she asked.

"No, Wanda, I'm fine."

She turned away and walked into the kitchen. I watched her walk. Even though we had spent the last nine hours together, this was the first time I noticed how pretty Wanda was. Not the tall skinny girl we used to tease as kids. Before yesterday, it had been ten years since I had seen her. And I probably wouldn't have called her if I weren't in this trouble. I felt pretty selfish. She had spent the night fencing with Kirk. I know she's tired, but she has no plans for sleeping until she has the whole story. Black posted a million dollars to bail me out. They were my family and I would never turn my back on them again.

"Sure you won't have some?" Wanda said, with a deep yawn.

"I'm sure. Why don't you get some rest? I know you must be tired. Get some sleep and we'll start again in the morning when you wake up."

"I don't think so, Nick. You wanna know why?"

"Yeah, Wanda, tell me why."

"Because as soon as I went to sleep, you would leave and I'd never get the whole story. And I need to know the whole story. You do understand that, don't you, Nick?"

"I understand, Wanda."

"Good for you. Which reminds me. Why didn't you tell me about killing André?"

"Black said not to. He said if you ever asked, to ask you if the words conspiracy to commit murder mean anything to you counselor?"

Wanda rolled her eyes. "That's the same ten cent answer I got from him. Even though it didn't turn out that way."

"What's that supposed to mean?"

"Nothing."

Wanda looked away. Whatever it was, it was something to her, but I didn't push it. "Black's always thinking ahead, ain't he? Always thinking about us."

"That's just how he is, you know that. He cares. Even though he'll never admit to it. That's why this thing with you and Bobby hurts him so much."

"I'm sorry."

"Why don't you tell him yourself?"
I didn't have a reason.

Chapter Six

Saturday, July 11; 3:28 PM

The next afternoon I drove to Brooklyn to see Ben Josephs. I gave some thought to what I was doing. I was driving to Brooklyn to see a blackmailer. In Brooklyn, of all places. I hate Brooklyn. I pulled up in front of the lot. I didn't want to just walk in there and ask for him. So I decided to call and pose as a businessman who wanted to buy no less then five cars for a Limo service. That should be enough to get him to meet me somewhere. "Ben Josephs, please."

"He's out on a test drive with a customer. Can one of our other salesman help you?"

"He's not the owner?"

"No, Sir. Can one of our other salesman help you?"

"No, that's all right, thanks."

Just a salesman, huh. Men will say anything to get some pussy. But the plan is still sound. What salesman could resist a five car afternoon? So I parked my car across the street and walked up on the car lot. When a short balding white man approached me, I went into my act. "Hi there." Big smile, hand extended, "My name is Patrick Mitchell."

"Well, Mr. Mitchell, what can I show you?"

"Those Cadillac's there. I need five of them. I was looking for Ben Josephs, is he around?"

"He's right over there. I'll get him for you, Sir."

He practically ran to tell him. And good ole Ben did a trot over to me. "Mr. Mitchell." Big smile, breathing hard, hand extended. "I'm Ben Josephs, what can I do for you?" After what Chesará told me about his performance in bed, I had to bite my lip to keep from laughin' in his face.

"Well, Ben. You don't mind if I call you Ben?"

"No, Sir. Not at all."

"I run a Limo service and I need to buy five of your Cadillac's there."

"I'd be happy to show them to you, Sir."

I'll just bet that you would Ben. To sell me five Cadillac's you'd probably kiss my ass from here to across the street.

I test drove one car, I liked it, I thought about actually buying it. Then reality set in and I remembered why I was there. I got out and picked another Caddy. Ben threw me the car keys.

"You drive," I said, throwing him back the keys.

"Huh?"

"I wanna see if it's comfortable in the back seat."

"Okay. Yeah, this is for a Limo, right?" Ben asked.

We got in and Ben drove away. "What do you drive, Ben?"

"Black Legend."

"Ooooh."

"Yeah, boy, the women really go for it."

"Probably the only way a *can't keep it up mutha fucka* like you can get a woman."

"What you say to me, nigga?" Old Ben turned around and looked into the barrel of my 9.

"I said, it's probably the only way a *can't keep it up mutha fucka* like you can get a woman."

"Yeah, man, whatever you say. You can have the car. Please, just don't kill me. I got a family."

"Calm down. I don't want the car, Ben. But there is something I want from you."

"What, man?"

"You have a picture I want."

"What picture?"

I hit him in the back of the head. Not hard. I didn't want him to wreck the car. "Don't insult my intelligence,

Ben. The picture of you and Mrs. Childers. You're gonna give me that picture, now. You're gonna give me any copies you have, and if there is a negative, I want that too. And if I hear of you ever tryin' to contact Mrs. Childers again, I'll kill you. Slow. You feelin' me, Ben?"

"Yeah, man, I feel you."

"But to show you what a nice guy I am, Ben, I'm gonna let you keep the money you blackmailed outta her. All I want is that picture."

"I don't have it with me."

"Well, where is it?"

"At my house. I can get it for you tonight and bring it to you."

"I don't think so, Ben. Let's just go there now and get it."

"I can't go now. I don't get off work until six."

I looked at my watch. It was almost four. "I guess we'll be test driving cars for the next couple of hours, huh, Ben."

For the next two hours, Ben chauffeured me around Brooklyn and we got better acquainted. He wasn't a bad guy, for a blackmailer. He was ex-army. If it wasn't for the fact that he was blackmailing Mrs. Childers, we could have hung out.

Once six o'clock rolled around we got in Ben's Legend and he drove to his house. He lived in a nice house in the East New York section of Brooklyn. "Wait here, I'll be right back," Ben said, and started to get out of the car.

"Yeah, right." I got out too.

"Wait a minute, man. My wife and kids are in there."

"What's your point?"

"I don't want her involved in this business."

"Good, then you'll be a good boy and get that picture. I'd hate to have to kill your wife and kids, but I will. Now let's go."

Ben unlocked the door to the house and we went in. The house was immaculate and smelled of dinnertime. "Your wife a good cook, Ben?"

"Yeah, good down home cook. Met her when I was stationed at Fort Mac in Georgia."

"Ben!" His wife yelled from the kitchen. "That you?"

"Yes, Renée."

"You're home on time for a change. You must not be feelin' well." She came out of the kitchen; she was a pretty woman. Naturally pretty, not done up, you know. No make up or fake nails. None of that. "I'm sorry, didn't know you had company." She came toward me with her hand out. "I'm, Renée, Ben's wife."

"Patrick Mitchell. It's a pleasure to meet you."

"We were just about to have dinner. Have some?"

"No, I just came to get something from Ben and then I have to go, but everything smells delicious."

"We're having fried pork chops, baked macaroni and cheese, candied yams, collard greens, corn bread and freshly squeezed lemonade."

"Mmm, sounds good, but I really can't. But maybe you'll give me a rain check?"

"That's right, honey, Mr. Mitchell has to go."

"Nonsense. You know you want to. I can see it in your eyes. You look like a man who appreciates a good meal. You married, Mr. Mitchell?"

"Please call me, Patrick. And no, I'm not married."

"When was the last time you had a home cooked meal?"

"I couldn't even tell you."

"Then it's settled, I insist."

"Well since you put it that way, Mrs. Josephs, I accept."

"Good. You just have a seat at the table. Ben, you call the children." I looked over at Ben as his wife went back in

91

the kitchen. The frown on his face let me know how he felt about me staying for dinner. He rolled his eyes and went to call the children to dinner.

Everything was wonderful; I made a complete pig of myself. She really was a good cook. Ben was pretty quiet during the meal, as one might expect for a man in his position. But Renée was a very entertaining conversationalist. Ben had a nice family, two very polite kids, Robert was ten and Grace was seven. After dinner, they excused themselves. Renée got up and cleared the table. "Ben always has a brandy after dinner. Would you like one?"

"Thank you."

"What you think you doin'?" Ben whispered.

"Having a brandy after dinner, - - - with Ben." As soon as his wife and the children were out of eye and earshot, I took out my gun. "You go get those pictures. I'll be in the kitchen with Renée."

Ben got up and walked away, while I joined Renée in the kitchen. "I just wanted to thank you for twisting my arm and having me to dinner, Mrs. Josephs."

"Please, call me Renée."

"Well, Renée, everything was wonderful. Where did you learn to cook like that?"

"I'm a country girl. My grandmother taught me. Didn't you know, all us country girls can cook like this."

"Where you from?"

"Flowery Branch, Georgia. I know you never heard of it."

"No, I can't say that I have." I laughed, as Ben returned with an envelope. He handed it to me and I opened it to verify the contents. I thought Ben was gonna faint. "Well, people, I really do have to go now, but, Ben, Renée, thank you very much for having me."

"It was our pleasure havin' you." Renée said, leading me by the arm to the front door. "Anytime that you're in the neighborhood, promise me that you'll stop by."

"I don't get out to Brooklyn much, but I won't hesitate to stop by if the need arises. Right, Ben?"

"Right," Ben said, as he walked out the house.

"Pleasure meetin' you, Renée." I smiled seductively, her left eyebrow went up, and she blushed.

Once we reached the sidewalk, I stopped and turned to Ben. "That's a real nice family you have there, Ben."

"Thank you. You got what you came for, now get out of here." Tryin' to sound tough.

"Renée seems like a good wife. Too nice for you to be cheatin' on her and blackmailing women."

"Yeah, sure."

I took out my gun again and pointed it at his head. "Don't act tough, Ben. You deserve to die for what you've done, and I will come back here and kill you if I hear that you've even called Mrs. Childers again. Get me?"

"You won't."

"When were you supposed to see her again?"

"Tonight."

"Where and when?"

"Ten o'clock at *Halcyon*."

And with that I walked to the train station.

Chapter Seven

Halcyon, on Smith St. in Brooklyn. I got there a little before ten and went inside. I looked around for Mrs. Childers, but she was nowhere to be found, so I took a seat in the back of the room so I could see the entrance. It was about eleven twenty before she finally showed up. She was wearing a powder blue dress that showed off her legs, naturally. Mrs. Childers had a seat at the bar, looking around for Ben. She ordered. For the next half hour I sat and watched her. I wanted to be sure that Ben didn't have a change of heart and show up. During that time I watched as she dismissed man after man who approached her. The list was long. Knowing I wouldn't fall prey to the same fate, I got up and approached her. I tapped her on the shoulder. "Mrs. Childers." She turned quickly and smiled when she realized who I was.

"Nick."

"Mind if I join you?"

"Well." She scanned the room again. "I was supposed to be meeting somebody here, but I guess they're not going to make it."

"Then this must be my lucky day." I sat down next to her and signaled for the bartender. "Johnnie Black, straight up. Can I get you something?"

"Hennessy Martini, with a twist."

"So tell me, Mrs. Childers, what man would be foolish enough to stand up a beautiful woman like yourself?"

Mrs. Childers turned away and made one last look around the room for Ben, shrugged her shoulders, and turned to face me with a smile. "Who said I was waiting for a man?" She lit a cigarette. "So, Nick, have you found out anything about Jake?"

"Not really. I did have a chance to look around his

apartment. Do you know if he was working on something?"

"No. I really didn't get into all that stuff he was into. A little too far over my head."

I reached in my pocket and took out the picture of Jake and the mystery woman. "Do you know who this is in the picture with him?" I handed her the picture. She glanced at it for a second.

"I've never seen her before. Where did you get this?"

"That doesn't matter. Has he ever mentioned dating any other woman, other than Lisa Ellison?"

"I'm not my brothers keeper. He's very private."

"So how do you know Lisa?"

"He's been seeing Lisa for years now. He brings her around to parties, family gatherings, things like that."

"Now let's talk about you, Mrs. Childers."

"Me? What about me?"

"You haven't exactly been honest with me."

"What do you mean? I've told you everything I know."

"About your husband, Mrs. Childers."

"Chilly. What about Chilly?"

"Well, Mrs. Childers, he's a little more than just involved with drugs. He controls most of the drug traffic uptown."

"And?"

"Don't you think that was worth mentioning?"

"Yes."

"Then why didn't you?"

"I didn't want to scare you off."

"I don't scare easily, Mrs. Childers. But that does change things."

"You want more money." She frowned and looked away, then turned back with fury in her eyes. "Is that what this is all about? Money?"

"No, Mrs. Childers, it's about you telling me what I

need to know to do what you hired me to do."

"What do you want to know?"

"Well, let's start out with what I know and you can fill in the blanks. Chilly was a forth-level dealer for André Hammond until him and Ricky Combs were assassinated ten years ago. Vicious Black declared a dead zone where he wouldn't allow them to sell drugs." Mrs. Childers sat up straight in her chair. I had her attention now. "Stop me if you want to add something."

"No, you're doing just fine." She lit another cigarette and played with the straw in her drink.

"When Jimmy Knowles, Charlie Rock, and Vincent Martin attempted to kill Black, that started a war between him and what remained of André's and Cazzie Riley's organizations. Well, Black was successful in eliminating his enemies and Chilly took over. He made peace with Black and agreed to respect the dead zone."

"How do you know all this?"

"I have my sources, Mrs. Childers. So with all that history out the way, let's begin again. Why do you think that Chilly has something to do with your brothers disappearance?"

"Like I said, it's just a feeling, that's all." I could tell that I was making her uncomfortable, but she was cute when she squirmed, so I continued my line of questioning.

"That's not good enough, Mrs. Childers, there must be something else. Something you're not telling me. I've heard that if Chilly had something to do with this, I should be looking for a body."

"Don't say that, please. Jake is not dead."

"How do you know that? You know how your husband works. Public execution is his style. So if he were involved, a simple kidnapping wouldn't cut it. Now you tell me, what did Chilly want to see Jake about?"

"I don't know!" she said louder than she needed to. I finished my drink and waved the bartender on to bring me another.

"And one for the lady?" the bartender asked.

"No, I've got to go," she said, standing up to gather her things.

"No, please don't go. I didn't mean to upset you, Mrs. Childers. I just need to know what you know. Please, have another drink with me. I promise I won't push you."

She smiled at me.

It made my heart beat fast.

"Okay, but just one, then I really do have to go." Mrs. Childers reclaimed her seat and ordered. "Bring me another Hennessy Martini."

"With a twist," I said and smiled. And she smiled back. "So tell me about yourself. Your sister tells me y'all are from Philly. How'd you get to New York?"

"I wanted to get out of Philly." She let out a little giggle. "Had to really. Our parents were really tough on us. Never let us go anywhere, do anything. It was like being on lock down. One by one, they drove us all out of the house. When Jake graduated from high school, he just never came home that night. No one knew where he was or what happened to him, he was just gone. About six months later he came to my school to let me know that he was all right and that he was going to college. He told me where, and he made me promise that I wouldn't tell our parents. Said they didn't have a son anymore."

"Kinda cold."

"They deserved it. They're dead to me now. Two years later, I left too. I hated to leave Chez, but she was too young for me to try to take care of both of us. So I did what I had to, to get enough money to get up here."

"What did you have to do?"

"That doesn't matter. I'm not proud of what I did. That was a long time ago. It's in the past and that's where it will stay."

"How'd you get hooked up with Chilly?"

"You really want to hear this, huh? - - - Okay. So I caught the first thing smokin' and came here. When I got off the bus at Port Authority, Chilly was the first person I met. I was young, barely sixteen. Never been anywhere and he offered me the world. He was nice at first, then." Her eyes dropped into her drink. "That war started and changed everything. Power changed him. I was just his showpiece, his toy. Something to show off to his boyz. But that was all show. Then the beatings started."

"Why don't you leave him? Get away, go somewhere, start a new life for yourself."

"Sure. Just like that."

"Leave New York.

"I have, a few times, but he always finds me. Brings me back," she said matterafactly. "Or he gives me a reason to come back."

"How does he do that?"

"He hurts the things that are important to me."

"Chesará and Jake."

"Once I thought it was over. I went to Kansas City. I didn't tell anybody where I was going. I got a job as a teller in a bank. They were even talking about promoting me to customer service. You know, sit at a desk, open accounts, that kinda stuff. I had been there for six months when he found me. I told him I was happy and I wasn't coming back. Usually he - - - yells, he grabs, shakes me, hits me. But I was ready for that. He was going to have to kill me. But he said okay and left. But it wasn't over."

"I didn't think so."

"The next day Chez called me crying. She said Chilly

brought Jake to her apartment and he had a gun to Jake's head. He told her that if I didn't say I was coming back right now, he was going to kill both of them while I listened. I said no. Then I heard the gun go off. Then Chez screamed and said he'd shot Jake in the leg. I was back the next day."

I didn't know what to say.

"You want more? I got more stories just like that one. That was just one of his masterworks. That's why you have to get proof that will stand up in court. I've seen him go to jail and come right back."

"Now you're talking like you think Jake is dead."

"I don't like to think about it. I know it's possible. The longer he's gone, the more I think about it." Her smile was gone. I thought I saw a tear run down her cheek, but she wiped it away quickly. "So, you tell me your story, Nick?"

"Well, there's not much to me. Ex-army, we've been doin' this for about a year now."

"We?"

"I have two partners."

"They have names I'm sure." Her smile had returned as quickly as it left.

"Monika and Jett."

"Monika? Lady private detective. I used to read Nancy Drew when I was a little girl."

"I used to read Mickey Spillane mysteries."

"You have any family?"

"Yeah."

"Doesn't sound like you guys are one big happy family."

"Not them, me."

"I see." She finished her drink. "Looks like there are some things you don't like talking about either. Good night, Nick."

"Good night, Mrs. Childers." What else could I say?

Chapter Eight

Sunday, July 12, 8:19 AM

The next morning I arrived at my office to find Monika waiting for me. She had followed Chilly, and I not only wanted, but needed to hear her report. On the way home the night before, and on the way there that morning, I gave some serious thought to this thing I was developing for Mrs. Childers and my promise to leave other men's women alone. No one really understood, and I never tried to explain it to anyone, except Monika. She understood. Over the years that promise has kept me from becoming seriously involved with many women. Seems like the women I take an interest in are all married, living with a man, got a man back home or whatever.

Thoughts of that night haunt me like a bad dream that never goes away. I know I'll never forget that night. Bobby with his gun in my mouth, screaming that he was gonna kill both me and Camille. It should have never happened. But I was gone too far gone. Camille had me, and I couldn't leave her alone. I knew when I met her that she was with Bobby, but it didn't seem to matter to me. It definitely didn't matter to her. I had never met any woman like Camille. She was fascinating to be around and to talk to. And her voice, the way she spoke with that Barbados accent, *Shit!* It simply blew me away. Her dark complexion, her flawless body, and those dark eyes. The way she'd look at me when we'd make love. For too long after that, when I'd close my eyes, I'd see those eyes looking up at me.

It began the first time I saw her. I was with Black in his office at The Late Night when she came in with Bobby. Camille walked right up to me. "Bobby, introduce me to this handsome specimen of a man."

Bobby's eyes narrowed when he looked at her. "That's, Nick."

That look was my first warning, but I ignored it and each warning that would follow. Camille stepped closer, put her left hand on my chest and looked up at me. "That's no way to introduce somebody, Bobby. My name is Camille Augustus. It is a pleasure to make your acquaintance, and what is your name?"

"Nick Simmons." I answered, and quickly backed up off her. But she had me then and she knew it. Each time I saw her after that, Camille made that point clear.

When she'd call me I'd come.

What she wanted, I got for her.

What she said, I did, without so much as a kiss.

I was riding with Black the night Camille decided she would have me. She paged me at 2:45 in the morning and I quickly called her back.

"Come see me, Nick. I want to talk. We never have enough time to sit and have a chat."

"Now?"

"Of course, now. Now is when I want you." Camille hung up the phone and I turned to Black.

"Booty call," he said.

"No, just a chat."

"Yeah, right. Nobody calls at damn near three in the morning to just talk. Talk about fuckin' maybe."

I don't know if he knew where he was dropping me off and at the time, I didn't care. I knocked on her door, but there was no answer. Maybe I had taken too long and she had fallen asleep. I waited awhile and knocked again. She opened the door dressed in a red gown and robe, which left nothing to the imagination. "Come in, Nick. I was beginning to think that you weren't coming."

We talked and laughed until the sun was shinning brightly the next morning. I admired her beauty, the way her dark skin over powered the red of her gown. Camille commanded my attention in more ways than one. Then she touched my hand and drew me to her. I ran my hand across her shoulder. "Kiss me, Camille." She patted my hand and stood up. "Stand up, Nick." I complied. Camille looked up at me and undressed me without breaking eye contact. I stood naked before her and she ran one hand across my chest while the other glided effortlessly along my length. She gently grabbed the back of my neck and drew our lips together, but only for a second. Camille eased me back down on the couch and ran her tongue over her lips. Then Camille introduced my length to her moistened lips. Her eyes still locked in mine. She slid her lips across what seemed to be every inch of it. Then she smiled and opened her mouth. It was soft and wet; if she had teeth I never knew it. She moved her head up and down in a very slow almost methodical motion. My excitement only intensified as I watched her, watching me. It was like slow motion, prolonging each stroke.

"Nick!" Wanda yelled.

"Huh?"

"Try to stay with me here. This is a little too important for you to be day dreaming."

"I'm sorry, Wanda, I was just thinking, that's all."

"You were just telling me that you went to your office to meet Monika and Jett. And - - - "

When I arrived at the office, Monika was there waiting.

"It's about time you dragged your ass in here," Monika said.

"Report."

"Yes, Sir." Monika smiled and rolled her eyes. "I followed them to *Aureole*, a restaurant on East 61st St. They met a man and a woman, both of Hispanic decent. The male was approximately five feet ten inches tall, dressed in a two piece dark blue suit, light blue shirt and enough jewelry to make you notice. The female, approximately five six, red dress, fuck me pumps. I got video and still pictures, they should be ready soon."

"Video?"

"Yes video. Jett gave me these photo sensitive sunglasses with a micro-miniature camera. The images are recorded using a standard video recorder, or it can be fed into a video transmitter in a remote location."

"Have to start callin' that boy Q."

"You keep givin' him money, he keeps buying new shit. Anyway, I was able to drop a bug on the back of Chilly's chair. There's the transcript."

"Anything we want?"

"Maybe. Page five. I circled it."

"Hispanic Male: *I took care of mine, Chilly. What about yours?* Chilly: *Not yet, should be another day, maybe two. But I don't see a problem here.*"

"It's pretty thin, right?" Monika asked.

"You're right. He may be talking about Jake, maybe not. There's just not enough here."

"The rest of the conversation was just small talk."

"Okay. You stay on Chilly. See where that leads us. Anything on those files. You find out what that formula is for?"

"Nothing yet. I should hear back from my guy sometime today I hope."

"Let me know as soon as you hear from him."

"What about you? What did you do?"

"Talked to the sister, Chesará. Other than trying to flirt, I didn't get anything we didn't already know. You heard from Jett?"

"Said he'd be here early. He could be here soon."

Almost on cue, Jett came through the door.

"Morning, people."

"Report."

"I'm fine, Nick and how about you, Monika?"

"I'm fine, Jett." Monika giggled.

"Report."

"Completed surveillance set up of the house. I was able to pick up cell phone frequencies for Chilly and two guy's that appear to be his top lieutenant's. I reviewed the tapes of the house. Noda. But that wasn't the highlight of the evening. I copied and reviewed the videotapes we found in Jake's safe. Bad boy, that one."

"Figures, watching other people fuck would be the highlight of the evening for a pervert like you," Monika said.

"That ain't it. I think I found something interesting." Jett handed me two pictures.

"Damn, she got a big mouth. Is that what I think it is?" They were stills he had extracted from the videos. "What's so interesting about this?" I asked, and handed the pictures to Monika.

"Look close. I don't think that's the same mystery woman from the first picture."

"I think he might be right, Nick. I saw a picture of this one too, but she had clothes on so I didn't pay her much attention. And there was a picture with the two of them. Looked like it might have been taken at the same party as the picture you been showing of Jake."

"Where is it?"

"I put it back in the safe."

"Great. I'd rather not show this picture around."

"Guess you gotta go back and get the other pictures,

Nick," Monika said. "Want me to go with you?"

"No, you stay with Chilly." I got up and started for the door.

"How are you and the Mrs. doin'?" Jett asked.

"There's more to this than she's tellin' me."

"How do you know?"

"Just a feeling," I said, closing the door behind me.

I drove back to Jake's apartment, let myself in, opened the safe and got the pictures that I had come for.

"That's Strange."

I was on my way out the door when I thought about the fact that we never found any camera equipment in either of our searches. I went through the apartment again. Nothing. So I walked out of the apartment and two white men in suits met me.

Cops.

"Shit."

"Hold it right there, pal."

"Can I help you gentlemen?"

"Yeah. Assume the position. I'm sure it ain't your first time."

I hit the wall with a little help from my new friends. One looked over my ID and the other looked at the pictures in my pocket. "You mind coming with us?"

"Am I under arrest?"

"No. We just want to ask you some questions."

"What type of questions?"

"We'll talk about that when we get there."

So there I was sitting alone in the interrogation room, waiting. It had been more than an hour before the door opened and Detective Kirkland walked in with that shit eating grin on his face.

"Nick Simmons. What's it been, ten years?"

"Ten years, Kirk.

"Pat, this is one of Vicious Black's old foot soldiers. But he dropped out of sight ten years ago."

"Where you been, Simmons?" Detective Richards asked.

"Army training, Sir."

"Oh. Another smart ass, huh."

"Yeah, yeah, Kirk. What's this all about?"

"I just wanted to see you, Nick. It's been a long time. So when I heard you were in here, I just had to stick my hand in. And what do I pull out? Do you know?"

"No. But I'm sure you'll enlighten me."

"Tell me something, Nick, what were you doing when the detectives picked you up?"

"Visiting a friend."

"They tell me that you're some type of private investigator. You working on something? Maybe something having to do with your friend?"

"Just visiting, Kirk."

"What's your interest in those women in the picture the detectives took off you?"

"They were cute. I happen to like women."

"Why do you say, were?"

"Excuse me."

"I'm sorry. I forgot you went to Vicious Black University. I'll break it down for you. Why are you referring to those women in the picture in past tense?"

"I didn't mean anything by it. Why?"

Richards dropped the pictures I took from Jake's safe on the table in front of me. "What's your interest in these two women?"

"Why?"

Richards drew back his hand to hit me, but Kirk grabbed him. Vintage good cop bad cop. Corny, but I played along. "What's with him, Kirk? I just wanted to know why. Am I being changed with something having to do with those two women?"

"Nick, I know you know something you're not telling me. I'm thinking that since you call yourself a private investigator, that you got a case and you're trying to protect your client."

"So far your right."

"I thought as much." Kirk pulled out a chair and sat down next to me. "But here's the problem with that, I know more about these two women then you do. So you need to know what I know."

"I'm still with you."

Kirk held out his hand and Richards handed him more pictures. He handed them to me. The same two women, but these weren't taken at some party. These were taken at the morgue. "Both of them died of an overdose of cocaine."

"You think I had something to do with it?"

"No. But one of them had your friends card on her person at the time of her death."

"Were they found together?"

"I will only answer your questions if you answer mine," Kirk said.

"Fair enough."

"What is your interest in these women?"

"I'm trying to find a missing person and I have, or should I say *had* reason to believe that these women may be able to help me find him."

"Jake Rollins, he the one you're looking for?"

"Were the two of them found together?"

"Answer his question!" Richards yelled.

"What's with him, Kirk?"

Richards came at me again, but good cop held him back. "They were found about two weeks apart. Now, Jake

Rollins, is he the one you're looking for?"

"Yes."

"Who's your client?" Richards asked.

"What's your interest in two women that died of a cocaine overdose?"

Kirk smiled. "These weren't your everyday overdoses."

"What do you mean?"

"Who's your client?" Richards asked again.

"That comes under the heading of privileged information." This time Richards swung on me, so I put him on his back.

Kirk grabbed me.

"Get out of here, Richards!" He picked himself off the floor and left the room. Once he was gone Kirk smiled at me like a kid who knew a secret. "What makes these different is that they had all the symptoms of a cocaine overdose, but there wasn't any trace of cocaine in their systems. And there are more just like them. We just found this one last night. Now, what do you know about that?"

"I don't know anything about it, Kirk. I'm just looking for Rollins. I found those pictures in his apartment, and I thought they might know where to find him. I don't know anything about any cocaine." I was lying and I knew it. I knew from the start that this had a cocaine flavor to it and it wouldn't be long before Kirk connected Jake to Mrs. Childers and then to Chilly. But now wasn't the time for me to tell Kirk that. Right now, I had to get out of here and talk to Mrs. Childers.

"Okay, Nick, you're free to go. But I need answers."

"Can I have my pictures back?"

Mrs. Childers had the answers we both needed.

Chapter Nine

I left a message on Mrs. Childers voice mail, telling her to meet me at *Jimmy's* on Fordham Road, "Now!" I drove straight there and waited. She arrived two hours and forty-three minutes later. I'd had dinner, Barbecue ribs with onion marmalade, autumn salad with raspberry vinaigrette and read over the transcript of lunch at *Aureole*, with the Hispanic couple, while I waited. The food was good, so the wait wasn't bad. Mrs. Childers arrived dressed impeccably, as usual. Her make up was flawless, but in good taste. Her eyes were ablaze as she came toward me. Each step she took was taken to send a message. She was mad at me.

"So what's with this *now* business?"

"You want to start telling me the truth now, Mrs. Childers?"

"This again." She gave me attitude and I loved it. "Look, I already told you, I don't know anything else to tell you. My brother is missing. I want you to find him. That's it."

"Good night, Mrs. Childers." I got up from the bar.

"Where are you going?"

She touched my hand. The helpless Mrs. Childers had returned. I continued the game. "I'll have a courier deliver a check for the refund of your retainer." I even started to walk off. She held my hand tighter.

"Please don't go. Sit down, please."

I sat down, trying my best to act like I was reluctant. "Now, you have to start telling me everything you know. Now."

"Nick, I have told you everything I know."

"Okay, lets start with what was your brothers involvement with your husband?"

"I don't know. Neither of them would tell me anything

about what they were doin'."

"What was your brother involved in?"

"This is stupid, Nick. How many times can I say this? I just don't fuckin' know any thing. Jake never told me anything about what the fuck he was doin'. Do you understand me now?"

"This picture was taken at the same party as the picture you gave me. I got it out of your brothers safe." I took out the pictures and handed them to her. "Who are they?"

"This one is Pamela Hendricks. And that looks like LaShawn. I don't know what her last name is. She came to the party with Pamela."

"Does your brother know them?"

"I don't keep up with all of Jake's friends."

"Does your brother know them?"

"I guess he does. I really don't know, Nick, please." I like the way she says my name. "He might have met Pamela at some party. And LaShawn runs with Rocky, so he probably knows her too."

"What were they doin' at the party, Mrs. Childers? Who invited them?"

"I did."

"Who are they? How do you know them?"

"I've known Pamela for years. She was my supervisor at the bank when I was in Kansas City."

"What does she do, fly in for parties?"

"No, Pamela got a job at Manhattan Bank as an Area Manager and she moved here years ago."

"Banker, huh. She have any involvement with your husband?"

"Not that I know of. She knows him, naturally. But I don't involve myself at all with Chilly's business. So even if she did have some business with Chilly, I wouldn't know it."

I was starting to believe her. She really didn't know anything or she was giving me an academy award winning performance. Either way, it didn't change anything.

"What's does any if this have to do with Pamela?"

"She's dead." I dropped the morgue picture in front of her for impact. I picked them up along with mine. I figured Kirk must have wanted me to have them since he left them sitting there.

"My God."

"The police think she died of a cocaine overdose."

"The police."

"Yes, the police, Mrs. Childers."

Mrs. Childers reached in her purse and fished out her cigarettes. Her hands were shaking. "Here, let me." I took the lighter and lit her cigarette.

"Thank you." Mrs. Childers inhaled deeply and blew the smoke in my face. "What do the police know about Jake?"

"They know he's missing."

"So they're looking for him?"

"In connection with these overdose's. Pamela had Jake's card on her when the police found her body. LaShawn, whoever she is, died about the same time Jake is supposed to have disappeared."

"And you think that has something to do with Jake disappearing?"

"I don't know, Mrs. Childers, I was hoping you would tell me."

"I don't know." She looked away.

"Well tell me something you do know."

Mrs. Childers looked back at me and smiled playfully. "I know how you know so much," she said, as if nothing that I was sayin' had any importance.

"Excuse me."

"I know some people too, Nick."

"And what are they telling you?"

"That you used to roll with Mike Black. Not only that, y'all came up together. Lived on the same block. They tell me that you were his enforcer. You were good at it too."

"Oh really."

"Yes, really. André's muscle. Let me see." She was having fun with this. Too much fun. But at least she had a playful side. She always seemed so distant. Like there was always something else she was thinking about. But she was all smiles now. "It was you, Vicious Black, Bobby Ray, Jamaica and Freeze. You and Freeze used to work together." She laughed. "So you're no stranger to how Chilly does his business. You used to work the same way. I heard you and Freeze were bad boys back in the day." She waved a chastising finger at me. "The story goes that you and Bobby Ray fell out over some woman and you cut out."

"True story." It made me a little uncomfortable that she knew.

"Tell me about it, Nick."

"You seem to know the story, so there's nothing to tell."

"There's more to your dark side. That the family you don't like talking about, Nick?"

"If you really gotta know, yes, Mrs. Childers, that's the family I don't talk about. I ran out on Black when he needed me most."

"Mike Black," she said in a way that made me a little jealous.

"You know him?"

"Of course I know him, everybody knows Mike Black. After Chilly made peace with him, we got invited to all his parties. He always threw the best parties. He used to have them at some mansion out on the Island."

"I remember those parties. Those were the days. But those days are dead and gone. You and I need to focus on the here and now. I need to know how to find Rocky."

"Rocky doesn't come around much. He just shows up when he needs to. I really don't know how to contact him. Even though he buys from Chilly, he doesn't like him."

"I haven't found anybody who does like your husband, Mrs. Childers. But we'll pass that for now. How does Rocky do business?"

"He usually sends somebody."

"Do you know if he knows Pamela Hendricks?"

"If he knows her, they met the same way, at one of our parties."

"It's not gonna take the cops long to put all this together and tie it all back to Chilly. But that's what you wanted, isn't it?"

"Yes, but there is no evidence. Nick, I've seen Chilly walk in and out of jail too many times to be excited about this. If they pick him up now, it will just make him mad and he'll take it out on me."

"You're right. Rocky is the one who's tailor made to step off for this."

"What do you mean?"

"Two women OD on cocaine, both of them know your brother. Rocky, his childhood friend is a dealer and one of the dead women works in a bank. It has money laundering written all over it. What is Jake's involvement in this? I know. You don't know, but if I do find him, he is poised to take a fall for conspiracy."

"I never thought about it that way. Nick, you just have to find him."

The longing in her voice set me off.

It made my will stronger, more determined to find him. Mrs. Childers was right about one thing, as far as the evidence went; none of this had anything to do with Chilly. The more I thought about the transcript and that thing about problems being taken care of, the more I was convinced that it was Jake he was talking about.

With all that had happened, I had completely over looked the one person who might be able to put all this together for me.

Lisa Ellison.

She would be my target for the night.

I looked at Mrs. Childers. I wanted to stay and talk to her. But I put aside that thought and focused on what I was doing. It was better that way.

"Tell me about Lisa Ellison."

Mrs. Childers rolled her eyes and called for the bartender. "Hennessy Martini with a twist."

Without answering my question, she lit another cigarette and waited for the bartender to return with her drink. I thought about asking my question again, then I decided to rephrase it. "Why don't you like her, Mrs. Childers?"

"Because she's a dizzy air head bitch, who thinks she's the shit, but she's not. She's just a stupid air headed bitch, who's so caught up in her own quasi bourgeois lifestyle, that she don't know her ass from a hole in the ground. The fake bitch."

"So you don't like her, huh?"

"No, Nick, I hate the fake ass bitch."

"What does she do for a living?"

"She works for Armstrong Direct."

"What's that?"

"It's some bullshit marketing firm. She's some type of bullshit director."

"Hmm."

"What's that supposed to mean?"

"It means, hmm."

"You know what I mean, Nick, don't be funny."

"I mean your brother seems to have a thing for professional women with lofty positions. They even look alike."

"That's just how Jake is."

I picked up my pictures. "Good night, Mrs. Childers."

"You're leaving?"

She didn't want me to go.

Maybe she wanted me?

What's more likely is that she's just lonely and wants to talk. I wanted to stay, but I couldn't. "I'm not gonna find your brother sittin' around here."

"Where are you goin' now?"

"Goin' to see Lisa Ellison."

"Well, I guess it is good night then."

"I guess so."

Chapter Ten

Monday, July 13; 1:27 PM

It wasn't easy getting to see Lisa Ellison. Mrs. Childers only knew where she worked and had no telephone numbers for her. First, I got the number and tried calling and was immediately pushed off to voice mail. Then I tried dropping by her office. I introduced myself as Calvin Bailey, but I couldn't get past Gilda, her administrative assistant. She was able to keep me at bay for hours with her enchanting eyes, her inviting smile and her engaging conversation. She also gave me a lecture about dropping by unannounced. "Next time, Mr. Bailey, please, call ahead for an appointment." After three hours, and reading the interesting articles in last months Essence, Gilda informed me that, "Ms Ellison is gone for the day."

Now what I wanted to know was how did she get out? She didn't come past me and I could see the elevator from where I was sitting. So I asked, "How did she get out?" I got more of a story then an answer. Gilda was good. I thought about hiring her. She'd be perfect. "Can I make an appointment to see her tomorrow."

"What time is good for you?"

"First thing in the morning. It has to be first thing in the morning. I have an appointment I have to keep in the afternoon."

"I'm sorry." Gilda smiled, and tipped head to one side. "Ms Ellison is busy in meetings until four."

"That will be fine. I'll see you then." I smiled at her. "Good night, Gilda. It's been a pleasure spending the afternoon with you." I left the office looking around for other ways out of the office. Sure enough, I rounded the corner and there it was. An unmarked door with easy access to the stairs.

Tuesday July 14; 3:00 PM

The next day I arrived at her office at three o'clock. More to talk to Gilda than anything else. I knew I wasn't gettin' in, appointment or not. She informed Ms Ellison that, "Mr. Bailey is an hour early for his four o'clock appointment."

Before I came in, I took the liberty of placing a small camera in position to see the outer door and the door to the stairs. I sat talking to Gilda and watching the view on my laptop. At three thirty, Lisa came out the door and went straight for the stairs. I quickly said goodbye to Gilda and followed her. By the time I got to the stairwell, she was gone. She had probably gotten on the elevator on the next floor. I ran down the steps to try to catch her in the lobby. When I reached the lobby I was exhausted. I used to run ten miles everyday, but not one step since I got out. The elevator doors opened and she came out with the crowd. I followed her outside where she caught a cab. I tried to follow her, but I was quickly reminded that Black men don't catch cabs easily in New York City.

Wednesday July 14; 3:00 PM

The next day I simply double parked across the street and waited for her, like I should have done in the first place. I would get the hang of this private eye thing sooner or later. She came out around seven and I followed her across The George Washington Bridge into New Jersey. Once she cleared the bridge, she headed north on Palisades Parkway and stopped at a little store. Then she headed back into New York to Spring Valley. Lisa pulled into the driveway of a very nice house on Harriet Lane. The garage door opened and closed behind her. No chance of catching her getting out of the car, so I gave her a chance to get settled before I rang the door bell.

"Yes," She yelled from behind the closed door.

"Ms Ellison, my name is Nick Simmons, I'm a friend of Jake's."

"He's not here."

"I know. That's why I'm here. Can I talk to you for a minute? I assure you, I mean you no harm." Reluctantly, Lisa opened the door. "Can I come in, Ms Ellison?"

"Like I said, Jake isn't here. So what can I do for you?"

"Well, that's just it, I can't find him."

"What did you say your name was?"

"Nick Simmons."

"I've never heard Jake mention you, Mr. Simmons."

"Actually, Ms Ellison, I'm not a friend of Jake's. I'm a private investigator and I was hired to find him."

"Jake's missing?"

"Can I come in, Ms Ellison? Really, I just want to ask you a few questions."

"Can I see some type of ID?"

I handed her my ID. She looked me and the ID over carefully before stepping aside to let me in. Lisa led me into the living room.

"Have a seat, Mr. Simmons. Can I get you something?"

"Water would be fine, thank you."

Lisa returned with my water and sat down on the couch. We sat on opposite sides of the coffee table. "When was the last time you saw him?"

"Is Jake in any trouble?"

"No, the person who hired me is just concerned about him, that's all. When was the last time you saw him?"

"Two weeks ago, we had dinner together."

"Did he seem upset or distracted about something?"

"No. Who hired you?"

"I'm not at liberty to say at this time. Have you heard from him lately?"

"I talked to him about a week ago."

"Do you know Alvin Childers? Calls himself Chilly?"

"Yes, I know him. He Jake's brother in-law. What does this have to do with Chilly?"

"As far as I know, nothing," I said very quickly, and with my best fake smile to try to put her at ease. It was obvious that the mention of Chilly's name had changed her mood. It was also obvious that Lisa, like everyone else involved in this thing, was afraid of Chilly. He was just that type of guy. These people hated Chilly. He had touched each of their lives and made it a livin' hell. Mike Black used to always say, "Make people fear, but respect you. Fear and respect last longer than love. People will love you today and hate you tomorrow." I still had another Chilly question to ask. But I decided to save it for later.

Then I changed my mind. "Do you know if Jake had any business with Chilly?"

"I wouldn't know."

"Do you know a woman named Pamela Hendricks?"

"I - - - I - - - never heard of her." Lisa said, then she turned away and began to twirl the ends of her hair with her fingers. "Why do you ask?" Then she flipped it. "Who is she?"

"Just a friend of Jake's." I thought about showing her the pictures. She was obviously shaken by the mention of her name. A picture of her on a slab in the morgue may push her to tell me the truth. And the truth was definitely in short supply with this bunch. The only one who was willing to speak freely was Chesará.

"I never met many of Jake's friends."

"What type of relationship did you have with Jake, Ms Ellison?"

"We've been dating off and on for the last five years. We're pretty close."

"But you haven't seen or heard from him in more than a week."

"Like I said, Mr. Simmons, that's just how Jake is."

"Does he like to travel?"

"Not really."

"So when he's not around for a couple of days, where does he go?"

"I don't know. With my job, sometimes I get very busy and I don't have time to call him either. That's just how we are. Two professional people trying to juggle a career and a relationship."

"Do you know what Jake was workin' on?"

"No. Jake never involves me in what he was doing."

There goes that twirling of the hair thing again. She's lying and I'm getting tired of being lied to. "You know a guy named Rocky?"

"Yes, he and Jake are good friends."

"You know where I can find him?"

"He hangs out at The Spot. It's his club actually. You can always find him there."

Finally, a straight answer. I decided to go for it. "You sure you don't know Pamela Hendricks?"

"No." I showed her the picture of Pamela and LaShawn from the party. "I said, no!" I dropped the picture of Pamela and Jake. She obviously recognized Jake. It hurt her to see it, but I had the feeling that she already knew about it. "I think you should go, Mr. Simmons."

I stood up and gathered my pictures. "One more thing, Ms Ellison. Did you know she was dead?" I dropped the slab shot on her. "Cocaine overdose."

"Get out, Mr. Simmons."

"Can I use your phone before I go? I promise it won't

take long."

"Go ahead."

I called Jett. "Jett, can you hear me?"

Jett had found a house with a basement for rent around the corner from the Childers house and had set up operations, complete with a satellite up link. I knew she was shaken, and as soon as I left she would call somebody, and I wanted to know who.

"I'm on it. Give me two minutes and I'll have it."

"I promised I wouldn't tie up this nice young lady's line for that long, so make it quick."

"I'm going just as fast as I can. Nice young lady, huh?"

"Yes."

"What does she look like."

"Nice piece of business."

"Can I fuck her?"

"I'm not sure at this point, but I'd be glad to make an inquiry as to the feasibility of your request."

"So does she have like big swingin' titties?"

"No. They're practically non existent."

"Flat chested, huh. Well, flat chested ain't bad."

"Maybe, but not my style."

"Probably skinny as a rail too."

"Exactly. But there's some form there."

"Well, you know what they say about skinny girls?"

"What's that, Jett."

"They're all pussy."

"You're too much. How much longer?"

"Almost."

"Heard from Monika?"

"No, but she's on Chilly. He can't fart without us knowin' it."

"She find out what's on those papers?"

"Not yet. But I did ID the guy they had lunch with. His

name is Diego Estabon. Peruvian, supplies Chilly. "

"Anything going on that I should know about?"

"She's at home in bed alone watching TV. She called her sister and they talked for an hour. Small talk. I'll have film and tape at eleven. Got it!"

"You're the man, Jett."

I hung up the phone and I looked at Lisa, she had been doing a small pace back and forth. More like a controlled two step, watching me the whole time I was one the phone.

"You made your call, now get out, Mr. Simmons," she said, as she walked toward the door. I smiled my best fake smile and followed her. "And I'll thank you not to bother me anymore."

"Goodnight, Miss Ellison." I stepped outside, but I couldn't resist sticking it to her one more time. "You sure you don't know Pamela Hendricks?" She slammed the door in my face. I got in my car and headed back to the city to find Rocky. After awhile, I called Jett.

"I don't know what you said to her, Nick. But whatever it was, it must have been one major mind fuck."

"She called somebody?"

"She's on the phone with Rocky as we speak."

"Can you hook me up so that I can hear it?"

"Is the Pope Catholic?"

The next voice I heard was Lisa's. She was practically hysterical. Screaming at Rocky, insisting that he tell her what was goin' on. *"Calm down, Lisa. I don't know what's goin' on!"*

"You know. I know you know. He had pictures."

"Pictures. What kind of pictures?"

"He had pictures of Jake with one of your girls."

"One of my girls? Who?"

"Don't play stupid with me, Rocky! You know who I'm talking

*about. The one that came with Pamela Hendricks to Jake's 30th
birthday party. The one he was all over."*

"Ooooh - - -, LaShawn."

"Yeah. LaShawn."

"Well what did he want?"

"He said Jake was missing and he was looking for him."

*"Wait a minute, wait a minute. Slow down. What do you
mean Jake's missing?"*

"I don't know. He just said he was trying to find Jake."

"He! Who the fuck is he!"

*"He said he was a private investigator, his name is Nick
Simmons. He said they were both dead and that she died of an
overdose."*

Then there was long silence. Like the line had gone
dead.

"What is it, Rocky? You know something. Tell me what is it."

*"Look, Lisa, I really don't know what's goin' on, but I know
how to find out. I'll call you back."*

"Where are you going? What are you going to do?"

"I'm goin' to see Chilly."

This is working out better than I thought it would. He
was going to use the direct approach and ask Chilly where
Jake was. "Call Monika and find out where Chilly is."

"No need, he's at home and Monika just came through
the door."

"I'm on my way." I drove as fast as I could to the
Childers house. All of a sudden, it occurred to me that
Mrs. Childers was in the house and Rocky confronting
Chilly about a private investigator asking questions about
Jake wouldn't go well for her. There was no telling what
Rocky knew. Nor was there any way of telling what Chilly
would do.

I got to the Childers house before Rocky, so I went to the house where Jett was set up.

"Didn't take you long," Jett said.

"What's goin' on in there?"

"The usual. Chilly talkin' shit with his boyz," Monika said. "I don't know if he knows anything about Jake, but I've got pictures and tape of him doing business. Enough that the police could arrest him in the morning for conspiracy to distribute cocaine."

"Nah." Jett threw in. "Any evidence we gave the cops would be inadmissible."

"Where's Mrs. Childers?"

"You can stop worrying, Nick. She went out before he got there."

"Where'd she go?"

"Gee, Nick, she didn't stop by and tell me. She got a call from her sister and she left."

All I could do was wait. Wait for Rocky to drive up and the drama to unfold. I was glad Mrs. Childers wasn't there. If things went badly, I could always stop her before she went in the house. The wait wasn't long. A convertible drove up and the driver got out and ran to the door. Another car pulled up behind him. Three men ran after him. I assume the first man was Rocky. And the men that ran behind him were his crew.

"Showtime," Monika said and leaned forward in her chair.

I was anxious. If Chilly had killed Jake he wouldn't have any problem telling Rocky he did, and kill him if he didn't like it or thought about doin' something about it.

We watched as Rocky pushed his way past Chilly's top lieutenant, Derrick Washington, when he answered the door. *"Rocky? What you doing here?"*

"Get the fuck out my way, asshole! Where the fuck is Chilly?"

Rocky made his way into the living room where Chilly's crew had gathered. Jett scanned the room, but Chilly wasn't in there.

"*Chilly, where the fuck are you? Chilly! Chilly! I know you hear me, you ugly black bastard.*"

"*What the fuck are you hollering about, Rock? And who the fuck you callin' ugly, you punk square head nigga?*" Chilly said, calmly walking into the living room.

"*What you do to Jake?*"

Rocky pulled out his gun and pointed it at Chilly.

"*So you gonna shoot me now, Rock? Is that what's happening here?*"

Everybody in the room pulled out a gun and pointed it at Rocky.

"*Put the gun down, Rock. You don't wanna die tonight. 'cause if you flinch, everybody in this room is gonna shoot you. So they can swear to me that they was the one to hit you with the first shot. Now put the gun down before they shoot you and get blood all over Gee's pretty white carpet. And you know Gee won't like it if we make a mess.*"

It was like watching a drama on TV. Rocky stood there and Chilly stared at him, smiling. Daring him to move. I knew by the look in his eyes that Rocky didn't want to die and Chilly knew it too. Rocky slowly moved the gun away from Chilly's face.

"*You're a smart man, Rock, but you always was. That's why I like you. You got heart, but you're smart enough to know when to back down. Now let's talk about this like you got some sense.*"

Chilly led Rocky into another room. Jett punched it up on screen.

"*Now what the fuck you want?*"

"*What did you do to Jake?*"

"*I ain't do nothin' to Jake. What you talkin' about?*"

"Lisa just called me and said that Jake's missing and somebody came to her house asking questions."

"Yeah. I'm looking for Jake."

"Why you lookin' for him?"

"I wanna ask him something."

"Like what?"

"That ain't none of your business. All you need to know is that if you see Jake, you make sure he sees me."

"It's about that shit ain't it? Told y'all that shit wasn't gonna work."

"Yeah, well. You just find Jake and bring him to me."

"Why? So you can kill him?"

"I ain't gonna kill him."

Chilly got up and stood by the door. Rocky got up and walked toward him. Chilly put his finger in Rocky's face. "Don't you mention anything about Jake bein' missin' or me lookin' for him to Gee. You feel me?"

Even though Rocky didn't answer him, I knew that he felt him. Rocky was scared of Chilly too. He walked out of the room quietly and headed for the door, signaling for his boyz to follow him as he walked out.

"Stay with Chilly," I said to Monika, as I hurried to my car to follow Rocky, and followed him on what turned out to be a slow roll down White Plains Road to Soundview.

Chapter Eleven

I looked at Wanda. Her head was back and her eyes were closed. She had stopped taking notes awhile ago. "Wanda."

"I'm still awake." Wanda answered without opening her eyes. "Where did Rocky go in Soundview?"

"He stopped at a house on Buckner Blvd. I don't know what he went there for, he was only inside for two minutes."

"Where'd he go then?"

"Back to his spot. I followed him there and talked to him."

"Did you find out anything?" Wanda yawned.

"You know, we can stop for awhile if you want to, Wanda. I can tell you're exhausted."

"I'm all right, Nick, really. I just need a quick shower and a cup of coffee and I'll be all right. So why don't you make another pot of coffee while I take a shower."

"Okay, Wanda."

"And, Nick."

"Yes, Wanda."

"Please don't leave."

"Yes, Wanda."

"All right now. I'm trusting you."

While Wanda showered, I made a fresh pot of coffee. While it was brewing I wandered around the house. It was fabulous. "I guess it ain't just drug dealers who know how to live." Just a house in the old neighborhood that Wanda had restored in grand style. Sometimes I used to wonder what my life would have been like if I hadn't cut out. Not that I regret the choice I made. The way things were, I didn't want to live like that, but I wonder. Would I be in jail or dead?

Or would I be as fortunate as my friends and grow old and respectable in the game?

I was starting to feel a little tired myself, so I poured myself a cup of coffee. I went back into the living room and stared out the large picture window. Wanda returned to the living room and stood next me. She looked at me and put her arms around me. Maybe I had that, *'I need a hug'* look on my face. "What are you thinking about?" she asked.

"Just thinkin' about the way things turned out."

"What do you mean?"

"You, Wanda. All this. You're a successful lawyer. You're all so respectable now. Black and Bobby married. Shit, Bobby's a father."

"He's a good father too. You should talk to him."

I chose to ignore her comment.

"Freeze walkin' around in a suit like a legitimate business man."

"That one wasn't easy."

"I can imagine."

"Cuisiné is a nice place. I thought Mike was crazy when he told me that he wanted Freeze to run the restaurant. But Freeze stepped up," Wanda continued.

"I don't think he's happy about it."

"Maybe. He may not be happy, but what he is, is fiercely loyal to Black."

"Unlike me, right?"

"You tell me, Nick? You're the only one who can answer that question."

I walked away from the window and sat down. Wanda followed behind me and reclaimed her spot on the couch.

"Regrets?" Wanda asked.

"No. Not really. I mean, the way things were. Everyday was the same, more violence and more murder."

"The only difference is, your life didn't change. You did

your violence and murder for the government."

"Yeah, right."

"Well, it's true. The Army recognized your skills. Enforcer, soldier, killer, assassin. Call it what you want to, Nick. But they programmed you with their objectives and put you right back to work. But you see, things changed here after André. We were out of the drug business and we started moving into more legitimate businesses."

"That's the part I didn't see coming. When Black said we were getting out of the drug business, I thought it would just be gambling and women and he'd just go right on highjacking trucks and robbin' warehouses. 'Cause let's face it, Black was a thief." I started laughing.

"Always was." Wanda joined me; laughing so hard she almost spilled her coffee.

"Damn the nigga could steal. So I thought that would be it and nothing else would change."

"None of us saw it coming, Nick. But Mike had a plan. Don't get me wrong, after the shooting stopped, he went right back to work, robbin' everything he could get his hands on. But we took that money and started buying property, opening businesses in the neighborhood. We tried to make things better."

"Just like that? Clean and easy?"

"Of course not. We were still running the women and the gambling houses. We still had enemies and Mike still dealt with his enemies in the same old way. But as time went on, that got to be less of an issue. Bobby met Pam, got married and opened Impressions. A few years later, Mike opened Cuisine, and they were both basically out. Freeze started running the day to day operations. And then Mike met Shy."

"Tell me about Shy?"

"She's all right," Wanda said matter of factly and looked

away.

"What?"

"What do you mean what?"

"You know what I'm talkin' about, Wanda. I didn't just meet you. Give it up."

"I don't know what you're talkin' about, Nick."

"Your whole facial expression changed when I mentioned her name." Wanda frowned up and looked away again. "You don't like her, do you, Wanda?" I said and laughed.

"I didn't say that. What I said was she's all right. Anything else you chose to read into my answer is pure speculation on your part."

"Whatever you say counselor."

"It's not that I don't like her, Nick, really. She's a nice person."

"But you're jealous of her."

"No I'm not," Wanda said, but her eyes told a different story. "Me and Mike had our time, remember. And we both agreed that we were better off as friends."

"You must not remember that I was there. So forgive me if I remember it a little differently from that."

"What do you remember?"

"I remember Black saying you two would be better off as friends. I also seem to remember you nodding your head on the verge of tears when he said it."

"You noticed that?"

"Yes, Wanda, I noticed that. I noticed a lot of things about you."

"I didn't think you noticed. I know Mike didn't."

"I always thought you and Mike would make it back, the two of you are like two halves of the same mind."

"I thought so too. But if you breathe a word of that to Mike or anybody else, I'll kill you ,Nick."

"You wouldn't hurt a fly, Wanda."

"That's what you think," Wanda said and smiled. "But anyway, I've adjusted and gotten comfortable with the fact that he's married now and that's that."

"Mike Black married and retired to the Bahamas. Hard to believe, that's all, Wanda."

"Make no mistake about it, Mike still runs things."

"Freeze said he likes to keep his hand in. I kinda figured that's what he meant. But you, Wanda."

"What?"

"I hear you're the mad scientist that made everybody rich."

"It wasn't just me, Nick. Sure, I handled the money, made some good investments, but everybody did their part. We changed with the times, Nick, that's how we all got respectable. Part of what we built here belongs to you. You just need to recognize. And ask for it."

"What's that supposed to mean? What am I supposed to be asking for, Wanda?"

"When you recognize, you'll know what to ask for. Now, let's get back to it. You followed Rocky to Soundview to some house and then back to whatever hole in the wall he hangs at. And - - -."

"And the whole time I couldn't stop thinking about what he said to Chilly."

"It's about that shit ain't it? Told y'all that shit wasn't gonna work."

What shit? What ever it was, it was the missing piece of this puzzle. Whatever it was, it involved this Diego Estabon guy that Chilly met for lunch.

"I took care of mine, Chilly. What about yours?"

Jake was Chilly's and he hadn't taken care of him. It was all starting to make sense to me. Jake wasn't missing, he was somewhere hiding. For all I knew, he could be out of the country. I called Mrs. Childers and told her to meet me later at my office. Then I entertained the idea that Mrs. Childers hired me to find Jake and she would turn him over to Chilly.

"Don't you mention anything about Jake being missing or me looking for him to Gee. You feel me?"

I remembered the fear in those eyes whenever she talked about him. I couldn't be sure. And that's when that programming kicked in. I wasn't there to choose whose right and whose wrong. Pick out the good guys from the bad guys. This was a mission like any other. Mrs. Childers was the client and my orders were to find Jake Rollins. What the client did with him once that was done, was their business.

With a newfound sense of clarity, I went inside to talk to Rocky. I could tell from the stares I got when I walked in, that this was Rocky's spot and I was the only one that didn't belong there. The Spot was crowded with Ballers, male and female, along with the usual array of wannabes and hangers on. Rocky was seated at a table in the back, surrounded by his crew. I stepped up to the table, and guns were drawn immediately.

"I want to talk to Rocky."

I put up my hands and allowed them to take my gun. Thinking that I could take out most of them, if not all them, before they got off too many shots. Unarmed would be little tougher. But I wasn't worried; I always carry a spare.

"Who are you?" Rocky asked smiling.

"I'm the guy Lisa Ellison called you about."

"Let him come!" He shouted, no longer smiling.

I sat down at the table across from him. "I'm looking for Jake Rollins."

"Haven't seen him."

"What was he involved in?"

"Who are you?"

"I told you, I'm the guy Lisa Ellison called you about."

"She said you were some kind of private investigator. Who you workin' for?"

I looked around the table.

With a wave of his hand, Rocky dismissed everybody.

"What was Jake doin' for Chilly?"

"I don't know what you're talkin' about. You got a lot of heart to be involving yourself in this shit. Who hired you?"

"Mrs. Childers."

"Gee hired you, huh? Well if I find out anything about Jake, I'll tell Gee myself."

"Fair enough." I got up from the table, unsure of whether he would he kill me as soon as I got outside. *It's about that shit.* Two women were dead, maybe another, at the hands of Diego Estabon.

I walked over to the guy that had my gun. "Can I have my gun back."

It was a statement, not a question.

The guy looked at Rocky, who shook his head no. So I rammed my left elbow into his face and took back my gun with my right hand. Just in case anyone in the room thought I was going to do something stupid, like try to shoot my way out of there, I held my hands up quickly. My finger was on the trigger just in case I had to. Rocky held up his hand and laughed, so naturally everyone else in the room laughed too. I pointed the barrel at Rocky. Once again, every other gun in the room was pointed at me. Rocky smiled at me and walked forward. He stopped before me. "I like you." He looked around the room. "You got heart." Repeating the words Chilly said to him. His crew laughed. "Let's see if you know when to back down."

I did. But this wasn't the time. I was a player in this game now. I couldn't fold. I had to stand, but not be stupid. I lowered my gun, but just a little, and started backing out of the room slowly. Watching Rocky's eyes. His eyes switched to the right. I felt somebody coming up on me. I quickly extended my arm and caught him in the neck. I was lucky, but they were impressed.

I made it outside without getting shot. I started for my car, but something told me to keep walking. I walked down to the store on the corner. I went inside and looked through the window. Rocky had sent three men after me. Two arranged themselves outside the store, while the third came in after me. Over the objection of the clerk, I went in the back room looking for a door. I opened the door and pushed down a trashcan before moving into the shadows inside the store. As the man ran pass me, I grabbed him. With my arm firmly wrapped around his neck, I had thoughts of breaking his neck, but I didn't. I hit him twice in the head with the butt of my gun.

I went out the back door and moved slowly down the alley. Staying in the shadows. The second man approached. I froze. He walked past me. I watched him pass and he went in the store. They both came out firing blindly down the alley. I aimed and fired a few near misses. They took cover. I continued to fire and moved very quickly out of the alley. I took the long way around the block to get back to my car. The third man held his post outside the store in spite of the shooting. I got in the car and drove away.

Chapter Twelve

When I got back to my office, I immediately checked my messages to see if Mrs. Childers had called, which she hadn't. It was late and she might not be able to get out of the house to meet me. What I had to tell her would keep until morning anyway, because to be honest, it wasn't much. And on top of that it was only speculation. I could only speculate that Jake was hiding. And if Rocky was a man of his word, which I couldn't count on, he would tell Mrs. Childers all about the events of the evening, anyway. Still, I decided to wait awhile, just to see if she would show.

It still bothered me that we never found any camera equipment in Jake's apartment. The pictures and the video were quality. It was obvious that Jake took his photo sessions seriously. I got the pictures from the file cabinet, along with my bottle of Johnnie Black. As I sat there drinking and looking at the pictures, two things hit me all at once. Some of the pictures appeared to be taken in rapid session. Maybe taken with a high-speed shutter. That in itself wasn't all that, but it was the angles they were shot from. The camera wasn't on a tripod, or some other stationary object. Somebody was taking the pictures. Pamela taking the pictures while Jake did LaShawn and vice versa?

"But, no it isn't."

I looked closer at the pictures. It was LaShawn in every picture with Jake. What little outfit there was, may have been different, but it was LaShawn. "Pamela Hendricks, you begin to interest me."

The second was a bit more subtle. The pictures were definitely taken in at least two different places. I popped in the videotape we copied from Jake's apartment. I sat watching, without really watching, fast forwarding for the most part. Comparing the video to the pictures, trying to get a sense of where they were taken. I turned off the video, I had seen enough. I began to sort the pictures into piles based on outfit or the lack of one. The difference in location was apparent now. So if it was LaShawn in every picture, what was Pamela's involvement in this? LaShawn came courtesy of Rocky.

Other than the one picture of them at the party, there wasn't anything to connect her with Jake. Mrs. Childers couldn't say definitely that Pamela knew Jake. The cause of death connected her to LaShawn, but not Jake. Now I needed to know where Pamela lived, and I didn't want to ask Kirkland. The need for Mrs. Childers to make an appearance just became more business than personal. It was better that way. Keep it strictly business.

By two in the morning I had given up on her, and had begun to nod out. "Time to get out of here." But I wanted to finish up my case notes with my new observations before I left.

But my chair was so comfortable.

Thursday July 15; 10:05 AM

The next thing I knew, the sun was shinning bright, and someone was knocking on the door. I had fallen asleep.

"Mrs. Childers?" I asked, as the door opened.

"I'm looking for Nick Simmons." The man said as he walked in the office.

"That would be me. Come in and have a seat, Mr.?"

"Douglas, Marcus Douglas."

"What can I do for you, Mr. Douglas?"

"I'd like to hire you."

"What exactly would you like me to do for you, Mr. Douglas?"

"It's a long story, Mr. Simmons. But I just need some

answers for my own peace of mind."

"You wanna tell me what happened?"

"I'm a lawyer in Atlanta, and about a year ago I ran into one of my old clients. She was in trouble."

"Her name?"

"Yvonne Haggler."

The name sounded familiar. "Go on, Mr. Douglas."

"I'll give you all the details at the appropriate time. She had gotten involved with a man named Paris. Yvonne was working as a courier."

"Drugs?"

"No, nothing like that, at least not to my knowledge anyway. On this particular occasion the package was money and some documents."

"How much money and what type of documents?"

"A hundred thousand dollars in cash and I don't know what was in the documents. They were in some foreign language. I don't know which. But something went wrong." Mr. Douglas told his story and I listened, but my mind was on Mrs. Childers. Wondering why she hadn't at least called. Maybe Rocky told Chilly that she had hired me to find Jake and he did something to her. I was surprised that he didn't want her to know anything about Jake being missing, or that he was looking for him. He didn't seem to be the type of guy that it would matter to. What was going on between Chilly and Jake? What shit wouldn't work? The answer to one would lead me to the other. And that would lead me to Jake. "- - - In your arms was the last thing she said to me. I don't know who the lady was or even if she was the one who did it."

"Have you gone to the police, Mr. Douglas?" It was becoming a standard question.

"Yes, and they can't, or won't help me. So I've spent the last year trying to find out what happened on my own. I found out that Paris was involved in some way with the CIA or some type of covert operation, I'm not exactly sure ---"

I held up my hand to stop him right there. "Mr. Douglas, if the CIA is involved in this, or it has anything to do with the government, my advice to you is to go back to Atlanta and forget any of this ever happened."

Mr. Douglas smiled and let out a little laugh. I didn't think I had said something funny, but he was definitely amused.

"He told me you would say that."

"Who did?"

"Bobby Ray."

"Bobby Ray? How do you know Bobby?" Now I was mad. The last time I saw Bobby, his gun was in my mouth and the last thing he said to me was, *I'll kill you*. Now he was sending me clients.

"I met Mr. Ray a week ago at my family reunion in South Carolina. His wife is my mother's cousin's, cousin's, goddaughter, I think that's how it goes."

"Why'd he send you to me?"

"Mr. Ray said you'd ask that. He said you know all about this black bag stuff."

"Look, Mr. Douglas, I don't know what Mr. Ray told you, but I can't help you. I've got no desire to get involved with anything like what you're talking about." He started that laughing shit again.

"Mr. Ray said you'd say that too. He said to tell you that he would consider it a personal favor if you would look into this for me. And he said if you did, it would make you two even."

Even? He was going to kill me and for all I knew, it was still on his agenda of things to do. But somehow, I still felt some type of loyalty to him.

A personal favor.

I sat back in my chair, scratching my fledgling beard and staring at Mr. Douglas. If I wanted to be honest with myself, I did betray Bobby's trust and I did owe him a debt, and it had to be paid.

"All right, Mr. Douglas. I'll look into it for you. My team is in the middle of something right now, but we'll start to make some inquiries. So let's take it from the top and I think this would be the appropriate time for you to give me all the details."

Once I got finished with Mr. Douglas, I left another voice message for Mrs. Childers. Since I hadn't heard from her, I didn't have much of a choice. I either had to ask Detective Kirkland for Pamela Hendricks address or make my third search of Jake's apartment. I chose the latter. This was starting to get old. I was on my way to search this apartment for the third time, and was starting to realize it took more than just the title to do this type of work.

But I liked it.

So if I was going to continue doin' it, I would have to be more thorough, more organized. As I drove to Jake's apartment, I tried to think where I'd heard the name Yvonne Haggler. It seemed familiar to me, but I couldn't place her. I arrived at Jake's apartment, but this time I was prepared to stay awhile. I brought a camera, tape recorder, and a pad. This time I went from room to room and took pictures of and cataloged everything. I wrote down and recorded my observations, no matter how small or insignificant. Everything mattered. I came across what I was looking for, Jake's address book. There under H, as it should be, I found Pamela's address. Determined not to have any need to return, I photographed the entire book. I was about to leave when I looked out the window. There they were. The police. I should have known that they would have the place under surveillance. I knew as soon as I walked out, they would take me into custody for questioning, and that would be the end of my notes, pictures and the tape would become evidence in the investigation. I turned on Jake's computer and scanner. I could scan the notes, make a wav. file of the tape and e-mail them to myself. But that wouldn't do me any good with the pictures I'd taken. I decided to take my chances with the cops. "Maybe I could put a banana in their tail pipe."

Not a bad idea.

I left the building and headed straight for my car, thinking that if I could get there before they took me, I could get the film into my tail pipe.

Wanda laughed. "Did it work?"

"Yeah. It did."

"I'm dying to hear this one, Nick." The look on her face screamed her disbelief. I'm surprised it worked without me getting shot.

"As soon as I got to the car they were on me. They identified themselves in their usual loud manner. I acted like they had caught me off guard and I dropped my keys. I put the film in the tail pipe and picked up my keys in one smooth motion, then I turned around with my hands up."

"Well you go, boy. Eddie Murphy would be proud of you." Wanda laughed. "Did Kirk give you much grief?"

"Nah, threatened to lock me up for breaking and entering. But he really just wanted me to give him something. Kirk already knew, but he made me tell him that Mrs. Childers was my client."

"Kirk's good, Nick. Very good. How long did they hold you?"

"A couple of hours, more or less."

"What did you give him?"

"Nothing really, 'cause that's what I had, nothing. He had connected Pamela Hendricks to Mrs. Childers and wanted to push the money laundering angle down my throat. But I got the feeling that he really didn't buy into it and wanted to know if I did."

"Did you?" Wanda asked.

"I was starting to, but I needed to be sure." I was starting to get a little tired myself. I closed my eyes and leaned back.

"What else?"

"The coroner still hasn't officially assigned a cause of death in any of the cases." I was getting tired of answering questions.

"Other than Pamela Hendricks and LaShawn, how many more were there?"

"Five."

"He share any of the details?"

"Just time frame." I opened my eyes and Wanda was staring at me. But she looked away quickly. "He said the first five died within a 48 hour time frame. LaShawn died two days later and Pamela died almost two weeks after that."

"I got the impression that Rocky didn't seem surprised to hear that LaShawn and Pamela were dead."

"I got the same impression. And after looking at the pictures, I needed to know what Pamela Hendricks involvement in all this was. I thought that if I knew more about her and why she died, I would be closer to the answers that I needed. Kirk let me go with his blessings to take a look around in Pamela's apartment."

"His blessings?"

"Crime scene. That's where her body was found."

"Ooh."

When I got there, I was met by a uniformed officer who let me in and told me that the scene had been tampered with once already.

"By who?" I asked.

"Seems she had a roommate." The cop said. "Chick named Felicia Hardy. She got in took her stuff, and disappeared."

"Any idea where she went?"

"Nope. She just vanished. She used to be a cop. Quit the force a few months back to go to school full time."

"Any relatives?"

"What do I look like, huh? Check with Personnel."

"Well, you knew all that other stuff." He unlocked the door and I followed him in.

"Yeah, well, Kirk told me all that stuff and said to help you anyway I can. So I figured he wanted you to know."

Kirk was helping himself by helping me. Nevertheless, I didn't think he'd let me have a look at an ex-cops file. I looked around the apartment. As promised, most of the roommates stuff was gone. The room looked like it had been hit by a very focused hurricane. Once I had my gloves on, I rambled through it, looking, but really not expecting to find anything. If she was a cop, she wouldn't leave any clues to where she was goin'. There wasn't so much as a piece of paper. I left the room and closed the door behind me.

Everything else in the apartment was untouched. I looked in the kitchen, there were signs of a struggle. Then at the spot where her body was found. "Do you know if they found any drug paraphernalia?" The officer checked the inventory sheet. "I don't see any." I went in Pamela's room and sat down on the bed. I was sure now that the pictures and the video hadn't been taken here.

Sitting on the dresser was a picture of Pamela and a

woman I'd never seen before. She was pretty, very pretty. It was taken in the living room. Maybe it was Felicia Hardy, maybe not. Since I was collecting pictures, I took the picture out of it frame and put it in my shirt. I would give it back to Kirk if he let me see her file. After one last turn around the apartment, I thanked the cop and left. I figured I'd check out LaShawn's apartment.

"Nick! Nick Simmons!"

I didn't recognize the voice. I turned around. The mailman was walking quickly toward me. "Nick Simmons, how you doin', man?" he grabbed my hand and shook it. It was obvious that he knew me, but I had no idea who this man was.

"I'm okay."

"You don't remember me, do you?"

"I sure don't," I said reluctantly.

"It's me, Reggie."

"Little Reggie McCray."

"Yeah."

"I sure didn't recognize you." Little Reggie McCray was now about six three and all muscle. "And look at you, Reggie. How you been?"

"Been doin' good, Nick. What about you? You look good, prosperous, you know."

"Thanks, man. I been doin' all right, Reggie." Seeing Reggie took me back to the old days coming up on the block. "You get around the way much? How's your mother?"

"She's fine, Nick. Still living in the same house. Me, my wife and my son live upstairs."

"How's that lyin' ass brother of yours?"

"Frankie's dead."

"I'm sorry, Reggie. I didn't know."

"Frankie got shot when Black took the neighborhood to war."

"I'm sorry." I didn't know if I was apologizing because his brother was dead or because I ran out on the war to fight someone else's. It didn't matter, it was probably both and I felt guilty for not being there.

"Don't sweat it, Nick." Reggie said, as if he were absolving me of both crimes. "It was a long time ago."

"Thanks, Reggie." It did make it a little easier. Everyone had moved past those years. Everyone but me. "Reggie, you know the girl that got killed in this building?"

"Yeah, real shame. Pamela was nice people."

"Did you know her?"

"Enough to know she was nice people. I been delivering her mail for seven years. We'd talk sometimes, you know."

"You know her roommate?"

"I seen her. She only been staying here for a few months."

I looked around to make sure the cop was gone and pulled the picture out of my shirt. "That her?"

"That's her. What's your interest in this, Nick?"

"I'm a private investigator. Somehow Pamela's death is tied up in a missing person's case I'm workin' on."

"Oh, yeah. I heard that you started doin' that after you got out the army."

"If I could find out a little more about Pamela, it might lead me to my guy. You wouldn't know if Felicia Hardy filed a change of address card?"

"Cops asked me that already. I told them no."

"I knew it was a shot in the dark."

"I said I told the cops that. And she didn't fill one out. But what I didn't tell them was that a couple of days after that, Felicia met me outside the post office."

"What did she want?"

"She said that she was leaving town and didn't want to leave a forwarding address, but she was waiting on some important mail and gave me a hundred dollars and an address if I'd send it to her and forget about it."

"Where'd she go?"

"LA."

"Can you give me the address?"

"I think - - - wait a minute." Reggie dug around in his bag and pulled out a piece of paper. He handed it to me. "That's the address."

"Thanks, Reggie. I owe you one."

"No you don't, Nick. That makes us even. I been owing you that one for years."

"For what?"

"You probably don't even remember this, but I was at Hafin Park the day that big fight broke out and the DJ kept playing through the whole thing."

"I remember that day. Me and Black were there, but we left before the fighting started."

"Me and some of the other kids from around the way were running around playing and I fucked around and accidentally bumped into some guy from the Valley. Before I knew it, they had snatched me up and was about to beat my ass. That's when you and Black walked up and you told them to put me down."

"I don't remember that."

"I didn't think you would, that's just how y'all was. Always lookin' out for everybody on the block. I remember running home with the other fellas and they was like, 'Yo! Nick and Black was there for you man.' I never did forget that. You know from that day on, nobody would fuck with me 'cause word got around that y'all had my back."

"I guess that does make us even, Reggie."

"One down, one to go. Still haven't figured a way to pay Black back. But he'll need me one day and I'll be there for him." Reggie said, as he walked away to continue his route.

"Hey, Nick!" he shouted. "Come around the way sometime."

"I'll do that. Hey, Reggie. Thanks for reminding me of what I should already know."

Now I had two reasons to go to LA. I also had to look into this Yvonne Hagler thing for Bobby. As I drove back to the office, I looked at the picture of Pamela Hendricks and Felicia Hardy. I didn't think her having to go to LA right away was a coincidence. I gave some thought to what was going on around me. If there was no drug paraphernalia found in the apartment, how did Pamela die? Kirk had to be thinking murder. In an ex-cops apartment.

Once I was back in the office, I left another message for Mrs. Childers that I would be out of town for a couple of days. Then, I called Chesará, but she wasn't home either. Next I called Jett to let him and Monika know what I had found out, which wasn't much, and told him I was going to LA. With that taken care of, I called to make airline reservations and got a room at the Marriott Courtyard near the airport.

Chapter Thirteen

While I was on the plane, I thought about the fact that I had been around the world a few times, but I'd never been to LA. So in addition to the two cases, I decided to do a little site seeing; play tourist. It was late when I arrived at LAX too late to try to see Felicia Hardy. So I rented a car, blue Mustang convertible, bought a map and rolled around to get the feel of the place. Since I was near by, my first stop was Bruce's Place in El Segundo. According to Marcus Douglas, this was the place where Yvonne Haggler settled her business with Paris. I still couldn't shake the idea that I knew Yvonne Haggler from somewhere or had heard her name tossed around. The bartender on duty wasn't working there then, so he had no idea what I was talking about. It had been over a year ago since it happened and I expected the trail to be cold. I had a friend or two out here who I figured might know something about Paris.

Friday July 16; 8:59 AM

By nine o'clock the next morning, I pulled up in front of the Victoria Ave address that I had gotten from Reggie. I walked up to the door and rang the bell. It wasn't too long before the door opened. But just a crack.

"Felicia Hardy?" When she didn't respond, I continued. "Miss Hardy, my name is Nick Simmons and I'd like to talk to you about Pamela Hendricks."

"Just a minute. I gotta put something on," she said and closed the door. I stood there thinking that she didn't have to go to any trouble on my account.

"Come on in." She opened the door a little wider and I stepped inside. I heard the door close and felt the barrel of what felt like a 44-magnum stuck in my back.

I naturally raised my hands.

147

"Just keep walking toward that wall and assume the position." I complied with her request. Felicia proceeded to search me, a very thorough search at that. Not the kind of pat down you'd get from a man. With her gun in her right hand, she ran her left hand over every inch of my body. Which included a handful of groin.

"Huh," she mumbled as she continued.

When she was finished, Felicia had relieved me of my ID and all three of my guns. Most people miss the holster that hangs midway down my back.

Felicia slowly backed away from me. "Now turn around. Nice and slow."

I complied.

Without breaking eye contact, she carefully picked up a set of handcuffs. I watched her move. Her picture didn't do her justice, even in a big tee shirt and sweats; she was much prettier in person.

"Hold out your hands."

Once again I complied with her request. I was impressed as she put the handcuffs on me. Still staring into my eyes. Still pointing that big ass gun in my face. "Sit down over there."

"Thank you," I said, remembering my manners. I sat down in the chair closest to me and Felicia sat across from me.

"Give me a reason not to shoot you and call the police."

"Believe me, Ms Hardy, I mean you no harm. I'm a private investigator. I'm looking into a missing persons case and I believe there is some connection to Pamela Hendricks."

"Who are you looking for?"

"Jake Rollins. Do you know him?"

"For the time being you let me ask the questions. How did you find me?"

"I'd rather not say." She raised the gun. "I saw your file," I lied.

"Bullshit! How'd you find me?"

"Change of address card."

"Bullshit! If you got the information from the post office, the police would be here." She pulled back on the hammer.

"Somebody owed me a favor."

"Reggie."

I smiled.

"I knew I shouldn't have trusted him."

"Don't be too hard on Reggie, he didn't tell the cops. Or anybody else."

"But you, he just up and told you."

"Like I said, he owed me."

"What do you know about Pamela?" Felicia demanded.

"I was going to ask you that."

"It's early and I'm not in the mood for games."

"I know she died of what appeared to be a cocaine overdose, but the police didn't find any traces of drugs in her system. I know you and her were roommates and that you most likely found the body and called the police. I know you used to be a cop." I raised my cuffed hands. "You quit the force to go back to school. How's that going by the way?"

"About Pamela." She lowered the gun, but just a little.

"I know she came to New York from Kansas City to work for Manhattan Bank. But what I'd like to know from you, is who she was, how and why she died, and who killed her?"

"What makes you think I could tell you that?"

"Well, your roommate was most likely murdered in your apartment. You called the police, but you didn't wait around to talk to them. Then you break into the crime scene, take your stuff and come out here. If I wasn't convinced by all that, then the fact that I'm wearing handcuffs and you're pointing a gun at me, pushed me over the edge."

"Is that a fact."

"Was it you who found the body?"

"Yes."

"Why didn't you stay?"

"Who hired you?"

"Jake Rollins sister."

"Which one? The wannabe lady or the tramp?"

"The lady. She used to work at the bank with Pamela."

"What makes you think Pamela knew anything about Jake's disappearing?"

"I've got pictures in my jacket pocket of her with Jake."

Felicia stood up and walked toward me. I was smiling, enjoying the view until she put the gun to my head. "Don't even think about doing anything stupid. I don't mind killing you."

"Believe me, that wasn't what I was thinking about." Felicia carefully removed the pictures from my pocket and returned to her spot.

She rested the gun on the table and glanced at one of the pictures. "LaShawn. I knew the girl was wild, but damn." She glanced at the rest and put them down.

I made note of the fact that even though she had only glanced at them, Felicia knew it was LaShawn and not Pamela right away. "She died two weeks ago under the same circumstances as Pamela. Pamela had Jake's card on her when the police found her body."

"How do you know that?"

"The police told me."

"You're working with the police?"

"Unofficially. I guess you can say that. My guess is they

weren't getting away with linking Pamela to Jake so they threw me the bone."

"Why you?"

"Other than Mrs. Childers being my client, I know a little something about the people involved in this."

"What's that supposed to mean?"

"How long were you a cop?"

"Four years. Why?"

"You've heard of Mike Black?"

"Vicious Black."

There it is again. Why does every woman say his name like that?

"Who hasn't heard of him."

"He's an old associate. Reggie owes him a favor too."

"So you used to run with Vicious Black, huh?"

"Yes," I said, with a newfound sense of pride. "But not for the last ten years."

"Why not?"

"Joined the army."

"So now you're a private investigator and the police have been feeding you information." Felicia stood up again. I was hoping she was coming to take the cuffs off. They were starting to hurt, but she picked up the gun, walked toward the window and looked out. "I didn't think the police had anything." She turned around and came back toward me. It produced the same response as it did the first time. She stood before me and raised the gun. "How do I know I can trust you? I mean how do I know that whoever killed Pamela didn't send you?"

"Then you do think she was murdered?"

"I know she was murdered. Pamela didn't do drugs."

"But that's not why you think she was murdered. Why'd you leave before the cops came?"

"Other than that innocent look in those brown eyes.

Tell me why I should trust you?"

"I can't think of any right now, but if I had to come up with something," I paused to give it the desired effect. "First of all, I wouldn't have come here alone. I wouldn't have let you take me without any resistance. And if I had come here to kill you, I would have just blasted you at the door."

Felicia smiled at me for the first time. She had a pretty smile. Then she laughed a little, but I guess it wasn't enough to make her take the cuffs off. She simply returned to her spot and put the gun down. I was happy for that much.

"Mind if I ask you a question, Ms Hardy?"

"Go ahead."

"You just glanced at those pictures."

"So."

"You can barely see her face in most of them. How did you know it was LaShawn?"

"LaShawn always wears her hair like that."

"So does Pamela."

"No, she doesn't."

"In one of those pictures. The one with two of them."

Felicia picked up the pictures and fanned through them until she found it. "This one?"

"That's the one. See, same ponytail. And the picture I got of the two of you out of Pamela's room. By the way, your picture doesn't do you justice, but she's wearing a ponytail."

"That doesn't mean that's how she always wore it. Both of those pictures were taken on the same day. I remember that day. She was going to Jake's birthday party and she didn't have time to get her hair fixed. I told her with her hair pulled back like that she looked like LaShawn."

"Why didn't you go to the party?"

"I knew the type of people that would be at any party

Gee was throwin'. Pamela would always ask me if I wanted to go, but I was a cop. I wouldn't be caught dead up in there."

"Mind if I ask you another question?"

"I'll save you the trouble. No, to my knowledge Pamela wasn't laundering money for Rocky. That is what you and the police want to know, isn't it? What is your name, again?"

"Nick Simmons. I'm pleased to meet you. And yes, that is what I was going to ask you."

"Cops think so?"

"I got that impression."

"That's why I don't want to talk to them. Once they figured out she was murdered and it was drug related, they'd start thinking money laundering and then they'd start looking at me. I'm sure someone has gone through my file and my arrest records looking to link me to this shit. And if they really want to, they'll find something, whether its there or not."

"Do you think that your leaving the way you did helped?" But Felicia didn't answer me.

"I used to tell her all the time that it didn't look good for her to be in her position at the bank and be associating with a known drug dealers wife, and goin' to their parties. But she would always say that for that to be a problem, she'd have to be doing something wrong, and her record at the bank would speak for itself."

"You mind if I ask you another question?"

"You don't have to ask me that everytime you want to ask me something. Go ahead."

"Have you had breakfast yet?"

"No." Felicia let out a little laugh.

"I haven't either. And I'm hungry, so can we finish this conversation over breakfast? I promise I'll behave myself even without handcuffs."

Felicia looked at me as if I had lost my mind. She picked up her gun and walked toward me again. She stood in front of me, not speaking. As if she was deciding right then how it was goin' to be between us. She looked into my eyes. I locked my eyes in hers. She exhaled and left the room.

"Shit," I said quietly.

For a second there, I thought we were having a moment. You know, the kind that James Bond always has when the girl kisses and then releases him. I felt the pain in my wrists. "Live in reality, Nick. This ain't no fuckin' movie." I didn't think she was going to kill me, so I didn't try to leave. I couldn't, not after coming all this way. She knows something. Something major, and she was scared because she knew it.

Twenty minutes later, Felicia returned to the room. She had changed into black jeans and heels. She still had on a tee shirt, but this one fit her. She had a holster on and had traded her 44 for a 9. "You better be real." She leaned forward and unlocked the cuffs.

"Thank you. They were starting to hurt," I said rubbing my wrists. I stood up and started walking toward the table to collect my hardware.

"Hold up," she said, as I reached. "We haven't gotten that far yet."

"No guns, huh."

"For the time being, I think it's best if I carry the gun. But I tell you what." She moved closer to me. "Pick one."

"One?"

"Yes. One. And I'll hold on to that. If you're a good boy and you don't give me any trouble, I may let you earn it back."

"Either one of the 9's will do." Felicia stuck the gun in

her jacket pocket and left the other two on the table. I stood for a second, looking at my guns. I wasn't getting a good feeling about leaving them.

"You coming?"

I turned around and she was pointing my 9 at me.

"Yeah, I'm coming."

I walked out of the house feeling naked. I tried, but couldn't remember the last time I went some place unarmed.

"Which one is yours?" She stopped and put my gun back in her pocket. "No, let me guess. First time in LA?"

"Yes." I stopped and frowned.

"Blue convertible." She was playing me like a tourist. Which I was, but she didn't have to play me. I unlocked her door and she got in. As soon as I got in she said, "Go ahead and drop the top. I know you want to."

She was right, so I dropped the top.

Once we pulled off, Felicia took my gun out of her pocket and rested it on her lap. "Where are we going?" I asked.

"Simply Wholesome on Sousean, make a left here."

We arrived at Simply Wholesome and were promptly seated. We sat quietly as our waitress arrived to take our orders. She filled our coffee cups and left us.

"You never did answer my question."

"Which one? I haven't answered several of your questions."

"I noticed. How is school going?

"It was goin' fine until all this came down."

"What were you taking?"

"Law school. I've been meaning to do it for years, but I got caught up in the job. Out there in the streets doin' the job."

"Do you miss it?"

"Not as much as I used to. I missed the feeling you get when you knock on a door or walk up on a car."

"What's gonna happen next. I know what you mean. You're excited and apprehensive all at the same time."

"That's right, you're ex-army. What did you do?"

"Special operations unit."

"Trained killer. Should I be scared?"

"No, you have the guns, remember." Felicia laughed. "What turned you? What made you decide to go back to school?"

"One day I had finally seen enough. Did enough. Too much."

"Sounds like you got a story."

"You don't want to hear about that."

"Yes I do, Felicia. I love a good story."

"Well, I'm not sure I want to tell you."

"What? You think it will scare me. I don't scare easy."

"No kiddin'." Felicia took a playful swing at me. "You could probably tell me stories that make mine sound like a church social."

"Maybe."

"I'll try and stick to the highlights, so stop me if I bore you."

"I'm sure I won't need to."

"Alrighty then. I've told this story so many times, one more time ain't goin' hurt. Officer Morgan and I, Morgan, that was my partner, we responded to a domestic disturbance call. When we got there, Officer Morgan knocked on the door and identified himself. They opened up on us right then." She giggled. "I mean, the suspects began firing at us through the door."

"All right now." I kept thinking Felicia was much too pretty to be a cop. "Try to keep it real for me."

"Anyway." Felicia cut her eyes at me.

"Why'd they just start blastin' like that?"

"Drug deal, in progress." She had pretty eyes, very expressive eyes. "I was goin' to call for back up, but Morgan kicked in the door and went in. By the time I got in there, one of them was tryin' to gather up the drugs from the table. He fired at me. I returned fire and hit him with two shots in his chest. I looked for Morgan, he was runnin' up the stairs. He yelled, 'They're goin' out the back!' I ran down the hallway. I could see the back door was open. Then I saw someone run out, but they were gone by the time I got there. I started back up the hall, when one of them came runnin' out. I shot him, kicked his gun away and kept moving up the hallway. I yelled for Morgan, but he didn't answer. Shots were still bein' fired. I heard footsteps coming down the stairs. When I cleared the hallway, I saw one on the steps. He shot at me, and I ducked back in the hallway. I shot back blindly. I hit him in the back before he got out the door. There was still shooting upstairs. I moved toward the stairs. I looked up and saw Morgan chasing one down the stairs. I fired at him, he went down and I took cover to reload.

"After awhile, Morgan came and sat next to me. It was over. I killed three people that day, Nick. Morgan killed two more. We just sat there looking at each other. Both of us knew we'd had enough. There was an investigation and it was ruled a clean shot. But it was ugly. Very ugly, what I had to go though before they cleared me. Two days later I quit. Morgan quit about a month after that."

The waitress returned with our meal. We ate, talked and laughed at this and that. I liked her laugh. I was starting to like her. Picture that, me liking somebody who wasn't married.

Finally the conversation worked it's way back around to the business at hand. "How long did you know Pamela?"

"We were play pen buddies."

"Really?"

"We go a long way."

"What was her involvement with Jake?"

"As far as I know, they were just friends. She met him at one of Gee's parties. There wasn't anything physical, if that's what you're asking."

"What about LaShawn? Were they close?"

"Yes, unfortunately. She met her at one of those parties and they became instant friends. LaShawn was nothing but poison. But Pamela seemed fascinated by that whole lifestyle. Not that she was a part of it or wanted to be. But she just liked being around them. She had never been around people like that and she just got caught up."

"Hmm. Growing up in LA, I would think she met plenty of people in the game."

"Pam's mom didn't play that. She kept a pretty tight reign on her kids. They weren't on lock down or nothing, they did stuff, but they did it as a family and her moms was always around."

"What about Mrs. Childers?"

"Her and Gee were close. Pamela looked out for Gee when they worked at the bank together. She said Gee was pretty helpless when she first got there. She'd never had a job before and she was a nervous wreck."

"By the way, you said those pictures were taken the same day."

"And?" Felicia leaned forward and smiled.

"Who took the pictures?"

"I was wondering if you had picked up on that. I would have been disappointed if you hadn't."

"Well?"

"Pamela did. Taking pictures was sort of her hobby."

"You think she took those pictures of Jake and LaShawn?"

"Maybe."

"You wanna tell me now?"

"Tell you what?"

"Why you left?"

"How long are you goin' to be here?"

"I'd like to say until you tell me why you left. But it'll probably be more like a couple of days."

"I don't know if I can trust you."

"Well, Felicia, you can tell me about it and I can go back to New York and do something about it. Or you can stay on the run until whoever it is you're running from, catches up with you."

"There in lies my problem, Nick. Even if I tell you, they still may come. I ain't trying to testify against nobody and live my life in witness protection. No, no, not a life for me."

I looked at my watch.

"What time you gotta be there?" Felicia asked.

"Noon. Gotta meet a guy who might have some information for me."

"If it's about Pamela, I wanna go."

"It's totally unrelated. Another case I'm working on."

"Tell me about it."

"Do you really want to know?"

"Sure, this stuff is fascinating to me. Ex-cop, you know. Maybe I might wanna do some private investigating."

I sat back and looked at her. I said to myself, what the hell. I might as well run this by her, maybe get some ideas. And maybe, just maybe, build a little trust. So I told her the story of Marcus and Yvonne. "- - - In your arms was the last thing she said to him. He can't say for sure who the lady was, or even if she was the one who did it. Since then, he's been poking around on his own, asking questions. He's got some idea that the CIA was involved."

"Mind if I tag along? I could back you up."

"Okay, come on. I'd be glad for your company."

I called for the check and we left the restaurant. Once we got to the car, Felicia handed me back my gun.

I felt better.

"Where are we going?"

"The post office."

"You want me to drive?" and held out her hand for the keys.

"By all means."

From then on I knew that she at least trusted me. It didn't mean she was going to tell me anything. But it was a start. We drove to the post office on West Century, by the airport. Felicia parked the car in front of the post office and we waited. "What are we doin' here?"

"Just waiting to see a guy."

We had been there for almost an hour when a late model dark blue Ford Crown Victoria pulled into the parking lot. A tall slender white man got out and went inside. "That's him. Wait here, I'll be right back."

"I'll be waiting here, *for you*," Felicia said and smiled.

It wasn't so much what she said, it was the way she said it. "In that case, I'll hurry back."

I got out of the car and waited for him to come out. I looked back at the car. Felicia waved to me and showed me her gun. I guess she called herself covering me.

As soon as he came out, I walked up on him. Fast. "Excuse me. Do you have change for a dollar?" he turned around slowly. "Gotta make a phone call."

"I don't have any dimes," He replied.

"Two nickels will do."

"That's an old code, Nick. I was about to shoot you."

160

"I am glad you didn't, Freddie. You still living dangerously?"

"Me, I should be asking you that. What are you doin' out here?"

"I need some help."

"Oh shit. I knew I was gonna regret not shooting you. What is it?"

"You ever hear of a guy named Paris?"

"Doesn't ring any bells. But meet me here same time tomorrow, I'll see what I can find out." He got back in his car and drove away.

I watched Freddie drive away and returned to the car. "What did you find out?" Felicia asked, as soon as the door was shut.

"Nothing. I'll meet him here tomorrow."

"What are you gonna do now?"

"That depends on you, Ms Hardy. What are you doin' the rest of the day?"

"Since you're out here, and it's your first time and all, I was gonna show you around. Maybe you'll like it enough to come back. Look in on a sistah every now and then. Make sure I'm still alive."

"I'd like that."

She caught me a little off guard with that one.

Maybe we did have a moment.

We talked about a little bit of everything while Felicia drove me around to all the tourist spots in LA. I felt comfortable talking to her. So for once, I let my guard down and opened up to her. "You've begun to interest me, Nick Simmons. Listen, I know a quiet little spot on the beach."

"I'm not dressed for the beach."

"That's why they made malls."

Felicia and I spent the rest of the afternoon and the early evening at the beach. Laughing and talking like neither of us had a care in the world. She sat with her head on my shoulder and watched the sun set. We drove to a Chinese restaurant in Torrance called *Szechwan*. I had Kung Pao. She ordered the Sweet and Spicy Shrimp. The food was excellent. After dinner, Felicia drove quietly back to her house. "I had a nice day, Nick," she said and got out of the car.

"I did too. But it's early, I was hoping you'd show me some of that famous LA night life."

"Not tonight, Nick. I'm tired. I got a lot on my mind and I wouldn't be good company. Will you come get me tomorrow before you go to meet your friend?" she asked, as she got to the door and unlocked it.

"Sure." I was disappointed for more than the obvious reason.

"Then I'll see you in the morning." Felicia kissed me on the cheek and went inside. I had just turned to walk away when I heard the door opened.

"Nick."

"Yes, Felicia," I said excitedly.

"Here are your guns." She handed them to me, one at a time. "Good night, Nick." And once again the door closed. I walked away thinking of my bad luck. I had just spent the day, a great day, with a woman I was really interested in, who seemed to be interested in me. The problem is she may be involved in a murder, not to mention that I lived six thousand miles away.

Chapter Fourteen

Saturday July 17; 10:59 AM

The following morning I picked up Felicia around eleven and went to the post office to meet Freddie. A bright red sundress and pumps was her attire for the day. "Not that I'm complaining or anything, but its kind of hard to hide your gun isn't it?" Felicia rolled her eyes at me, and without hesitation, pulled up her dress. Just enough to show me that she had a 25 strapped to each thigh.

When we arrived at the post office, Freddie was there waiting for us. I got out and began walking toward him. "How's it goin', Freddie?"

"First of all let's get one thing straight. You never saw me. So I never talked to you, not today or yesterday. We clear on that?"

"That bad?"

"Are we clear, Nick?"

"I never saw you, Freddie, so we never talked. Now, what you got?"

"Nothing. That's what I got, nothing. All my inquiries were met by a polite brush off or the word classified."

"You have anything for me?"

"Some advice, and this came from Walter."

"How is Walter?"

"Still pissed at you about Beirut. He sends his regards, and said to get yourself a new client."

"Can't do that, Freddie, but thanks anyway for your help. See ya." I started to walk away.

"Back off this one, Nick, it's political. Whatever this Yvonne Haggler was involved in with Paris - - -"

I stopped in my tracks and walked back to Freddie. "I never said anything about Yvonne Haggler. You know something, Freddie. Give it up."

Freddie stood and looked at me. "All right, Nick. Paris did some work for some people we know in Virginia. And this Yvonne was one of his mules. All I know is she shot him."

"Shit, I knew that."

"Sorry you came all this way for nothing. When you get back to New York, give Sal my regards." Freddie said, and got back in his car.

"Sal? Sally Fitz? What's he got to do with this?"

"I didn't say he did. Understand. See ya, Nick." I watched Freddie drive away before rejoining Felicia in the car. I was glad to be leaving with half of what I came for. Now it was Felicia's turn.

"Well?"

"I got to go back to New York."

"Now?"

"Not right away, but I gotta see a guy I used to know. My flight leaves in the morning."

"That's all?"

"The less you know, the better."

"See how you do me?"

"Believe me, it's for your own good. You've got enough problems. Which does bring us back to you, Ms Hardy. Tell me what's going on."

"Well, since you're leaving in the morning, I was hoping we could spend the rest of the day together."

"That wasn't what I was asking and you know this."

"I know that, Nick. But trust me."

"Okay."

I didn't really want to leave her and I didn't want to leave without hearing her story. What else could I do. I put on my seatbelt and relaxed. We did lunch at a place called *Killer Shrimp*, on Colfax Ave and Ventura Boulevard. After lunch, Felicia drove out of LA on the 101 until we got to the Town Center Drive exit. "Where are we going?"

"Back to LA," she said, and got on California state route 1. "I wanted to share one of my favorite places with you."

"Where is that?"

"Shhh. You just trust me. I trusted you. You're not afraid, are you?"

"No," I said louder then I needed to. "I just like to know where I'm goin' that's all." My sixth sense was kicking in. For all I knew, she could be taking me some place secluded so she could kill me. Wasn't like she couldn't do it. After all, she was an ex-cop on the run. But on the run from what?

"I've never taken anybody here before." She smiled a very soft and satisfied smile. It caused my apprehension to subside, but just a little. Apprehension. The rush. Something else we shared.

We had driven a short while when Felicia said, "This is part of what I wanted to show you."

I looked and saw what was probably one of the most beautiful sites I'd ever seen. The Pacific Ocean on one side of the highway, and the mountains on the other. Felicia tapped me on my thigh. "How do you like it?" she asked me, as she drove down the curvy stretch of highway.

"It's breathtaking." I replied, thinking that she either needed to slow down or drive with two hands.

"No, breathtaking comes a little later."

"Well are we in a hurry to get there?"

"Kinda, well yeah, we are in a hurry. Why, you a nervous passenger? I mean you're not scared or anything?"

"No. I just want to enjoy the view. You did want me to see this, didn't you?"

"Yes. But there's more. You just gotta trust me."

"That's funny coming from the woman who had me in

handcuffs first thing yesterday morning."

"Stop being such a punk. I gave you back your guns. You'll be all right."

Felicia slowed down, but only a little. We drove for awhile longer until she got into Malibu. She made a left off the highway and started to drive up into the hills.

"Excuse me, that sign says private property."

"And?"

"Where you takin' me?"

"Trust me, Nick. If it makes you more comfortable, - - - " Felicia let go of the wheel, reached between her legs and handed me her guns. "There, that should help."

It did.

"Thank you. But I still want to know where we're goin'?"

"Some place breathtaking."

I decided to relax and roll with it. If I couldn't take her, and whatever she had waiting, I deserved whatever I got. Before too much longer we passed a sign that read, *SERRA; A Franciscan Retreat.*

I was more curious now. She parked the car and led me by the hand toward the building. As we walked past the building, I followed her up a small hill, Felicia said, "Now this is breath taking."

And she was.

She walked ahead of me and sat down on a bench at the edge of the mountain. "I used to come here all the time. Get away from it all. Gives me a chance to think."

From where we were, high in the mountains, the view was spectacular. Surrounded on three sides by mountains and the ocean was dead ahead. It was breath taking. The only sound was the sound of her voice. And to top it off, the sun was setting. "I've been out here every night since I've been back."

"Guess you got a lot to think about?"

Felicia smiled that smile I was getting fond of seeing. We sat there in silence for the next hour, until the late summer sun dropped out of sight. I don't know what she was thinking about, but I couldn't stop thinking about what she knew. I played out several scenarios while I took turns admiring Felicia's profile, painted with a backdrop of sunset. Then she got up abruptly. "You ready to go, Nick?"

"No." I stood up and faced her. "I could stay out here and look at you all night."

She turned and walked away, and I followed her back to the car. Once we were back on the highway I thanked her for bringing me. She didn't answer. She turned onto Sunset Blvd. and took the scenic route back to her house. She invited me in this time and offered me a drink. "Johnnie Black, if you got it."

"A glass of white wine will have to hold you."

Felicia returned with two glasses. She handed me one and took a sip of hers. "When are you going to tell me what you know?"

Felicia put her drink down and then she put her arms around my neck and kissed me. There was real passion in her kiss. More passion then I'd felt coming from any woman I'd kissed in a long time.

"I will tell you everything you want to know," Felicia said then kissed me again. "In the morning."

She kissed my lips and then down to my neck. I unzipped her dress and allowed it to fall to the floor. I paused to admire her body. Felicia was beautiful. I ran my tongue along the edge of her bra, reaching behind her back unhooking her bra at the same time. Her breasts were firm and her nipples grew harder when I ran my tongue across them. Felicia moaned quietly, wiggling her way out of her panties.

We kissed our way into the bedroom and we fell on

the bed. I kissed her calves. The closer I got, the more Felicia squirmed. I started working my way up to her thighs. I slid my tongue around the edges of her pubic hair, then spread her lips. Her back arched as I stuck my tongue inside of her. Her stomach muscles tightened, her thighs pressed together as her back arched, and she screamed in ecstasy.

I stood up took off my pants, and laid down next to her bed. I rolled on top of her, and put the weight of my body on my arms. I entered her slowly. She arched her back slightly and began to rotate her hips. We began to move slowly, then faster and then slow again. Her body began to quiver again. I placed my hands gently on her face and kissed her. We continued to make love until we both passed out.

Chapter Fifteen

Sunday July 18; 5:27 PM

I was tired when I got off the plane. I was up all night with Felicia and I got up early again in the morning. But it was worth it. In more ways than just the obvious. I wanted to go home and get some rest, but I went to the stake house first. Things were quiet when I arrived at the house. Monika was sitting in front of the console, but not really looking. Jett was sitting on the floor, goin' through the paper. It didn't matter where in the world we were or what language it was in, Jett always went through the paper, page by page. You never know what's goin' on unless you read the paper, he'd always say.

"Evening, people." I said and made myself comfortable.

"Where you been?" Monika asked excitedly.

"California."

"California?"

"Yeah. Jett didn't tell you?"

"Oops," Jett said, and buried his head back in the Times.

"What were you doin' in Cali?"

"I went to follow up on a lead I got on Pamela Hendricks. Why? Did something happen?" My first thought was for Mrs. Childers safety. "Is Mrs. Childers all right?"

"Nick, take your head out that woman's ass for a minute and take a look at this," Monika said, and handed me a piece of paper.

I looked at it and shrugged my shoulders. "Is this supposed to mean something to me?"

"I'll say," Jett said. "That paper is the missing link. It puts it all together. It's the answer we've been looking for."

"Are you gonna let me in on it or do I have to guess?"

Felicia was true to her word. She told me everything she

knew once she got me up this morning. But they seemed so excited, why blow it for them.

Monika smiled. "That is the formula for what appears to be some type of synthetic cocaine."

"Synthetic crack to be exact," I said. "Jake developed it for Chilly."

"How did you know?" Monika asked.

"That's what I was doin' in California. Chilly got the formula from a chemist named Rodrigez who used to work for the Peruvians."

"Used to?" Jett asked. "I didn't know that was possible."

"He was on the run. There was a bounty out for him. He had started a new life, quiet and low profile. But Chilly spots him at some mall upstate. Rodrigez gave Chilly the formula so he wouldn't give him up. But it didn't work."

"Damn right, it didn't work," Jett said. "It was killin' people, and dead customers are bad for business."

"After the first five died from smokin' it, Chilly gives him up to the Peruvians. That's what Diego Estabon was talking about when he said I took care of mine. Apparently, they agreed that everyone involved had to die."

"So what do we do now?" Jett asked.

I looked at Jett and Monika. Jett dropped his head.

Monika shook hers in semi disgust. "I told you that this wasn't something we needed to be fuckin' around in. I say we back all the way up off this. Shut all this down and go back to doin' what we do. Jett hacks our way in, you kill them, and I blow it up so there's no trace."

"Jett?"

"I think she's right, Nick. The shit didn't work, so if Jake ain't dead, he's gonna be."

"How 'bout it, Nick?" Monika asked.

I didn't want to admit it, but they were right. If Jake was still alive and he had any sense, he'd be so far away that

Chilly would never find him and neither would we. "I'll call Mrs. Childers and give her back her money."

"Why?" Monika asked.

"We earned our money," Jett said. "Her brother took off before her husband could kill him. Case closed."

"You're right, Jett, all this set up does cost money."

"And our time." Monika added.

"All right, case closed," I said. "Now, we have a new client."

"Who's that?" Monika asked.

"His name is Marcus Douglas."

"Not another missing persons case?" she asked.

"No, just information." I told them Marcus's story. They wanted no parts of that one either. I couldn't say that I blamed them, 'cause I didn't either, but a debt is a debt. I left out the part about it being a personal favor for Bobby. Or that somehow Sally Fitz was involved. That would have really set Jett off.

"Nick, I think you can handle this one on your own. Doesn't seem like you need us," Jett said, as he started to tear down the set up. "Just ask a few answers from the right people, and tell this Douglas guy what happened. What was her name again?"

"Yvonne Haggler."

"That name sounds familiar," Jett said.

"I've been thinking the same thing. But I just can't place her."

"Well, whoever she is, you shouldn't need us," Monika said, and she started helping Jett pack it up. I got up and started to help. "No, no, Nick, you just go on and tell Mrs. Childers what ever you need to tell her. We'll take care of this. You give me a call when Felix has something for us."

"So, like, what are you sayin'? I can't call you until then?"

"That's not what I'm sayin'," Monika said, shaking her hands. Monika walked over and put her arm around me. "Don't stand there lookin' like we're runnin' out on you, 'cause we're not. You can call me anytime, Boo. But this private eye stuff, ain't for me."

"She's right, Nick. This is too much like work," Jett said. "But if you're diggin' it, hey, that's cool too."

"Okay. I'll get with y'all later."

What else could I do? I was diggin' this. But I had to keep my prospective clearly in focus. Jake was gone, long gone. And if he had any sense, he would stay that way. The only thing left to do was to break it down for Mrs. Childers and move on. But there were still some things about all this that I couldn't shake. Something about Pamela Hendricks, or maybe it was just the personal feelings I had developed for Felicia Hardy that was clouding my judgement. Either way, I knew it wasn't over. At least not for me.

So I drove to Rocky's hang out. I wasn't exactly sure why I was going there, much less what I would say when I got there. I walked in and got the same reception as the last time, it seemed like every eye in the house was on me. That's when I saw him, Chilly, the man himself. He was standing at the bar enjoying the company of two very attractive young ladies. Rocky was seated in the back at what I assumed was his regular spot. As soon as he was alerted to my presence, he made a B-line straight to Chilly.

I went and sat down at a table as far away from them as I could and still keep them in sight. A waitress came to take my order. "Johnnie Walker Black, straight up." I started to ask her if she would tell Rocky that I wanted to see him, but I kinda figured that he'd get around to it sooner or later. Chilly looked over his shoulder as Rocky pointed me out to him. I didn't think he'd do that, but fuck it. It was time I got this over with. Chilly dismissed Rocky with one hand and patted one of the ladies he was with on the ass, then started for me.

"Mind if I sit down?" Chilly asked.

"Be my guest," I replied, as the waitress returned with my drink.

"No check for this table, Cat. His money's no good here." Chilly said, as he took a seat. "Nick Simmons. I haven't seen you since the old days. I thought Bobby killed you and that army shit was just a cover."

"No, Chilly, I'm still alive."

"Rocky's snitchin' ass told me you're a private investigator now. That's a long way from where you came from. What's the matter, Freeze and them ain't got no spot for you, or is Bobby still tryin' to kill you?" Chilly laughed. "Let me quit fuckin' with you. Shit, if Bobby really wanted you dead, you'd be dead."

"Good point."

"So what brings you here?"

"Stopped in to have a drink." I raised my drink and downed it. Chilly smiled and motioned for the waitress.

"Ain't too many of us old heads left in this game. Mutha fuckas now ain't got no honor. No respect for the game. Niggas like you and me got to keep it real, you know what I'm sayin'?"

"Yeah."

"What's up with you? Like you mad at me bout something. That shit between me and Black is over with. I got nothing but respect for him. He did right by me."

Damn right, Black let you live to make all that money. "There ain't too many like Black."

"That's what I'm sayin'. These young bucks like that bitch made nigga there." He pointed at Rocky. "Ain't loyal to shit but money."

"It's a new day. With new players."

Cat served us another round of drinks. Chilly raised his glass. "To the old days."

"I'll drink to that." All that talk about honor and loyalty was starting to wear on me for personal reasons.

"Let's cut the bullshit. I know why you're here. Same reason I'm here. Jake. I know Gee hired you to find him."

"Rocky tell you that?"

"Naa. But that's exactly what I'm sayin'. He got no idea who you are or where you come from. That bitch ain't have no business tellin' me that you was a private eye. Him and Gee go back some years. He should be loyal to her over me. But as soon as you came through the door, he comes runnin' to me like a little bitch and told me everything. But you see, Nick, I already knew all about that."

"Did you?'

"Shit yeah! What, you think I just let Gee run wild, doin' whatever she wants? Hell no! I keeps her on a long chain. I knew she wrote you a check for ten thousand dollars. So I did some checkin', that's when I found out you was a private investigator. I figured she hired you to look for Jake. I got me a little honey at the bank. She keeps tabs on Gee's account for me. Gee will fuck up some money if you let her. But that's my fault. She was a young girl when I met her. Didn't know her ass from a hole in the ground. I should have taught her the value of money, instead of just throwin' it at her. But that's my problem."

"It's probably too late now."

"You got that right. You have any luck findin' Jake?"

"Not a clue," I lied. I started to lay it all out for him. Cut the bullshit. But I thought better of it. "I figure he's some place hidin' out, what I don't know, is why. What was he into Chilly? Was he doin' something for you? The way I get it, you were the last person to see him before he dropped out of sight." I was pushing my luck and I knew it. But I had that *I don't give a fuck* attitude in full effect.

"You take chances, Nick. But I know what kind of nigga you are, so fuck it. I respect a mutha fucka that gets right to it."

"I'm glad to hear that. So what was he doin' for you?"

Chilly laughed. "He wasn't doin' nothin' for me. I just wanted to talk to him about some shit I been hearin', that's all. I want you to find Jake. And I want you to let Gee know where he is. After you tell Gee, then I want you to tell me."

"Why, so you can kill him." It was a statement, not a question.

"No, I'm not going to kill him. You have my word on that. I just want to talk to him. He was into something, I just want to know what."

He reached in his pocket.

I put my hand on my gun.

He dropped a stack of money on the table in front of me. "That's five thousand dollars there. Take it."

I complied.

"I'll give you five more when you tell me where he is. And there's something else I want you to do for me."

"What's that?"

"In the last three weeks, Gee's been takin' a lota money out her account. Cash money, twenty thousand dollars. You tell me where that money went, and that twenty is yours."

I thought about making a quick twenty grand right there and tell him about how Ben Josephs was blackmailing his wife. But what honor I had left, and my loyalty to his wife stopped me. "I'll look into it."

"You know me, Nick. I'm a man of my word and I pay."

"Thanks for the drink." I got up and walked out, with the five grand in my pocket. I got in my car thinking how things had just taken a weird turn. At this point, I was sure that Jake had just taken off. I decided to turn my attention to this Marcus Douglas thing and Sally Fitz.

Salvatore Fitzpatrick was his real name. Italian, Irish. Me and Sal did some work together when he used to run with Angelo Colette back in the day. Our lives took a similar turn when he joined the army. Only difference was he joined because he killed somebody. Sal was always trying to put a deal together. The last time I saw Sal was in Turkey. He was trying to sell some weapons back to the guys he'd stolen them from. Over the years, Sal had made a reputation for himself as being able to get anything for anybody, as long as they could pay his price. Which naturally made Sal very popular in some circles. I didn't know if he was back in New York, or where to find him. So I drove by Cuisiné to see if maybe Freeze could help me.

Cuisiné was crowded and I couldn't find a place to park. So I drove around finally finding a spot about two blocks away. I had walked about a half a block when I heard somebody say, "Got a light, man?"

I turned around and was met immediately by a fist in my face. There were three of them, one grabbed me from behind and held me while the other two hit me repeatedly. I recognized one of them from Rocky's joint. I fell to the ground and they started kicking me. Once that was over he said, "Chilly sends his regards."

They left me lying there and walked away laughing. I struggled to my feet and breathed deeply. I would have to repay their kindness. I started walking the rest of the way to Cuisiné. I made it as far as the lobby before I passed out.

When I came to, I was lying on a couch, Alexia was tending my wounds and Freeze was standing over me. "What happened to you?"

"Some of Rocky's boyz tried to warn me off and blame it on Chilly," I said, and stood up slowly.

"How you know it wasn't Chilly?"

"'Cause Chilly just - - -," I got up and reached in my pocket. I still had the money. "Chilly gave me five thousand dollars to find Jake."

"I thought you was workin' for Gee?"

"I am. He still wants me to tell her where he is, as long as I tell him too." My head was still spinning, so I sat back down.

"I told you not to fuck with this, now look at you." Freeze laughed. He walked over to the desk, put the phone on speaker and dialed a number. "Fucked around and got your ass kicked."

"I think my ass was the only thing they didn't kick."

Freeze just shook his head. "This is Freeze, let me speak to Rock."

"This, Rock. What's up, Freeze? I ain't - - -"

"Shut the fuck up nigga and understand what I'm tellin' you. You sent your boyz after Nick Simmons tonight."

"I didn't have nothing to do with that, Freeze. I - - -"

"Shut the fuck up, bitch! Nick Simmons is family to me. You feel me, Rock? So I'm tellin' you now, if that shit happens again, fuck peace. I'll kill you and your whole set. Got that!" Freeze hung up the phone and started laughing. I laughed too, but it hurt.

Freeze took me out to Perry's house so he could check me out and give me something for the pain. Perry grew up with us on the block. Now he was a doctor. It was damn good seeing Perry again after all these years. Like everybody else, Perry treated me as if I never missed a day.

"I brought somebody by to see you, Perry." Freeze said.

"Yeah, who's that?" Freeze stepped aside. "Nick! Damn

its good to see you. Y'all come on in. Hold up, neither one
of y'all shot or bleeding?"

"No, man. We just came to visit." Freeze said as we went
inside Perry's house.

"Okay, 'cause I still remember the last time you two
came to my house this late."

"So do I. How could I forget," I said to Perry. I looked
at the smile on Freeze's face and I could tell he hadn't
forgotten either.

"Couldn't forget what, Nick?" Wanda asked. "Y'all were
just full of stuff I didn't know about. I'm starting to feel like
an outsider."

"Don't feel like that, Wanda. We never even told Black.
But you know Black, he found out anyway."

"Found out what, Nick?"

"Back in the day, me and Freeze did a little freelancing."

"What kind of freelancing, Nick?"

Even though we still sorta worked for Andre, who was
one of the biggest drug dealers around those days, Black
absolutely forbid any of us to have any direct involvement
with drugs. Black made his money highjacking trucks,
robbing warehouses and payrolls. We all made crazy money,
but me and Freeze wanted to, needed to, make some money
on our own.

"So what we gonna do, Nick? We can't roll, so how we
gonna get paid?" Freeze asked.

We kicked around a bunch of stuff, but everything we
thought of either wasn't worth the risk or wasn't enough
paper to make it worth the effort. It all came back around
to the fact that fast, easy money was spelled D-R-U-G-S.
Then it came to me. "Look, who's making the money?"

"Dope boyz," Freeze replied.

"Right, so why can't we get that money?"

"'Cause Black will kill us if we started rollin', that's why. And don't you say that he'll never find out. That mutha fucka is psychic about that shit. You ain't forget what we did to Banks when Black found out he was dealin'?

"No, I ain't forgot. But who said anything about us dealin'?"

"You did."

"No, I didn't. I said why can't we get that money, there's a difference. You interested?"

"I'm listening."

"Dope boyz rollin' around everyday with stupid cash on them. I'm talkin' about rollin' up on them, and robbin' them niggas while they laid back."

"You talkin' about rollin' up on a bunch of heavily armed mutha fuckas while they do business? That ain't no plan, that's suicide."

"You ain't scared are you, Freeze?"

"Hell no!"

"I didn't think so. But I ain't talkin' about hittin' them while they doin' business, that would be suicide. I'm talkin' about catchin' them comin' out they cars. They get out the car. Bam, we hit them quick and bam we out."

"That could work. I mean we know who they are. I don't like most of them niggas anyway. And as long as we don't take their dope, Black won't have shit to say."

So it was set.

Me and Freeze became stick up kids. We'd hit two or three a night some times. And the money was good, three, four, five grand a pop for a minutes work. Most times we never had to fire a shot. But after awhile, word got around and things started to dry up. The money was less and the security was more. But we were addicted to that cash. So the plan changed. We started robbin' them while they were selling quantity. Things were going good, it was easier than we thought. Except this one time. We over heard a guy, used to call himself Forty-eight, who had a real high, squeaky kinda voice, talkin' about he had some white guys on the hook and he was gonna retire on the money he was gonna make.

"You mean we gonna take," Freeze said to me, making fun of the way Forty-eight talked.

We sat and watched as the players went into a motel room on Boston Road. Once the deal was in progress, we busted in.

"Nobody move! Nobody get hurt!" Freeze shouted.

I looked at the guy carrying the briefcase with the money. Forty-eight and his boy raised their hands and backed away from the dope. But the two white guys with the money started beefin'. "If you know what's good for you, you'll walk out that door quietly." And then he made a play for his gun. Freeze wheeled around, "Shut up, white bread!" and caught him in the mouth with the pump. "You're speaking out of turn."

I covered with the semi while Freeze closed the case and we backed out of the room. It wasn't long after we got out of the room before somebody started blastin'. I fired back while Freeze headed for the car. The fire fight continued until we were in the car and away.

We both looked at each other and started laughin'. "That was gettin' kinda hectic," Freeze said as he drove away. "Must be a lotta money in that case for them to have backup outside."

"I think this is the biggest score we ever had," I said, as I opened the case. "Maybe we can retire." Making fun of Forty-eight. We were both laughing so hard that neither of us noticed the black Ford that pulled up along side of us. Until they started blastin'. With the first shot, they busted out the back window on the passenger side. "Where the fuck did they come from!"

"I don't know!" Freeze yelled as he floored it. He sped away down Boston Road with the Ford on our tail.

"Get us out of here, Freeze!"

"What you think I'm doin', writin' a love song?" Freeze turned sharply against traffic, but they stayed right with us. He turned on 222nd and then back on to Boston Road. "You see them?" Freeze demanded to know.

"No, I think you lost them."

"Damn right, I did! I told you I'd lose them!" That was when the back window got shot out.

"Shit!"

Freeze turned on Eastchester Road and kept going until he hit Laconia Ave. "I thought we lost them?"

"You did. These are different guys."

"What do you mean, different guys?"

"That it's not the same guys. It's a different car. Blue Chevy, coming up on your right." I began firing through the now opened back window. Trying to get them off us. But they kept coming. "Turn here! Try to lose them in the projects!"

Freeze turned on 229th street and drove thru Edenwald Projects. "Damn! These guys are good." But he couldn't shake them. We came out of the projects and back onto Laconia, up 219th and onto Bronxwood Ave.

"Who the fuck are they?" I asked.

"I don't know. How the fuck should I know?"

"You just lose them." A car pulled out in front of us and we crashed into a parked car. We got out blastin'. "This way!" I yelled.

"I ain't goin' down there, there's dogs down there!"

"Shoot them! Lets go!" I yelled as I started running down the alley.

"Look out!" Freeze yelled. I turned quickly, in time to see that two more guys were shooting at us. I caught one in the shoulder. "Ahhh! Shit!" If I hadn't turned when Freeze yelled it would have hit me in the chest.

"You hit?"

"Yeah, in the shoulder! I'm all right, keep goin'!"

I could hear the dogs barking in front of us and the guys firing behind us. I started firing in both directions. The barking stopped and the dogs ran in the opposite direction. But the guys kept coming. Freeze ran toward the building and shot the lock off. We ran through the building and out the front door. A car came down the street. Freeze stood in the middle of the street with his gun drawn.

The car stopped in front of him.

"Get out!"

Both doors swung open and the people ran away from the car.

The guys came out the door and opened fire on us again. This time it was Freeze who got hit, he went down.

"Freeze!"

I ran toward him, shooting that semi-auto wildly in their direction.

They took cover.

I kept shootin'.

I pulled Freeze up and pushed him in the car, got in and drove away.

I looked over at Freeze. "Where you hit?"

"In the gut! Shit that hurts. They got me in the leg too."

"Who the fuck are they?"

"How many times you gonna ask me that shit? I told you I don't know!" Freeze shouted.

"They still on us?"

Freeze struggled to turn around, he was bleeding pretty

bad. "I don't see anybody."

I drove around for awhile to make sure we'd really lost them, who ever they were, this time. Then drove as fast as I could to Perry's house. Freeze had passed out at some point, so I had to carry him. He was in pretty bad shape. Perry said if it had been any longer he'd be dead. He took care of our wounds and I made him promise not to tell Black, but he found out anyway.

"You saved his life, and he saved yours."

"That's just one more reason why we're so tight."

"You ever find out who those guys were?" Wanda asked.

"Yeah. They were cops. They had a string set up on Forty-eight. We just picked the wrong guy to rob that time."

Chapter Sixteen

After we left Perry's house, we spent the rest of the night hangin' out. My boy Freeze was still wild as hell, in spite of the suit. Freeze rolled us around to all the spots we used to go. Not much had changed, except now, Freeze was the man.

Monday July 19; 4:42 PM

I slept late the next day. It was well into the afternoon before I finally rolled out of bed. It was almost five and I was still feeling a little groggy from the pain pills I had gotten from Perry. I thought about going back to bed, but I picked up the phone and checked my messages.

Felicia had called and left me this message;

"The least you could have done was call me and let me know that you made it back safely. Anyways, I didn't call to fuss. I just wanted to say that I miss being with you. Bye, bye, honey."

I was really starting to like Felicia Hardy and I missed being with her too. I started to call her back, but then I remembered the last time I started feeling this way about a woman. I hung up the phone and called Mrs. Childers instead. It had been more than a week since the last time I saw or talked to her.

I left a message on her voice mail and asked her to meet me at *Sparks Steak House* on 46th St around nine. I was a little late getting there and much to my surprise she was there, looking impeccable as usual, when I arrived. "Hello, Nick."

"Hello, Mrs. Childers. I hope I didn't keep you waiting very long?"

"I've been here about a half hour. But that's okay, I wanted to get out of the house anyway. Have a seat."

"Thank you." Once I was seated, her smile turned to a

frown. I guess she noticed the cuts and bruises on my face.

"What happened to you?"

"I ran into some people who had something to prove."

"It looks like they did a good job. Are you all right?"

"I'll be fine."

"What have you found out for me, Nick?"

"Well, Mrs. Childers, I don't think your brother is missing, or that anything happened to him. I think Jake is somewhere hiding."

"What makes you say that?"

"He was involved with Chilly in some type of scheme to develop synthetic crack."

"Synthetic crack?" she looked at me strangely and lit a cigarette. "I've got a good idea, but just what exactly is synthetic crack?"

"Basically, Mrs. Childers, it's crack without the cocaine."

"How is that possible?"

"I really don't understand how the formula works, your brother's the chemist. But the long and short of it is, that it didn't work. At least seven people have died from it."

"Pamela?"

"Yes."

"That's not possible. Pamela didn't use drugs."

"I know that, but I believe that anybody who knew anything about it had to die. Pamela was just runnin' with the wrong people."

"I'll try not to take that personally." She rolled her eyes at me and turned away, but she turned back quickly. "If that's the case, then what makes you think that Jake isn't dead too?"

"Because Chilly is still looking for him."

"How do you know that?"

"Trust me." I thought about telling her that he gave me five grand to find Jake, but she didn't need to know that.

Or the fact that he had somebody keeping tabs on her account and that Chilly wanted to know about the money she gave Ben Josephs. "Anyway, as far as I could tell, Chilly hadn't killed him. But he is nowhere to be found."

"Did you talk to Rocky?"

"That's something else I wanted to ask you."

"What's that?"

"What type of relationship do you have with Rocky."

"He's a friend of Jake's. Why?"

"Your friend?"

"Well --- "

"Well?"

"Well, not really. Me and Rocky don't speak to each other anymore. We haven't spoken since before I left Philly."

"Why?"

"I don't think that's any of your business."

"Mrs. Childers, you made all this my business. What happened between you two?" She frowned up and looked away. The waiter finally came to take my order. "Hennessy Martini for the lady, and I'll have Johnnie Black, straight up." Once the waiter departed to get our drinks, I went back to the question. "What happened, Mrs. Childers?"

She rolled her eyes and looked away. "Do you remember me telling you that I did some things that I'm not proud of to get away from Philly?"

"And?"

"I asked Rocky for the money so I could get away from there. He told me he would give me the money and that I should come by his apartment to pick it up. When I got there, Rocky and five of his boyz were waiting. I didn't think anything of it, Rocky always had a crowd around him."

"So I noticed. Go on."

"He tells me to come in the bedroom 'cause he don't want his boyz to know what he was doin'. When we get in there, he tells me that I could have the money, but I had to fuck him first."

"Pathetic."

"I was a virgin, Nick, so I told him that I couldn't do that, and I started to leave. He grabbed me and raped me. I cried and I screamed, but he didn't care. When he was finished, his boyz came in. They tied me spread eagle to the bed and stuck a sock in my mouth. They took turns raping me for the rest of the night."

"I'm sorry. I shouldn't have pushed it." What else could I say?

"No, you shouldn't have." When the waiter returned with our drinks, Mrs. Childers drank hers down like water. "Can we get out of here?"

"Sure. Where do you want to go?"

"I don't care, anywhere." She put her cigarettes in her purse and threw some money on the table. "Just come ride with me." She got up without waiting for an answer. I shot my drink and headed out the door behind her.

We rode in silence while Mrs. Childers drove us nowhere fast. I couldn't think of anything to say after the gang bang story, so I sat quietly. She drove out of the city, across the Tappanze Bridge to a small house in Nyack. When we went inside the house, the first thing that hit me was the smell. It didn't smell bad; it was more like the stale odor of some place that had been closed up for awhile. The living room was well furnished and none of it looked like it had much use. Mrs. Childers turned on some music and went around the house turning on ceiling fans and opening windows.

"This is my little hide away," she said, opening the French doors that led to the deck.

"Hide away?"

She smiled and went out on the deck, seemingly to avoid my question. So I followed her outside and asked it again. She looked irritated by my question as well as my presence on the deck. "I come out here to get away."

"Get away from what, Mrs. Childers?"

"More to get away from all the stress and pressures, you know, and be by myself. It's so peaceful out here, it gives me a chance to relax and think."

"Bullshit." I said to myself. "Yes, It's very peaceful."

She went back in the house and I followed behind her. "Can I get you a drink?"

"Thank you. Do you have Johnnie Walker Black?"

"No, will Hennessy do?"

"Hennessy is fine."

I sat on the couch and watched her as she poured. She looked in my direction, but she dropped her eyes when she saw I was looking at her. I had noticed that she wasn't making eye contact with me when she talked. There was fear and uncertainty in her eyes. She handed me my drink and sat down across from me and started to talk. Talk about nothing, really, just a lot of reminiscing about her, Jake, and Chesará growing up dirt poor in Philly.

We drank, and like I said, she talked for over an hour and then she stopped. She got up and walked over to the French doors. I walked over to her and touched her arm. It seemed to startle her.

"Is something wrong?"

"No, just wondering what you must think of me."

"What do you mean?"

"I mean what do you think of me, Nick?"

"I don't know, I think you're nice. Very pretty."

"Is that all you see in me, Nick. A pretty face, - - - nice. Nice to look at, but not much more, right?"

"I didn't say that."

"You don't have to, because it's the truth. That's all I've ever been, pretty. Oh, look at Gabriel, she's so pretty. All my life I've gotten by on my looks."

"You ain't all that now." I knew I had touched a nerve, so I tried to make light of it. "I was just being nice when I said you were pretty."

"Very pretty, that's what you said, Nick." She laughed. "You said I was very pretty."

"I was lying, 'cause you look like you been hit in the face with a bag of quarters. I bet little children scream and run to their mothers when they see your ugly ass."

"Stop it, Nick. I'm not that bad. And besides it wasn't a bag of quarters, it was a fist."

"I know, I was trying to be nice about it. But I can see. And I see that make up doesn't hide everything."

She looked away from me and stared into her drink. "I've never been in control of my life, Nick. I went from my father's house to Chilly's. The first day I met him, he told me that I was the prettiest woman he'd ever seen. From that day on, I never wanted for anything. After a lifetime of being told no, you can't, that's not for you, Gabriel. Everything was yes. All because I was pretty. But that's all I was. All I've ever been. I was just something for him to show off to his peeps. To look good on his arm. I don't have a life of my own. That's Chilly's wife, Mrs. Childers, even to you, Nick. To you I'm Mrs. Childers. Well I'm not, my name is Gabriel, my friends call me Gee. Since I'm not your client anymore it's time you started calling me Gee too."

"Okay, Gee. Why don't you get me another drink?"

"I didn't say you could start ordering me around," she

said, snatching the glass out of my hand. "Want any ice?"

"No, just Hennessy will be fine." Mrs. Childers handed me my drink and sat down next to me. "You've never told Chilly that story about you and Rocky, have you?"

"He'd kill Rocky if I told him. I never told anybody. Not Jake, not even Chez. You're the first."

"What makes me so special?"

"I don't know. I've told you a lot of things about me, Nick. Shame that none of it is good. But that's the way it is."

"There must be some happiness in your life."

"You tell me what there is to be happy about? I live in fear, Nick. I never know when Chilly's gonna snap. Sometimes he can be so sweet to me and other times he's like a nightmare."

"Maybe it's time you wake up."

"Maybe. Maybe it is time to get my life back."

She began to cry.

"I never meant for things to turn out the way they did. You have to believe that, Nick. It was never supposed to happen."

"What are you talking about?"

"Huh?"

"What are you talking about?"

"Nothing." She got up and poured herself another drink. "I've been babbling on like a fool. I am a fool."

"When are you gonna tell me what's really goin' on, Mrs. Childers? I mean, Gee."

"I have told you everything, Nick." The tears were gone.

"I don't think so. You're lying about something, or at best you're not tellin' me everything. I can't help you if you don't tell me the truth."

"There's nothing else to tell. Jake is gone. You said it yourself, it was all about this synthetic crack."

"Okay, if that's the way you want to play it." I finished my drink. I was ready to go. I wanted to call Felicia. But she took the glass from my hand. I looked at her. I mean really looked at her for maybe the first time. She was miserable. The more she talked about her life, the more I wanted to, needed to talk to Felicia, hear her voice. Hear something positive. Mrs. Childers returned my glass to me full. I sat back and took a sip of my liquor. "Who's that?"

"What?"

"The music. Who's singing?"

"*N'Dea Davenport.*"

"Never heard of her."

"She used to be the lead singer for *The Brand New Heavies.*"

"Oh yeah, I like them."

"Really, what was your favorite?"

"What's the name of that song? *Never Stop,*" I said.

"You go way back."

"I'm old school. What about you? What's yours?"

"*Mind Trips.*"

"Any reason why?"

"What do you mean?"

"Think about the words."

"Yeah. Maybe that is me. Chilly sure has played some mind trips on me. I remember the first time I caught him with another women. I was so mad, I wanted to kill him. We were at a party at one of his friend's houses. It was the usual dope boy party. People doin' drugs, listening to music, and having sex all over the place. The place was packed, and it was so hot in there and the air wasn't doin' any good. After awhile I noticed that I couldn't find Chilly. So I went looking for him. I looked outside, didn't see him. Then I started going from room to room, that's when I saw him coming out of a room with some ho. Both of them still putting their clothes back on."

"The least they could have done was get dressed before they came out of the room."

"I thought so too."

"What did you do?"

"I slapped the shit outta him, cursed both of them out and left."

"That was it?"

"No. Chilly ran after me, and started with the, you know, 'Baby I'm sorry, I didn't mean for you to see that, she didn't mean nothing to me' and all that shit."

"The usual."

"But I was young, stupid, and in love. A deadly combination. So I bought it, I went back inside with him, and everything was cool. We hung out the rest of the night like two lovebirds. Until most of the people left. So there I am standing by the kitchen, right." She lit up a cigarette and blew the smoke in my direction. "Chilly was sitting on the couch. So I waved to him and smiled. He got up, walked over to me, and back handed me down to the floor. He yelled for me to get up, I tried to crawl away from him, but I couldn't. He grabbed me and pulled me up by my hair. This time he punched me in the face, but he didn't let go of my hair. He kept on punching me. I don't know how many times he hit me. Then he stopped. He looked at me and said '*bitch don't you ever raise your hand higher than your waist to me,*' and he walked away. Here's the funny part."

"There's a funny part?"

"So there I am lying on the floor, crying, face swollen and bleedin'. Blood all over my clothes. People walking by me. The only one who helped me was that same ho he came out the room with. She helped me up off the floor, took me into the same room they were in, and cleaned the blood off my face. She even gave me some clothes to put on. After awhile Chilly knocked on the door, wantin' to know if I'm ready to go home."

"I guess I don't have to ask if you went with him."

"What else could I do? I was scared to death of him. On our way home he was just as nice to me like nothing ever happened."

Just when I was starting to have a little respect for the brother, she goes and lays this on me. "Why do you stay with him?"

"Please, Nick, where am I goin'? What am I gonna do? I tried to get away before and he always comes after me. There's no telling what he'll do to me or Chez if I try it again."

"What about Jake? I noticed you didn't mention Jake."

"Jake is gone. Chilly can't bother him now." The tears began to flow again. "Can't you just listen to what I say without trying to read something into it? But no, you have to analyze every word I say? Can't you stop being a detective for awhile? Can't you just hold me?"

She moved closer to me and put her head on my shoulder and she continued to cry. I felt her heart pounding in her chest; I felt the wetness of her tears, along with her hand on my chest. I wanted to say something to comfort her, but nothing came to mind so I put my arm around her.

After awhile she stopped crying and had fallen asleep. I sat there holding her for awhile. Suddenly she jerked away from my embrace and grabbed a pillow from the couch. "Maybe she can't stand to be held either." I thought about Felicia, how she slept peacefully with her head on my chest. I got up from the couch and looked around for something to cover her. I wandered around the house until I found my way to a bedroom. Not bothering to turn on the light, I found the bed and took the sheet off. When I turned around, I was startled to see her silhouette leaning against the door. The light from the hall seemed to cling to each curve of her body. "Are you lookin' for something, Nick?"

"I was just getting something to cover you with." I said holding up the cover. "You were asleep," I said as she walked toward me.

"I was. But I'm awake now." She stopped in front of me. "I don't think we'll need this." She took the sheet out of my hand and let it drop to the floor. "Maybe now that you don't work for me, you'll start paying me some attention."

"Just what makes you think I haven't been payin' attention to you?"

"I see the way you look at me."

"I ---" she put hand over my lips.

"I'm hot." She stepped closer, resting her chest against me. I took a moment to contemplate the way her moods took dramatic swings. Not five minute ago and for most of the night, she'd been crying. Now she was almost predatory. "And I'm sticky. I'm goin' to take a shower." She stepped away and turned around. "Unzip me." I unzipped her dress and she walked away as I lost site of her in the darkness. The light came on in the bathroom. I stood motionless, watching as she turned on the shower. Then she looked back at me. I took that as my invitation to join her.

She kissed me. Then she put her arms around me and kissed me again. "Undress me, Nick."

I took my time undressing her slowly. Once I was done, she stepped into the shower. "Aren't you coming?"

I undressed myself very quickly and followed her into the shower. My presence was met immediately by her arms around my neck and her tongue in my mouth. I picked her up by the waist, and she wrapped her legs around me. I angled her back against the wall and entered her. Despite the lack of foreplay, she was dripping wet. I like it like that.

"Harder, Nick! Fuck me harder!" I pounded her furiously against the wall. "Yes, Nick! Yes!" she screamed her delight. We went at it in the shower for awhile before we got out. Without bothering to dry ourselves, she hopped up on the bathroom vanity and spread her legs. "Come here," she said, motioning with her finger. I quickly complied. I placed my hands on the mirror to steady myself as well as get some added leverage. She lifted her legs and grabbed her ankles.

For reasons which I can't explain, Ben Josephs crossed my mind. I thought about what Chesará said, *"'Cause he can't fuck. Gee said that he couldn't keep it up long enough to do anything for her. Gee said she rocked the house two times and he came."*

Well, she was rockin' that house with a vengeance, but I was hanging right in there with her. Then her eyes bucked open, her body began to quiver, and her mouth opened as if she wanted to scream, but no words came out.

Mrs. Childers picked up a towel and walked out of the bathroom without a word. I grabbed a towel and followed her out, drying myself as I walked. She wrapped the towel around her and headed for the bar. She poured a drink for each of us and handed me one. I drank mine, and watched as she came from behind the bar. She poured her drink across my chest and then she proceeded to lick it off. Once she was satisfied that she had gotten every drop, she led me into one of the bedrooms, and we went for it again. "Your turn now."

Mrs. Childers laid me down on the bed and she climbed on top of me. I felt her ease herself down on me. She grinded her hips into mine, pinning my shoulders against the bed and stared in my eyes. I felt paralyzed, I couldn't move and I didn't have to. She rode me furiously until I felt myself expand and explode inside her. I had to laugh, because when I came, she screamed louder than I did.

Chapter Seventeen

Mrs. Childers dropped me off at my car and I finally made it home about two in the morning. She was nervous during the ride about what Chilly might do if he were home when she got there. I had drank my share of Hennessy and could feel the makings of a serious hangover coming. I popped a couple of aspirins, took a shower, and crawled into bed. I went to sleep thinking, not only about what I just did with Mrs. Childers in the shower and in just about every room in the house. But I thought about Felicia mostly. Although I found Gee, *now it felt funny saying it*, very attractive, I missed Felicia. I just had sex with her and it was great, but in some strange kind of way, Gee's sex made me long for Felicia's touch even more. I wanted to see her face, hear her voice, to see her smile and be excited by her touch. I rolled over, I didn't understand it and I was too buzzed to try.

Tuesday July 20; 8:03 AM

The sound of somebody's fist or maybe it was their foot, I'm not sure which, woke me from my sleep, around eight the next morning. "Stop fuckin' bangin', I'm coming!"

I dragged myself out of bed and made my way toward the door. What I found was two uniformed cops informing me that Detective Kirkland wanted to see me at the station right away. Once I got through cursing them out for makin' all that noise so early in the morning, I told them to wait, and I would be right out. I gave some thought to getting back in the bed. But that would only make them bang on the door some more. Still, I took my time about getting ready. And an hour later, I found myself sitting alone in an interrogation room waiting for Kirk to show up. But as luck would have it, Richards walked through the door.

"What happened to you, Simmons?" Detective Richards asked.

"I walked into a door?"

"Yeah, right. Looks to me like that door worked you over pretty fuckin' good, Simmons."

I didn't see any point in commenting, so I didn't. Richards was an idiot anyway. Finally Kirk came in and slammed the door behind him. "Sorry to keep you waiting." He stopped in his tracks when he saw me. "Shit, what happened to your face? No wait. Let me guess, you cut yourself shaving."

"No, he walked into a door." Richards laughed.

"Had to be one or the other." Kirk said, and took a seat next to me. "Anyway Nick, I had you brought down here to see if you found out anything more about Jake Rollins."

"Why do you want to know, Kirk? What do you care about my missing persons case?"

"Because your missing persons case may be tied to several drug cases and a murder."

"I know about the drugs. What murder are you talking about?"

"Pamela Hendricks," Kirk said.

"Wasn't that one of the people who you told me died of this mysterious drug overdose?"

"That was our first impression." Richards chimed in.

"Why are you calling it murder now?"

"Nick, in case you haven't noticed, we are the police. That means we investigate." I guess Kirk was trying to be funny, but he wasn't successful. "That investigation has led us to come to a different conclusion."

"What brought you to that conclusion?"

"As near as we can tell, this Hendricks woman didn't use drugs." Kirk asserted. "There were signs of a struggle in the general area where the body was found. So, I'll ask you again, what have you found out about Rollins?"

"Nothing really. I've been working on another case. The more I talk to you guys, the more I'm convinced that I don't want any parts of this. As a matter of fact, just last night, I told my client that I don't think Jake wants to be found."

"You can say that." Richards laughed, and Kirk shot him a look. The more he talked the more the sound of his voice annoyed the shit out of me. Maybe Kirk felt the same way. "Your client thinks her husband, Chilly is involved, doesn't she?"

"I'm not at liberty to say."

Richards jumped out of his seat. "You're startin' to piss me off with that privilege shit, Simmons."

"So."

Kirk looked at him and shook his head. "Sit down Richards."

"Like I said, Kirk, that's all I know."

"What about Felicia Hardy?" Kirk asked.

"That's the roommate, ain't it? Wasn't she a cop?"

"Yeah, you talk to her?"

"No."

"What were you doing in California?"

"I told you, I have another case. Why, is she in Cali?"

"We think so," Kirk said. "Her and the Hendricks woman grew up there. I think maybe she went back there."

"Hmm. Sorry I can't be any more help to you Kirk. But like I said, I backed off of this."

"Then you wouldn't be interested to know that Jake Rollins body was found last night. He was shot, once in the head with a heavy caliber weapon. At fairly close range."

"Has anyone informed my client?"

"Somebody is taking care of that as we speak."

At least I didn't have to be the one to tell Mrs. Childers

that I was a fool. Or at the very least, I was a lousy detective. Yesterday I told her that her brother was alive and hiding somewhere from her husband. Now the cops were there to tell her he's dead. She's probably screaming Chilly did it, right now.

Maybe I was just kidding myself into thinking I could be a detective. I had to start facing the reality that I'm not a detective. I'm a trained killer, that's what I am.

If it wasn't for Reggie, I would have never have found Felicia, and I wouldn't know anything about this whole synthetic crack thing. "Where was the body found?"

"Behind a dumpster at a restaurant on Third Ave. The body had been there awhile."

"You know how long?"

"Not yet. Few days at least. People at the restaurant said they'd smelled it for days before they finally checked it out. Here's what makes this whole thing a little more interesting. It seems that Rollins worked for the same company as another body we found three days ago with his throat slit from ear to ear."

"Coincidence?" I said nonchalantly. As far as I was concerned, I was out of it. I had one more so-called case to investigate, and that was this Marcus Douglas, Yvonne Haggler thing for Bobby.

"I don't think so. They were both chemists, working for the same company. They didn't work together, but still, I'd say that was a bit more then just a coincidence. Wouldn't you say so, Nick?"

"Maybe." The shit was starting to get deep now. The other guy was probably this Rodrigez guy that Chilly's Peruvian friend, Diego Estabon, was supposed to have taken care of. If that was the case, maybe Chilly did take care of his, as promised, in a couple of days. I began to consider the possibility that maybe Chilly had found and killed Jake days ago and he was just setting me up to be part of his alibi.

"You ever seen this guy before Simmons?" Richards asked.

He walked up to the table and handed me a picture of the dead man. "His name is Norman Vogel."

My heart stopped.

"We fished him out of the East River near Pier 17."

The shit just went from deep, to fucked up. If Rodrigez and Norman Vogel was the same person, then we delivered him gift wrapped to the Peruvians. And if that was the case, we were in this up to our necks. I picked up the picture as causally as I could. "No, never seen him before." I dropped the picture. "You finished with me?"

"No, Nick, we're just getting started," Kirk said.

"You think I killed them?"

"Not necessarily. But I'm not ruling you out. I'll tell you what I do think though. I think you know exactly what's goin' on here."

"What makes you say that?" I tried to laugh it off, but he was right. I knew exactly what was goin' on here. I just wasn't about to tell him.

"These are your people, Nick. Scum bags and drug dealers, all of them. So let's start with what happened to your face?"

For the next hour, Kirkland and Richards asked me questions that I knew the answer to, but refused to tell them. Anything I said at this point would lead right back to my front door. So my answer to every question was the same. "I don't know anything about it." I knew they had nothing to hold me on, not yet anyway. The only thing that was on my mind at that point was Felix.

As soon as the police released me, I called Monika.

"Monika, this is Nick."

"No need to be so formal, Nick. How you doin'?"

"Not good. I'm on my way over there now. Call Jett and tell him to meet us there as fast as he can."

"My house? What's goin' on, Nick?"

"We have a problem. Jake is dead. Police just found the body."

"Good for them. How is that a problem for us?"

"I'll explain everything when I get there. Just call Jett. I'll be there in about twenty-five minutes." I must have been driving faster than I thought, 'cause I was there in fifteen minutes. Jett was there when I got there, which would save me the trouble of telling the story twice.

"Are you sure it's the same guy?" Jett asked pacing back and forth around the living room.

"Yeah, I'm sure."

"Something ain't right about this. It's too messy too public. The police can tie this back to us. Felix should never have put us in this position," Monika said.

"Have you tried to call Felix?" Jett inquired. "Find out what the fuck is goin' on?"

"Not yet. And if I did, what's he gonna say? I don't know anything about it, this shouldn't have happened. Best he doesn't know that we even suspect he had any part of this."

"If the cops connect us to Vogel, the shit is over. Fuck Felix. He set us up to take this fall," Monika said.

"We don't know that," Jett said.

"The hell we don't, who else could it be? I never did trust Felix," Monika said as she got up and looked out the window. "I mean what do we know about him anyway?"

"It all goes back to that last mission."

"What are you talking about, Nick?" she asked.

"The way the whole thing went down. I mean what were

we really doin' down there?"

There was silence.

"We've all thought about it. I know I have. There we were in South America killing drug dealers, blowing up drug plants and seizing their financial records. We were small teams, each working independently. But all of a sudden, the entire unit is needed to take out one plant. Then boom, everybody dies."

"Except us." Monika asserted.

"And we'd be dead too if you didn't fall on approach and break your ankle."

"I never will forget searching the area for survivors." I looked over at Jett; he looked like he was in another world, sitting there in the middle of the floor. "Knowing that there wouldn't be any. But the whole time, I'm thinkin' Nick. I'm thinkin', something ain't right. Something in the milk ain't clean."

"I hate it when you say shit like that, Jett. Like white milk is so pure, so clean that - - - "

"Give it a rest for now, Monika. Okay! We pick up the whole Black, White thing at 0700 tomorrow," Jett said and bounced up from the floor. I had to agree. This wasn't the time.

Jett resumed his pacing routine. "Then the way they got us out of there. Quick and quiet. Like we were down there doin' somethin' we didn't have no business doin'. But shit went wrong and everyone died but us. Well shit, we don't know what we know, so what could we tell anybody. And who's gonna ask? You have to know what was goin' on to even ask the damn questions."

What he said was confusing at first, then I realized just how right he was.

"Then we get processed out. And the very next day there's Uncle Felix. But the money's been good so I ain't sayin' nothin'."

"Imagine if we had told Felix no," Monika said

"Like I said, it's not like all of us haven't thought about it. But that's the case with any of the shit we've done, in or out. If we become expendable, we die. More so now."

"We don't know who the fuck Felix is. He never identified himself as a representative of - - - shit, anything!" Monika exclaimed. "We all just went along with it for the money. The fact of the matter is that we're mercenaries."

"She's right, Nick."

"Don't you think I know that? We aren't some kinda high-powered secret government agents. They didn't recruit us into the CIA or any shit like that. They pushed us out and threw some bones our way to keep us happy and quiet."

"I need a drink." Monika picked up a bottle of gin. "What do we do now?"

"Make it two." Jett got up and followed Monika to the kitchen. She poured herself and Jett a glass. "You want one Nick?"

"Hell no. I don't know how y'all drink that shit anyway."

"Like this!" they both said almost at the same time and drained their glasses. "I got some Johnnie Black for you, Nick."

"Thanks."

Monika handed me a glass. "So what are we gonna do?" she asked.

"For the time being I need to stay as far away from this as possible."

"You a suspect, Nick?" Jett asked.

"And I quote, I'm not ruling you out."

"That's not good, Nick," Monika said.

"Jett, start diggin' into Felix. Find out everything you can about him, bank records, property he owns, the whole nine."

"I'll crawl up his ass with a microscope."

"That's disgusting gray boy," Monika said.

"We got to start covering our tracks. But first we need to be sure that Vogel is the one that Estabon was talking about."

"How we gonna do that?"

"Monika, I want you to talk to Chilly, see if you can't get him to confirm that Rodrigez and Vogel are the same person."

"Why me? What makes you think Chilly will tell me anything? Why can't Jett go?"

"We can't send Jett."

"That's right, Monika, he won't tell this gray boy nothing." Jett laughed. "But you, on the other hand, with all them lips, tits and hips you got. Shit, he might confess to murdering 2Pac and Biggie Smalls."

"So what are you trying to say?"

"Just that he's more likely to talk to you, because you're a woman. Just tell him that you're my associate," I said, and they both looked at me.

"Excuse me," Monika said.

"Oh, I forgot to tell you, Chilly gave me five thousand dollars to tell him where Jake was after I told his wife."

Monika poured herself another shot of gin and shook her head. "This shit gets weirder and weirder as we go along."

"Tell me about it."

Chapter Eighteen

Wednesday July 21; 7:21 AM

With nothing else to do, I decided to concentrate my efforts for the day on finding Sally Fitz. I didn't get a chance to talk to Freeze about where I could find him, but if Sal was in the city, he wouldn't be hard to find. There was nothing low profile about Sal.

I went by Freeze's apartment and beat on the door. For fifteen minutes. It was early, but I knew he was there. He opened the door and put a gun in my face.

"Why all the tension and animosity? Show me love, nigga."

"Fuck you, Nick. What you doin' here? You know what fuckin' time it is?" he walked away from the door and then flopped down on the couch.

"Which question do you want me to answer first? What am I doin' here, or what time is it?"

"Start with what time it is."

"It's almost seven thirty."

"Now, what the fuck are you doin' here so fuckin' early in the morning?"

"I came to visit you, man."

"You know, Nick, it ain't that I'm not glad to see you. But, shit, most people don't beat on the door for fifteen minutes. After a minute or two they just go away."

"I knew you were here."

"How you know I was here?"

"The rug. You still turn the rug over when your home."

Freeze looked at me and frowned. Slowly, the frown became a smile and turned into a laugh. "Glad you back, Nick."

"You hungry?"

"Why, you gonna cook?"

"Hell no. But I'm buyin'."
"Good, 'cause there ain't no food here anyway."
"Well, get dressed then."

About a half-hour later, Freeze came out of the back, escorted by a very attractive young woman. I stood up to meet her. "Nick, this is Paulleen. Paulleen, that's Nick."
"Nice to meet you Paulleen."
Judging only by the way she rolled her eyes and sucked her teeth, I could tell that Paulleen wasn't glad to meet me.
"I'll be right back, Nick. I just need to roll her home."
"How long?"
"Fifteen minutes."

Once Freeze got back from droppin' off Paulleen, we set out to eat breakfast. While we ate, Freeze told me about his night. *Before Paulleen, I mean. She was the closer.* There was a problem at Cuisiné. A customer had a complaint with their meal and the manager had gone home sick. The only one left to talk to him was Freeze.
"So, Nick, the guy starts yellin' at my ass, talkin' bout how the service was fucked up and the food was cold. Nick, I'm talkin' bout right up in my face."
"I know you can't stand that. What did you say?"
"I was cool. So I back up off him and I go through the whole nine, apologizin' for the food, and the service and shit. I tell Alexia, no check for this table. Then I tells him, get this, to call ahead for a reservation the next time he wishes to dine with us, and he would be my personal guest for the evening."
"You said that shit?"
"Shit yeah! I'm fuckin' tired of hearin' Wanda's mouth bout this customer service shit. But I ain't feelin' that shit, Nick."

"Why you do it then?"

"That's where Black wants me," Freeze said quietly.

"End of story. So what happened with you and old boy?"

"Okay, after I told him all that shit, he jumps up in my face again. Only this time he got his finger in my face. Now it's all about how I better be glad I did that, because he's some fuckin' body and what a word from him would do to my business. Then the mutha fucka poked me in the chest. Nick!" Freeze started laughin'.

So I laughed too. "What?"

"Nick, I reached for my four five."

"No you didn't."

"Nick, I was about ta pull and blast, but my girl Lex said, '*Freeze*', and I chilled. But I was about to drop his ass. You know I hate that shit, all up in my face and shit."

"At least you didn't do it. Maybe you should take one of them sensitivity classes or something."

"Fuck you, Nick."

"Just tryin' to help."

"So what's up wit you? You find Jake yet?"

"No, not exactly."

"What's that suppose to mean?"

"I mean Kirk found his body."

"So that's it, right? You through wit that shit, right?"

"No, not exactly. Freeze, there's a whole lotta other shit goin' on with this."

"Like what?"

I leaned forward. "It's all about this pipe dream Chilly had about synthetic crack."

"Pipe dream is right. Mutha fucka been talkin' about that shit for years."

"Jake developed it, but everyone who smoked it died."

"Chilly kill him?"

"I don't know."

"What all that got to do with you bein' through with that shit?"

"Cops found a guy we snatched with his throat slit. He might be the one who created it and gave it to Chilly's stupid ass."

"Cops know you killed him?"

"We didn't kill him. We just dropped him off on Pier 17. But that ain't gonna matter now 'cause we all up in this."

"Yeah, I can see where it could all turn on you," Freeze said. "Maybe you should talk to Wanda about this."

"Maybe I should."

"So what are you gonna do?"

"Do you remember Sally Fitz?" I asked.

"Hell yeah, I remember Sal. Why?"

"I need to find him."

"For what?"

"That thing for Bobby."

"What thing for Bobby?" Freeze asked.

"I didn't tell you about it?"

"Naw, you missed that."

"I'm doin' a favor for Bobby."

"When you talk to Bobby?"

"I didn't. Bobby sent this guy, Marcus Douglas to see me."

"Bobby sent you a client?"

"Picture that."

"That should, if you was payin' attention, let you know that the only one carryin' that Camille shit around, is you," Freeze blasted. "But you ain't payin' attention, so fuck it. What's up with this Douglas guy?"

"He got hooked up with some woman that was workin' as a courier for some guy named Paris. Things went south for her and he wants to know why."

"What Sal got to do with it?"

"I was talkin' to a guy I know that runs in those circles. He couldn't or wouldn't tell me anything, but he put me on to Sal."

"He in the city?"

"That's what I hear."

"I'll call around, see what's up wit that."

"That's why you my nigga, Freeze."

"So what you doin' now?"

"Nothing, til I find him. I'm keepin' a low profile today."

"Fuck that, Nick. Hang out with me."

"Where we goin'?"

"I don't care. You drivin'. Check!"

We hung out the rest of the day. It's funny; me and Freeze are so different now. But it felt like I never left.

We finally rolled up at Cuisiné about seven and Freeze hit the phone. He still knew everybody. *Some thing's never change.* By nine thirty he had found out where Sal had been hangin' out lately and we were on our way to see him. We fell up in Some Joint in Queens, glad that we were both heavily armed. I spotted Sal at the bar, surrounded by four women. Talkin' loud, drink in one hand, money in the other. Nothing low profile about Sally Fitz. I made my way toward him. "Yo, Sal, Sally Fitz!"

He looked around to see who called him Sally Fitz. He only lets certain people call him that. "Nick! That fuckin' Nick!" he came toward me and shook my hand. "Good to see you Nick. How you been? Where's Jett?"

"Jett's workin' on something."

"What you doin' in here?"

"Lookin' for you."

"For me? You didn't fall up in this joint by yourself, did

you?"

"And suppose I did." I looked around the room. "I can drop every ass in this *joint* if I had to."

"I fuckin' know you can, Nick. I fuckin' know you can."

"Don't worry about it Sal, Freeze is with me."

"Freeze! Shit, I haven't seen his ass in years. Where's he at?"

"Over there." I pointed at Freeze.

Sal threw up his arms. "Call him over."

"He's watchin' my back."

"This sounds fuckin' serious."

"Some place quiet we can talk Sal?"

"Outside. Come on."

I followed Sal and Freeze followed me out the club. Sal walked across the street. Once again Freeze decline Sal's invitation to join us. "So what's up, Nick?"

"You know a guy named Paris?"

"Paris, yeah I know him. We did a lot of business together. Why?"

"You know a lady named Yvonne?"

"Yvonne Haggler. I know her. She used to carry for him. You know her too, well, at least you met her."

"I been thinkin' the name was familiar. Where did I meet her?"

"A little club in Istanbul."

"Istanbul? I remember. I came there with Jett, and as usual, you were surrounded by women. Which one was she?"

"The one with the body beggin' to get out that blue dress. Kept sayin' she was waitin' for somebody."

I smiled. "I remember her."

"Hard to forget them when they come like that. What's you're interest here?"

"I'm doin' a favor for a friend. But I already forgot

about talkin' to you."

"Fair enough. What about him?"

"How do you know Yvonne carried for him?"

"I saw who she was meeting, so I checked her out. Paris told me to fuck her quick."

"Why?"

"Nick, that's exactly what I said. Why?"

"Well?"

"Paris used to take her around with him. Show her off to people. You seen her. He was in love with her. He was thinkin' about askin' her to marry him. So he feels her out first. She tells him that this life was nothing but a part time job for her. That she was plannin' on retiring when she turned thirty and could collect on some trust fund. He said he couldn't let that happen. Yvonne met too many people, saw too many things she could talk about. That's all I can tell you. And I didn't tell you that."

"Thanks, Sal." I shook his hand. "Freddie sends his regards." And walked across the street.

"That lyin' fuck!" Sal yelled.

Freeze came up and talked to Sal while I watched his back. I would call Marcus Douglas in the morning and tell him what he wanted to know. And why. But I could have told him why right after he told me his story. There's usually only one way out of that game.

Freeze dropped me off at my apartment, before goin' back to the club. I tried to call Felica, but I got voice mail. I left a message and then I called Jett. He had been trying to get information about our Uncle Felix. "I'm not gettin' anywhere with this, Nick. At this point, I can't even tell you if Felix is really his name. But I'm on it, I'll get him."

"I know you will. You heard from Monika?"

"Not since this afternoon. She said she was goin' to

meet Chilly. What's goin' on with you?"

"I saw Sally Fitz tonight. He asked for you."

"Oh did he. Where?"

"Some *Joint* out in Queens. I'm not sure where we were, Freeze was driving.

"The slimy bastard didn't give you the money he owes me."

"No, sorry."

"I didn't think so."

"He did remind me of where we know Yvonne Haggler from."

"Where?"

"Istanbul. Remember, me and you went to that little club and Sal was there."

"He bet me five hundred that he could fuck one of them honeys he was with. He fucked around all night tryin' to get her drunk. She drank him under the table and left. So I know it wasn't her. Which one was she?"

"She was the one in blue dress."

"Nervous broad, always lookin' around. Yeah, I remember her. Nice tits. Sally was at her first. But she kept playin' him off sayin' she had to meet somebody."

There was a knock at the door.

"Hold on, Jett. Someone's at the door."

"Hope it's some pussy!"

"Let's hope." I thought about Felicia, but that wasn't about to happen. But fantasy is a good thing.

"See if she got a friend." I heard Jett holler though the phone. I went to the door. And looked thought the peek hole. The hallway was filled with cops. I went back to the phone.

"Jett, a whole group of cops are at the door."

"What do they want?"

"Whatever it is, it ain't good." The knocking began

again. "I'll call you back."

The banging got louder as I walked back to the door.

"Police!"

I opened the door and was met by Kirk.

"Nick Simmons?" An uniformed officer said while Kirk smiled at me.

"What's goin' on, Kirk?"

"We have a warrant to search these premises." The officer said.

"You gotta be kiddin' me." He handed me the warrant. I looked at it. Maybe I shoulda called Wanda. Thinking that I had nothing to hide, I let them in. Cops seemed to swarm all over the place. Kirk was still standing in the hallway by the door. Smiling.

"What's goin' on here, Kirk?"

"We found Lisa Ellison, Jake Rollins girlfriend, dead in her living room. Shot at close range with the same caliber weapon that Rollins was killed with."

"What does that have to do with me?"

"Your fingerprints were found on," Kirk broke out his notepad, "on a glass, the coffee table, the phone and the inside door knob."

"Am I under arrest?"

"No. And that's only because I don't think you'd be stupid enough to shoot her and leave prints everywhere."

"So what's goin' on here?"

"Well, Nick, you searched Rollins apartment on more than one occasion, and your prints puts you at the Ellison murder scene. This makes you a suspect in both murders, as far as I can see. We're just looking for what you found and aren't telling us about, that's all, Nick. After we're finished here. You are going to ride with me down to your office, where we'll execute this warrant to search your office."

"This is fucked up, Kirk."

"Maybe. But just for laughs, why don't you explain to me when you were there and what you talked to her about."

"I was there last Wednesday night about eight. I asked her a couple of questions about where I might find Jake. I had a glass of water. I used the phone and I left."

"This may sound like a stupid question, but you never know. Was she alive when you left her?"

"Of course she was."

Once they finished terrorizing my apartment, we went to my office and they did the same. Since I didn't kill Jake or Lisa and there was nothing in either place to connect me to Vogel or Rodrigez or who ever he was, I wasn't sweatin' the search. Until - - -

"Detective Kirkland, I think we got something here." Kirk looked at me, smiled and walked away. I had no idea what they had, but I was goin' to see. I fell right in behind Kirk.

"Take a look at this."

The officer had Jake's file in his hand and gave Kirk a piece of paper. At least it wasn't the murder weapon. Kirk looked over the paper carefully, and then handed it to me. It was the formula for synthetic crack. What a time for Monika to start filing.

"What is this?" Kirk asked me.

The officer gave Kirk another piece of paper. It had to be the analysis that Monika's friend had done.

I waited for Kirk to finish reading before I answered. Kirk handed me the paper. "Does the phrase withholding evidence, or obstruction of justice mean anything to you."

"They do now."

"Book him."

215

Chapter Nineteen

The more I thought about it, the surer I was that Monika and Jett were right. This private investigating stuff sucked. I hate cops. And I had been spending too much time with them fuckas. Now I had to help them. It just went against everything.

Me and Kirk had a long conversation, during which he threatened to charge me with murder if I didn't start cooperating. I knew he couldn't make a case there. However, withholding and obstruction they had me on, but I still stuck to my story. "I don't know anything about that." I still felt like a snitch sittin' there. This shit sucks. He wanted to know how I got the formula. No biggie there, since he already figured I got it from Jake's safe. I gave him that and told him that I had only got the analysis back yesterday. "Jake was already dead. Case closed, so we filed it."

We danced around the same points for hours and then he had some uniforms take me to the holding cell. The benches were cold and hard. Naturally, it was crowded with just us.

Thursday July 22; 12:45 PM

Jett arranged my bail, and I was out by lunchtime. When we got back to my apartment, Monika was there waiting for us. Not only had she cleaned up after the cops, but she had cooked. Monika never cooks. She hates it. So even though I was skeptical about eating it, I know it was made with love. For the rest of the afternoon we sat around and talked about our situation until the sun went down. Monika got up to leave. "Where you goin'?" Jett asked.

"I'm goin' to meet Chilly," she replied, heading for the door.

"I thought you got with him last night?" I asked, gettin' up to see her out. "You ain't fallin' in love with him, are you?" Me and Jett laughed, but Monika, on the other hand, saw no humor in it at all. She stopped dead in her tracks.

"You two silly ass mutha fuckas done lost y'alls *gotdamn* minds! This is strictly business, understand!" she said with her finger on my nose. I still was laughing. "Business that you're sending me on. So remember that." And with that, she left.

"She's kinda touchy. Must be that time of the month," Jett said as he got up. "I'm outta here too, Nick. I'll catch up with you tomorrow."

"I'll git wit ya, Jett."

With the house now empty, I gave some thought to sleep. Which I hadn't done since the day before. So I put on some music. Freeze had been bumpin' some bootlegged 2Pac, and he let me borrow it. "I should have taken that N'Dea Davenport CD from Mrs. Childers."

Jake's funeral was the next day, so I thought about whether I would make a cameo appearance. I took a shower and fell asleep to the sound of Pac tellin' me how I was fuckin' wit the wrong nigga.

I don't know how long I had been asleep; it was quiet, but that quiet was soon replaced by somebody bangin' on my door. My first thought was that it was Freeze, exacting a measure of payback from the day before. I picked up my gun and opened the door, prepared to shove the gun in his face.

"Remember me?"

"Felicia."

"Surprise!" she threw her arms around my waist and kissed me the kiss I'd been dreaming about since the last time she kissed me. I responded in kind.

"What are you doin' here?"

"I missed you." Felicia kissed me on the cheek. "Did I come at a bad time?"

"No, not at all."

"Can I come in?"

"I'm sorry. Of course you can come in." I stepped aside and closed the door behind her. "I'm just surprised, that's all. Have a seat. Can I offer you something?"

"No I'm fine. Nice place, mind if I look around?"

"No, be my guest."

Felicia wandered around the apartment with her hands on her hips. Lookin' over her shoulder to see if I was watching. Which I was. She swung her hips harder and I smiled. "What you smiling about?" she asked as she walked past me.

"Just happy to see you, Felicia. What made you come back here anyway?"

"You did."

"I did?"

"Yes, you, Nick."

"How did I do that?"

"Two ways. First, I missed you and I wanted to be with you." She went into the kitchen. She looked impressed. It was clean for a change, thanks to Monika. She came out. "Seems you got a sistah a little dick whipped."

Felicia wandered into the bedroom.

"Nice bed," she said and came back out, carefully closing the door and tapping the doorknob. Felicia turned around and came toward me. "And second, you gave me a shot of your courage. So I decided to come back and face things head on, you know, take a more proactive approach to this thing."

"Well, it's pretty much over."

"You solved the case?" Felicia's face lit up. She was

excited for me. I thought that was sweet of her.

"Nope."

Man I was diggin' her. Look at her eyes, her smile. I took a step closer to Felicia.

"Cops found Jake dead a couple of days ago."

"Oh really."

"Yes really. Cops searched here and my office last night. They found the formula and the analysis of that synthetic crack. So I'm done with it."

"Good, what about your other case?"

"Done. I just need to call Mr. Douglas in the morning and tell him the deal."

"Even better. That means you'll have some time to spend with me." She reached for my hand and squeezed it. Then she touched my face with the other hand.

She kissed me on my cheek.

She started to walk away, but I pulled her back toward me.

I touched her face and kissed her lips. It was more like I pressed my lips against hers. I started to walk away but she pulled me back toward her and she kissed me. Believe me, it was more fun this time. I liked it and I wanted more.

She kissed me again.

We stood awkwardly looking at each other for what seemed like a long time. And then, almost at the same time, we both started taking off our clothes. I felt the vibration of my pager, but I didn't seem to care.

Friday July 23; 1:17 AM

When I woke up, it was past one in the morning. I looked at Felicia; she was out for the count. I got up and put on my pants, and once again, I felt the vibration of my pager. I checked the number, "Monika." It was late but I called anyway.

"This is Detective Richards."

"I'm sorry, wrong number." And I hung up quickly. What was Richards doin' there? I called again.

"Hello," Detective Richards answered.

"Richards, this is Nick Simmons. Where's Monika?"

"You're her partner, right?"

"Yeah, where is she?"

"She's been shot, Nick. Shot five times. Doesn't look good for her."

"When was this?"

"Around ten, we figure." While I was busy laying down my mack. I cursed myself for not answering.

"They took her to the hospital."

"What hospital?"

"Lebanon."

"What happened?"

"I'm not at liberty to say. Was she working on the same case?"

"I'm not at liberty to say."

"Come on, Nick, give me a break, anything you can give us would help."

"Come on, Richards, give me something, That's my partner." My friend. My family.

"You know I can't do that," Richards said. I could hear Kirkland's big mouth in the background. I couldn't make out everything he said, but I did hear him say, "There was no sign of forced entry. Nothing appears to be missing. So we can assume it was someone she knew." Which answered all my questions. When I heard him say, "Pick up her partner, Nick Simmons, see what he knows." I knew it was time to hang up. "I'm going to the hospital, Richards. You can catch me there."

I went to Monika's room in the intensive care unit.

The nurse stopped me from going in the room. "I'm sorry sir, family members only."

"I am her family." And pushed by her.

Jett and I are the only family she has, or at least that she communicates with. Monika and her mother fell out long before she joined the army. When she was fifteen, her mother's boyfriend grabbed her ass when she walked by him. She told her mother what happened. But she didn't believe her. She accused Monika of flirting with him and told her that's what she got for dressin' like a tramp. They haven't spoken since.

A doctor came in to check on her. To be honest she didn't look old enough to be a doctor. She told me that Monika had been shot five times. Two shots in the chest, two to the head, one hit her above the left ear. She caught the one in her eye. They were not able to save her eye. The other one was in her hand. Knowing Monika, she was probably trying to stop the bullet with her hand. I felt my eyes began to water.

I sat there with her, holding her hand and talking. I didn't know if she could hear me or not, but I didn't care. I wanted her to know that she wasn't alone. That I was there with her and that she was going to be all right. If 2Pac can take five shots and live, she could too.

"Nick, 2Pac is dead." Wanda asserted.

"Freeze say's he ain't." I replied.

Monika was strong, in both mind and body. Next to Mike Black, she is probably the strongest person I've ever met. I sat there wondering how it happened. Was her attacker there when she paged me? Was there something I could have done to prevent this from happening? Even if I left right then, the best I could have done was get there in time to talk to the police. "I still should have answered." There was nothing I could have done. But still, I felt like shit. I should have been there. I should have been there watching her back.

"But no, fuckin' Felicia seemed a little more important."

The chair began to feel harder than it had all night, so I walked to the window and watched the sunrise. I don't know how long I stood there, but when I turned around Jett was sitting there.

"How long you been here?" But he didn't answer. He just sat there, kinda stone faced. He was pale. Paler than he usually is. He just sat there staring at Monika, he didn't even blink. Since he wasn't talkin' I went and sat down.

Finally, after about an hour, Jett finally spoke. "I love Monika."

"I do too." I replied.

"I don't think you understand Nick. I really love her. I love both of you. You and Monika are closer to me than my own family, man. --- I was there, Nick. I was right fuckin' there, Nick. Right there."

"What happened, Jett?" But he didn't say a word. He just kept on staring at Monika. Since he wasn't talkin' again, I told him what the doctor said. I couldn't tell if he was listening or not. I'd never seen Jett like this and it worried me. Jett was always live. This wasn't good. They had been my two closest friends, my only family for years. Now one may die and Jett, I couldn't tell where he was. But it wasn't good. I had a pocket full of questions and no one to ask.

"She called me, Nick. She said things didn't go well with Chilly. She said to meet her at her house. When I got there I heard the shots. I ran to the door, yellin' for Monika. I went inside and saw her. Lying there. I picked up the phone and called the cops. She tried to talk. But I couldn't hear what she was sayin'. I did what I could to stop the bleeding and make her comfortable." Then he stopped talking again. He still hadn't taken his eyes off Monika. He still hadn't blinked. Another ten minutes or so went by before Jett started talkin' again. "I heard a noise in the back. I got to the back door in time to see someone drive away. I got to my heap and I followed him. He didn't pick me up. He stopped at a house on 229th street. I put on my gloves and went in after him. He didn't hear me come in. Caught him in the bathroom pissin'."

"Who was he, Jett? Was he black, white, what did he look like?" No answer. Just that pale, glassy eyed look. Like my questions annoyed him. I decided I would save my questions until he was finished. He looked back at Monika. I watched the tears roll down his cheeks. My eyes began to water again. I got up and walked back to the window.

"I popped him in the back of the neck and dragged him into the living room. I put him in a chair and tied him up. I slapped him around until he came out of it. I took out my knife. He tried to get free." Jett shook his head. "That wasn't happening. The more he moved the tighter they got. I asked him who he was and why he shot Monika. But he didn't answer, so I cut him. Just a little cut on the arm to get him bleedin'. But he didn't say shit. Didn't even finch. And told him I would cut him everytime he didn't answer me. He just looked at me. So I cut him again. But he wasn't talkin'. I worked him over pretty good, but the bastard wasn't sayin' shit. So I went back to cuttin' him."

"How many times did you cut him, Jett?"

"I don't know."

I forgot my promise not to ask any more questions. At least he answered me. But he stopped talkin' again. Just starin' at Monika. It took almost a half-hour before Jett spoke again. "We had been there for hours, Nick. Blood was all over the floor. He was shakin' and shit. I was really fuckin' pissed when I saw the sun coming up. I walked up to him and cut his throat."

"You killed him?"

"That's what I fuckin' just said. I cut his fuckin' throat."

I sat down in that hard ass chair and buried my head in my hands. "Jett you killed the only person who could tell us who tried to kill her and why."

"He wasn't gonna talk, Nick, so he had to fuckin' die."

"You're probably right."

"We don't need him to tell us shit, Nick." Jett finally faced me. The expression on his face didn't change. "That fuckin' Chilly knows why."

"What did you do with the body?"

"I left him there."

"Come on." I got up and walked out of the door. Jett was right behind me. He drove me to the house and we went inside. There he was. The sunlight was shining brightly through the window on him. A pool of blood surrounded the chair. Jett stood there and looked at him, while I searched the house. It was empty. No clothes in the closets, no food in the refrigerator. Nothin' to go on. "Lets go."

Chapter Twenty

I drove Jett's car back to the hospital and left him there to be with Monika. In the condition he was in, that was the best place for him. He would be of no use to me and maybe just a little out of place where I was goin'. My destination was Woodlawn Cemetery, for Jake's funeral. I drove back to my apartment to pick up my rifle. Felicia was gone when I got there.

I stood quietly off to the side and watched Mrs. Childers and Chesará hold one another and cry. But my eyes were on Chilly. There he was, standing there with that smug look on his face. Not consoling his wife in her time of loss. That's because the ugly fuck did it. He probably had Lisa killed, figuring that Jake must have told her what was up. And Monika. I was gonna kill him. I looked around the crowd. There was an older couple watching from the other side as Jake's casket was lowered into the ground. The woman was crying and the man just held her close to his chest. I figured that was their parents. I wondered who called them? Chez most likely. Mrs. Childers, I mean Gee, wouldn't call them. She said they were dead to her. Maybe she felt they should know their son was dead.

I thought about losing my parents, when I was eleven. No one really knew what happened to them. One day they just didn't come home. They sent my brother and sister to Mississippi to live with my fathers brother and his wife. They didn't want me. My uncle said they were just babies, they would raise them in the church. They would be all right. But I was into too much trouble and he wasn't havin' it. Not in his house. Said I was probably the reason my parents didn't come home.

He didn't know I was listening.

I never saw my brother and sister again. I don't think

about them much. But I was feelin' kinda family. Maybe I would go to Mississippi and try to find them. What would I say to them? They probably don't even remember me. It was decided that I would go live with my grandmother. And after awhile, it didn't matter as much. My grandmother was good to me. Showed me much love. She died five years later. But I had a new family by then. And after Black kicked my ass on my first day on the block, they showed me much love too.

While I was daydreaming, the funeral party had broken up and Chilly was safe inside the limo. I followed the limo to their house. I had no idea what I was goin' to do. Would I simply ask him what happened with Monika the night before? Or would I just drop him because he deserved to die. When the limo arrived at the house, it was crawling with cops. I parked the car down the street. As soon as the limo stopped, the cops opened the door and took Chilly into custody.

"Shit!"

The cops put him in the car and I watched as the police car drove past me. I looked at Chilly, he looked at me. The feelings were mutual. I drove away thinkin' about Monika and before I knew it, I was back at the hospital. When I got to intensive care, Jett was gone and Detective Richards was there.

"What happened, Richards?"

"Simmons, I'm sorry about your partner. I know how it feels to have a - - -"

"Fuck all that! What happened to her!" I yelled and I pounded my fist against the glass. It frightened the nurses, so I tried to calm down. "Just tell me what happened." I expected Richards to be his usual arrogant white boy cop self, but he was cool.

"She was shot in the living room, there wasn't any sign

of a struggle. Her gun was still in her shoulder holster. We figure she either knew the guy or he caught her off guard. He came in, she turned, and he shot her. Your other partner," Richards checked his notes. "James Bronson, says the door was opened when he got there. Paramedics told me he probably saved her life, stoppin' the bleedin' before he left the scene. He wasn't real clear about why he left the scene. Says he went after the guy who did it. He was pretty shook up, so I didn't press him about it. But we're gonna need to talk to him."

"Where is he?"

"He left about fifteen minutes ago."

I started to ask if he said where he was goin', but I knew better. I knew Jett. The only thing on his mind was finding who was involved. And kill them. And he wouldn't be invitin' the cops along. "Thanks."

"Like I was sayin', I know what it feels like when your partner gets shot." Richards walked away. Maybe be wasn't such an asshole.

I talked to the doctor before I left the hospital. She told me the Monika's condition hadn't changed. "It's all up to her now." She promised that she would do all she could. I thanked the doctor for everything she had done. My mind was on finding Jett.

Where would he go? I drove by the house he followed Monika's assailant to. Looking for anything that might lead me to who was responsible. No cop cars, no yellow crime scene tape. Just in case somebody was watching the house, I parked a couple of blocks away and walked back. When I went inside the body was gone. All the blood was cleaned off the floor. There was no trace that Jett had tortured and executed a man there. I went through the house anyway. Nothing.

"What now?"

I didn't feel like sitting around the hospital, so I drove by Rocky's spot. I didn't think he was involved in Monika's shooting, but I was mad. I had a little payback I wanted to deal out.

When I got there a crowd had formed. The police were standing around a convertible Impala stopped at the light. I parked and approached the crowd. I watched as they took two bodies out of the front seat. "What's goin' on?" I asked an old man in the crowd.

"Somebody shot those three men in that car." The third body was removed from the car. It was Rocky. My first thought was Jett.

"You know if they saw who did it? Was he white?"

"I don't know."

I thanked the man and returned to my car. With nowhere else to go, I went back to my apartment. Quietly I was hoping that Felicia had come back. I needed to see her, but that wasn't happening. The place was in darkness.

The phone rang.

"Listen, Nick," Jett said, he still didn't sound good.

"Where are you?"

"I'm at the stake house, by Chilly's. I know who did it."

"Who?"

"I can't talk now. Meet me here."

"Jett, wait!" I yelled, but he was gone. I drove as fast as I could to the house. When I got to the house, Jett was gone. I walked outside and got back in my car. I drove down the street slowly. I saw Jett's car parked on my right. I parked up ahead of him and walked back to his car. I came around to the driver's side. "What's goin' on, Jett?"

"Jett!"

I looked in the car. His eyes were wide open. "Jett!" I shook him. That's when I saw the trail of blood coming from his ear. I opened the car door and Jett fell into my arms.

He was dead.

I asked a lady walking by to call the police. I sat there in the street holding Jett until the paramedics came. I talked to the police and was doin' an excellent job of telling them as little as possible, until Richards showed up. "What's goin' on, Simmons? First one of your partners, then the other. What are you involved in?"

"I don't know. My case was closed when you found Rollins dead body with a bullet in his brain."

"I didn't tell you this, but Rollins was already dead when he was shot. His neck was broken, that's what killed him.

"How he died don't matter, he's dead. You found that formula and arrested Chilly."

"You think he's involved in this?"

I looked at Richards like he was stupid. Of course I think he's involved. Monika met him last night. Whatever happened, happened and she wanted me and Jett to meet her. Now Jett gets popped a block from the fuckas house.

"What happened here?" Richards asked, taking the hint that I wasn't goin' to answer his question.

"I don't know."

"Were you with him?"

"No. He called me and said to meet him here."

"Did he say why?"

"No. He hung up before I could ask him."

"Look, Simmons, I'm really sorry for you. I know you think Chilly is involved in this. It's pretty funkin' obvious that your partner here did too. We're a block from his house for Christ's sake. But please, let us handle it."

"Yeah right." I turned and started back for my car.

"Where are you goin'?"

"I need a drink."

Chapter Twenty-one

There was no doubt about it, I was drunk. Trippin' over the rug by the door was a real indicator of that. Staggering the way I was, the couch was as far as my drunk legs would carry me. I disarmed myself and sat down. Fell down actually. Fortunately for me, I had left a bottle of Johnnie Black on the coffee table. I picked up a glass and started to pour. I decided that was too much trouble. So I raised the bottle to my mouth. I could actually feel the liquor flowing through my body. The only problem was that it wasn't helping. I had just returned from the hospital, Monika hadn't regained consciousness and was still in intensive care. It didn't matter. I still had to tell her that Jett was dead.

For the second time, I faced myself with the same question. "If I had only got there sooner, could I have saved him?"

I didn't know.

The only difference was that this time I wasn't fuckin' Felicia, or some dumb shit like that. I was on my way. His body was still warm when I got there. "If I had only - - -"

No point torturing myself about it now. Jett was dead and Monika was fighting for her life. I slammed the bottle down on the table. This game had gone on long enough. Somebody was going to have to answer for both of them. But who?

I wanted to hurt somebody, make somebody feel my pain. But who? I was sure that Chilly ordered up both hits, but he was in jail. I gave serious thought to getting myself arrested so I could kill him. But the thought faded quickly. I could get Freeze to arrange it, but I wouldn't get any satisfaction from just knowing he was dead. I had to do it. I wanted him to feel all my pain. I wanted to look in his eyes before I pulled the trigger. "Say Good-bye." I wanted him to know why he had to die. Not just for me, but for everyone he terrorized over the years. Johnnie Black called out to me, as if he wanted to drink to it. I gladly obliged him. "A drunk never argues with his bottle." It was almost a rule. A good soldier always follows rules. No, a good soldier always follows orders. "What do drunks do?"

They drink!

Stupid!

Saturday July 24; 11:19 AM

When I woke up, the bottle was empty and I was on the floor. I stood up slowly, and looked around the apartment. I took a moment to think about how I got that far away from the couch and who made this mess. I needed someone to blame. I looked at the empty bottle. "Had to be you."

I was hungry, but I didn't feel like cooking, so I grabbed my keys and looked around for my guns. I didn't see them and I didn't care. I would find them when I got back. The liquor store was my first stop. My first drink of the day convinced me that it wouldn't be my last. I walked to the bar on the next corner. "Might as well kill two birds with one stone." Since it wasn't quite time for lunch, and a little too late for breakfast, I had steak and eggs. Johnnie Black replaced the orange juice. While I sat there gettin' my eat and my drunk on, I gave some thought to, you know, stop feeling sorry for myself and doin' something about it. All this drinking wasn't gonna bring Jett back from the dead or make Monika open her eyes. And on top of that, it wasn't making me feel any better, just drunker.

With that thought in mind, I was able to keep the

drinking to two shots. On my way out of the restaurant, a man asked me for some spare change. Freeze told me that was the line Shy used on her boy E. But since that wasn't the case here, I made his day with a picture of Alexander Hamilton.

When I got back to the apartment, I put my bottle down on the coffee table, headed for the shower, and tried to pull it together. I love long hot showers. With my head clearing, I began to think about how I was goin' to exact my revenge. I might not be able to get Chilly, but I would tear threw his whole set. I would be the nightmare now, but they wouldn't be wakin' up.

All at once, I became very conscious of the fact that I was just one guy and he had an army. But I knew in my heart that I wouldn't be alone. Freeze had my back, just like the old days. And for that, I felt like shit. I would be draggin' Black's organization into a war. Maybe even, Black himself. "How could I do that after what I did." I turned off the shower and came back to reality. If it was gonna get done, it would be me doin' it. I would have to have a plan. Pick them off, one by one, in methods that were more creative. I put my pants back on and resumed the search for my guns. It wasn't like I didn't have an arsenal here. But it was the principle of the thing. There was a knock at the door. I looked out the peep hole and didn't see anybody. "Who is it?"

"It's Gee, Nick. Please let me in." I looked again and still didn't see her. I opened the door, stepped aside, and prepared to receive her. She took a step inside. I looked at her face. Her jaw was swollen and - - -

"Get in there!" the door swung open and there was Chilly. Gee stumbled to the floor. Chilly pointed the gun at me and grabbed her, jerking her back to her feet.

"I'm sorry, Nick." Gee whimpered.

"You stay right where the fuck you are! You move and I'll kill you."

"You're gonna try to kill me anyway, what's the difference?"

"Right."

Chilly fired at me.

I didn't move. It came close to hitting my arm. I don't think he meant to hit me with that shot. It was meant to get my attention.

It did.

I wasn't afraid to die. I just didn't want to die like this, half-naked and unarmed.

Chilly looked at me and then at his wife. "Get over there with him. You two belong together." He pushed her in my direction. "Ain't neither one of you worth a shit."

"You all right?"

"I'm okay," Mrs.. Childers said softly, not taking her eyes off Chilly.

"How'd he get out?"

"Bail," She whispered.

"Don't ask her nothin' mutha fucka! You wanta know how I got out, you ask me!" Chilly screamed. "Cops can't hold a mutha fucka like me on some bullshit tip like this! You two think you're slick. Had this shit all worked out. Neither one of you mutha fuckas can be trusted. Your ho ass, out there fuckin' everybody. And you nigga, everything they said about you is true. But I thought that was all bullshit. I thought you was old school. I came to you on the real, straight up business. Showed you more respect than you deserved. You took my money!"

"You took money from him?" Mrs. Childers looked puzzled at me.

"Oh, he didn't tell you? That wasn't part of y'alls little plan? Stupid bitch! You always was a stupid bitch, Gee.

This nigga been playin' you! I gave him five grand to tell me where Jake was. But the difference between me and this nigga, is that I have honor. You ain't loyal to shit are you mutha fucka? Fuckin' my wife. You a dirty mutha fucka. Bobby shoulda killed your ass." He spit in my face and then moved the barrel of his gun against my forehead, in case I wanted to do something about it. "You two dirty mutha fuckas set me up!"

"Set you up?" I had to laugh. It might have been foolish to laugh at a man that's pointing a gun at you, but that shit was funny. "You killed Jake."

"Wasn't me. Up 'til the day before the cops found him, I was still lookin' for him. Don't you remember? I gave you five grand to find him. For all I know you killed."

"Jake develop that killer crack for you? All those people dyin' is on your head."

Now it was Chilly who was laughing. "I didn't kill nobody. That's on Jake's. Who knew his sorry ass was a sorry ass chemist?"

"You practicin' for your day in court?"

"I ain't goin', you are."

"Who killed Pamela Hendricks?"

"Let's see, - - - didn't she die from that bullshit *her* punk ass brother cooked up?"

"What about Lisa?" I asked him quietly.

"You killed her. Your finger prints was at the murder scene."

"Rocky?"

"You killed him too, 'cause he sent his boyz after you."

"What about Jett and Monika?"

"I don't know no damn Jett. And Monika," He licked his lips and smiled a smile that annoyed the fuck out of me. "Shit! I had other plans for her fine ass. So you see my nigga, you the one gonna die for this."

Although I hated to admit it, he had a point. He could still walk away from all this. Leaving me to step off for it.

"Get me a drink, Gee."

"What?"

Chilly slapped her to the floor and quickly returned his gun to my forehead.

"I said get me a fuckin' drink."

Figuring it was best to stay low, Gee crawled over to the coffee table and poured him a drink. Gee got to her feet and walked slowly toward him. she reached out to hand him the glass. He took his eyes off me to reach for the glass.

"Don't even think about it."

Gee threw the glass in his eye.

Chilly grabbed his eye.

I went for the gun.

I kicked it out of his hand; the gun fell to the floor. He punched me in the face; I fell to the floor. Chilly backhanded Gee and she went down too. He was strong as hell. I got to one knee, but before I could get up, he was on me. He rammed his knee into my face and I fell back. I hit my back against the coffee table and rolled over. Chilly came at me fast, kicking me in the back. Gee got up; Chilly kicked away. She jumped on his back and scratched his face. In one smooth motion Chilly shook her off of his back; Gee hit the floor hard. Chilly turned to look at her; it gave me enough time to get to my feet.

I rushed at him. Clinching both of my hands together, I hit Chilly in the face. He fell back and stumbled over Gee. I went straight at him, hittin' him again and again. Chilly swung at me and missed. I got one arm around his throat and the other around his head. I squeezed with everything I had. He struggled, I squeezed harder. He tried to get my arm from around his neck. I squeezed harder. I could feel him gasping for air. I jerked his head as hard as I could to the side. Chilly stopped strugglin'. I looked at Gee, she hadn't moved.

I let his body down to the floor.

My back was killin' me.

I looked around for his gun. Conveniently, it had fallen by the couch. I picked it up, sat down, and look at their bodies on the floor.

Gee began to move and I got up slowly. I helped her to her feet and over to the couch. "Are you all right?" I sat down next to her.

"I think so." Her hands were shaking, so I held them.

"You were all right back there."

"Huh?" she looked at me like I was stupid.

"I mean you didn't just stand back screamin'. You came through for me. Thank you. You saved my life."

"It wasn't all that," she smiled. "My back is killin' me."

"Mine too."

She looked at Chilly. "Is he dead?"

"I don't know. And I'm not all that interested in goin' over there to find out. If he moves, I'll shoot him."

Chapter Twenty-two

"Was he dead?" Wanda asked.

"Yeah, Wanda, he was dead."

"What did you do then?"

"I called Freeze and told him where I was and what happened. He said he was gonna call you. Then I called the cops. They came and arrested me for murder."

"What happened to Mrs. Childers? Was she taken in too?"

"No. The cops talked to her, took her statement, and then they had an officer take her home."

"Do you know what she told them?"

"We went over our story before the cops came. It was pretty much the truth.

"Did you talk to anyone before I got there?"

"You asked me that already, Wanda. No, I didn't talk to anybody."

"Good."

"How did Black find out I was in jail?"

"Freeze told him. Freeze has been keeping Mike up, all of us really, keepin' us up on what you've been doin'."

"Bet you've all been havin' a good laugh."

"Why do you say that?" Wanda said and laughed. "We all care about you and what you do, Nick." Turning serious, Wanda continued. "I don't know how I can get you to see that. Whether you accept it or not, whether you accept us or not, Nick, we *are* your family."

I didn't say anything.

What could I say?

I'd been fighting that war within myself for years. "Chilly was right about one thing."

"What do you mean?"

"When he said Bobby shoulda killed me about

Camille."

"Camille. Not Camille again. You need to let that go, Nick. She wasn't worth it then, and she damn sure ain't worth it now."

"You've never met Camille, have you, Wanda?"

"Yes I have, twice actually." Wanda smiled and I wondered why.

"When?"

"Before you or Bobby met her."

"Where?"

Wanda took a deep breath. "I met her in Mike's bedroom."

I guess Wanda could tell by the look on my face that I wanted to hear the story. Needed to hear it. "Mike was supposed to be going with me to a fund raiser."

"Black? Back then, at a fund raiser?"

"You know Glynnis Presley?"

"Ain't she an aid to some congressman?"

"Senator now. But yeah, that night began our long association. Anyway, I went there to pick him up. He wasn't ready when I got there, so he got in the shower and told me to pick him out something to wear. I walked in the room and Camille was in the bed. I apologized for walking in on her, she didn't seem to care." Wanda let out a little laugh. "She invited me to join her."

"That was Camille."

"She was poison, Nick."

"You couldn't possibly understand."

"Yes I can, Nick. More than you know."

"I was sick when I left there that night, Wanda, can't you see that?"

"I know. I don't think I'll ever forget that night. Bobby with his gun in your mouth. Screamin' he was gonna kill you. Mike with his gun to Bobby's head. He just kept sayin',

'Bobby put the gun down.' I remember lookin' at his face, his eyes. I could see the pain he was in."

"My two best friends. Bobby was ready to kill me. And Black, shit! I can't even imagine where his head was, with a gun to Bobby's head. Him and Bobby are like brothers."

And the reason was Camille.

"I called her when I left there. Told her what happened. She didn't care. She laughed at how she had us. And she had us. She told me to come fuck her. I was on my way, but I needed a drink first. Three really. Camille was dead when I got there. Two shots to the head."

"Camille," Wanda said as she got up from the couch. She walked slowly, thoughtfully toward the window. Wanda looked out the window and said without looking at me. "There is so much you don't know about that night."

"Why don't you tell me about that night. I've been talking all night. You talk for awhile, Wanda."

"Do you remember passing Freeze on your way out?"

"Yeah."

Wanda turned around. "I mean really, remember, Nick? Do you remember him carrying a large envelope?"

"I remember."

I remember it all.

"Bobby put the gun down," Black yelled.

I felt Bobby's hand tighten around my throat.

"I'll kill you!" Bobby screamed.

Black put his gun to Bobby's head. "Bobby please," he said quietly. "Take the gun out of his mouth and put it down."

Black moved his gun away from Bobby's head. Bobby let go of my throat and slowly eased his gun out of my mouth.

I reached for my throat and took a step away from Bobby.

Bobby stared at me. "Don't think this is over."

I started to walk away, trying to catch my breath.

"I'm kill you!" Bobby shouted. "And that bitch!"

I left Black's office at the Late Night and walked across the dance floor on my way out the club. Wanda ran after me. "Nick wait." she said.

I saw Freeze coming, "Yo, Nick, I gonna wanna to see this."

"I remember."

Wanda walked toward me and held her hand out. "There's something I want you to see." I accepted Wanda's hand, and she led me into the bedroom. "Don't even think about it."

"Furthest thing from my mind." I looked Wanda up and down, I smiled. "Not until you brought it up."

Wanda led me to her dresser and let go of my hand. She removed the picture from the wall and opened her safe. She took out an envelope and handed it to me. "This is what he wanted you to see."

I sat down on the bed and Wanda left me alone. The envelope had a notebook in it. I sat quietly and began to read. It was a journal. A very detailed account of all contact Camille had with any of us. All about our operation. Where our gambling houses were, and who ran them. Everything. From the first time she met Freeze at the Knicks game. *She fucked him too.* She wrote at length and in great detail about Black. How it troubled her that she never could get Black to talk to her, much less tell her anything important. She wrote, "Black would say just enough to get me out me dress."

Which is how I coulda played her.

Camille wrote about her and Bobby. About how she was so turned on when she met me. She wrote everything, every conversation she'd heard, everything she saw.

Everything I ever told her. She even described her desire to seduce Wanda.

I sat there reading for hours. Was she Five-O? Couldn't be. No cop would keep this type of journal and leave it around to be found.

Wanda was back in her spot on the couch and I joined her there. "Where did Freeze find this?"

"After Bobby saw you leaving her apartment and went after you, Freeze went in and searched her apartment."

"What was he doin' there?"

"Mike sent him."

"Why?"

"Why do you think Mike would? She was a cancer growing in his organization."

"What happened that night?"

"After we read the journal, Mike made Freeze take Bobby home. Then me and Mike went to see Camille."

"To kill her."

"No, Mike offered her twenty thousand dollars to go back to Barbados. She refused. He asked her to explain herself. She said it was just to protect herself. And that she had another copy of that book and she would use it when she needed to and for more than twenty thousand dollars."

"So Black shot her."

"No. You know Mike would never shoot a woman."

I looked at Wanda.

"I shot her Nick."

"You."

"Yes, Nick, I shot her. It had to be done. She was poison, and she was eating her way through our entire organization. There's enough evidence in that journal she was keeping to put all of us in jail for long time. I know how you felt about her and I hope you can forgive me, but I did what had to be done."

"All these years I thought Bobby killed her."

"No Nick, he didn't. I killed her. Bobby said he felt like a so stupid to be so fooled by her. Camille had you all fooled."

"That's all well and good, but it doesn't change the facts. I betrayed Bobby."

"Whatever, Nick. I'm goin' to bed. You're welcome to stay here, if you want. I have plenty of room."

"I might take you up on that." I yawned.

"I hope you do. We still have things to talk about. So I hope you're still here when I wake up. Good night, Nick."

"Good night, Wanda. And thanks."

"For what?"

"For being there." I stood up and hugged her.

"I wouldn't miss it for anything in the world. Just don't run away from us this time. We love you." She kissed me on the cheek. "Good night, Nick."

I watched her walk into her room and close the door behind her. I could use a drink, but I really didn't need one. I went to the bedroom next to Wanda's. Kicked off my shoes and laid down on the bed.

I had talked out the whole story and I still didn't get it. I thought about what Wanda told me. I tossed and turned, trying to get comfortable. But I couldn't. Everything kept rolling around in my mind. I just kept thinking about Chilly. And Camille. And Bobby. And Gee. Nothing is as it seems.

And then it all came together.

I put my shoes on and left.

Chapter Twenty-three

"Hello, Gee."

"Nick!"

"Surprised to see me?"

"Yes."

"I just bet you are. Mind if I come in?"

"I'm sorry, Nick, come in please."

"Thank you." I stepped inside the house. Mrs. Childers was dressed to kill as usual. "You look very nice today. Were you on your way somewhere?"

"No, I just got back actually. Have a seat. Can I get you a drink?"

"Thank you."

"Johnnie Walker Black, straight up, right?"

"You remembered, I can not help but be touched."

"When did you get out?"

"Yesterday."

"Well, what happened?"

"I'm out on bail." She returned with my drink. "Well, what about you? How are you doin'?"

"I'm okay."

"You should be happy. The nightmare is over. Chilly's dead. That's what you wanted, isn't it?" When she didn't answer, I finished my liquor and said, "Now that it's over, don't you want to tell me what really happened?"

"What do you mean?"

"I didn't stutter, what the fuck really happened?" She just sat there and looked at me with those eyes. Those eyes that got me into this mess in the first place. "Look, Mrs. Childers, I mean, Gee, I killed Chilly, he's dead. It's over. So, why don't you tell me the truth?"

"Nick, I don't know what to say. I - - -"

"You knew where Jake was all along, didn't you? You

knew all about this synthetic crack shit."

"Yes."

"That seems like a good enough place to start."

"Chilly wasn't there the night Jake came looking for him. I asked him what he wanted to see Chilly about."

Wednesday June 30; 9:15 PM

"Come ride with me, Gee. We need to talk," Jake said.

"What's the matter with you?"

"I'm in trouble, Gee. Maybe we all are."

"That's nothing new. What's wrong now?"

"Three months ago Chilly came to me with this formula. Says it gonna make all of us rich, and he wanted me to develop it for him."

"What kind of formula?"

"For synthetic crack."

"What do you mean, synthetic crack?"

"It's a chemical compound, that has the same effect as crack, only there's no cocaine in it. All the ingredients are legal, and it is twenty times cheaper to produce. Only problem is people died from using it."

"You did it? You made it for him?"

"That's what I'm trying to tell you, Gee. LaShawn gave some to some people she gets high with, and they all died."

"My god, Jake, why did you do it?"

"Why do you think? He said he would kill Chez if I didn't do it. What else could I do? Now he says he's got to start covering his tracks. He said there can't be any trace of this that will tie it back to him. That includes me, he's gonna kill me, Gee. He's got to, I would be the only one who can connect him with all of it."

"You've got to get away from here, Jake. Far away, where he'll never find you."

"Live in reality, Gee. Didn't you try that? Didn't he find

you? Didn't he shoot me in my fuckin' leg until you said you would come back? You remember that, don't you?"

"All right! All right, Jake. What are you gonna do?"

"I don't know."

We rode in silence for awhile. And then it hit me like a shot. "Jake, you got to disappear."

"No Gee."

"Yes Jake, listen to me. What if the cops could tie all this back to Chilly? They have him for murder. And we'd be free, Jake."

"You want me to go to the cops?"

"No, but the cops need the evidence, and it has to be solid enough so he doesn't get off."

"How we gonna do that without going to cops? And I'm not going into witness protection. He'll find me and kill me. He'll kill all of us."

"What happened then?" I asked.

"I told Jake that we're not going to tell the cops a thing. That he had to disappear, go to the little hideaway he had in the Hamptons. Chilly doesn't know about the place. Then I told him that I'd hire a private detective to find him. That you would get the evidence we needed and turn it over to the cops."

"So you hired me. And led me into all this."

"I didn't mean for anybody to get hurt."

"Except me."

"This is your business, Nick. You were getting paid to take the risk."

"Who hit me that first night in Jake's apartment?"

"Jake. He went there to put the formula in the safe so you would find it. But you got there first. He thought Chilly sent you so he took off your glove to get your fingerprints on something, so the police would connect you to Chilly."

"How did Jake break his neck?"

"The night that you went to see Lisa Ellison."

"Yeah, what about it?"

"After you left her house, she went to see Chez to find out what was goin' on. They argued, but Chez didn't tell her anything."

"Chesará was in on it too."

"Of course she was. Lisa told Chez that she thought she knew where Jake might be and she was goin' out there in the morning. Chez called me and I went out there to warn him."

"Why?"

"She didn't need to know. Lisa is weak. If anybody put pressure on her, she'd give the whole thing up and that would ruin everything. So I went out there to tell Jake she was coming and not to let her know he was there."

"What happened?"

"When I got there, I told Jake that Lisa was coming out there and that he shouldn't talk to her."

Wednesday July 14; 9:15 PM

"Why not, Gee?"

"Jake, don't you see how that will ruin everything? If she knows where you are, she'll give you up the first time somebody asks her any thing. You know how she is, Jake. If Chilly steps to her, you know she'll drop the whole thing."

"Okay, okay. Anything else I need to know about?"

"Yes."

"What now, Gee?"

"There is something else I have to tell you." I stood up and walked to the window. I didn't want to be the one to have to tell him, but he needed to know. I took a deep breath and turn to face Jake. "I don't know how to say this any other way, so I'm just gonna drop it. Jake, LaShawn is dead."

Jake jumped up from the couch. "What?"

"She's dead, Jake. And so is Pamela."

"What, how?"

"They both OD'd on that stuff you created."

"That's not possible!"

"I'm sorry Jake."

Jake ran up the stairs and I went after him. He stopped at the top of the steps. He started to cry. "Why?"

"You said it yourself, everyone who knew about it had to die."

"But Pamela didn't have anything to do with this. Why did Chilly have to kill her?"

"I don't know, Jake."

"You didn't say anything about that. They weren't supposed die. That wasn't part of your great plan, Gee!" He grabbed me by my shoulders and started to shake me. "Why ,Gee, why? Why did they have to die?" Jake screamed.

"Stop it, Jake, you're hurting me."

"Why?" Jake screamed and kept shaking me.

"He was hurting me! So I pushed him off. I didn't think I pushed him that hard, but he lost his balance and fell down the steps. I tried to grab him, Nick, but I couldn't hold him. As long as I live, Nick I never will forget how he looked. Head tipped to the side, lying there like he was staring at me. I ran down the steps, I shook him, screamed his name, but he was dead."

She started crying.

I didn't sweat her about it. She killed her brother. I couldn't even imagine the burden she must be carrying around with her. "I didn't mean to kill him. Really, I didn't push him that hard, I didn't! He just lost his balance."

I put my arms around her and held her, trying to give her a chance to compose herself. I still had a lot more questions to ask. I didn't want to, but I had to. "What did you do then?"

She tried to pull herself together enough to answer me. "I panicked, Nick. I ran out of there."

"Where'd you go?"

"I went to Chez's apartment. I told her what happened. I was practically hysterical. But Chez was calm. Calmer than I was anyway. She cried a little and said that we would deal with it in the morning. Then she gave me some of her sleeping pills and made me go to bed. We went back out there early the next morning. We both cried when we first saw him laying there, staring at us. Chez rushed over and closed his eyes. Then she turned to me."

"We got to move the body, Gee."

"I can't, Chez. I can't, Chez, I killed him."

"Gee, you got to pull it together."

"No! We have to call the police."

"Don't make me slap you, Gee. It's too late for that now. This has gone too far. Jake is dead, Gee. You goin' to jail for life ain't gonna change that. Now help me get him to the car." Chez went and got a blanket, and we wrapped him up in it. It wasn't easy, but we dragged him out to the car and into the trunk. "We'll make it look like Chilly killed him."

"How we gonna do that?" Chez didn't answer me. She went back in the house and came back with her purse. Chesará pulled out a gun with a handkerchief wrapped around it. "What are you doing?" She walked up to the car and shot Jake in the head. "Are you crazy?"

"Chilly always carries a 9. Do you remember when Chilly shot Jake in the leg?"

"Yes."

"This is the gun that he used. He left it there. He said it was so I'd know that he will come back and kill me with it. It's his gun, Gee. The cops will think that he shot him."

"We heard a car pull up in the driveway, we turned around and Lisa was getting out of her car. She ran toward us screaming. She saw Chez shoot him. We tried to explain, but she wouldn't listen. She just kept screaming 'You killed him!' Then she ran back to her car and drove away. We went after her; she drove to her house and went inside. She had calmed down a little by that time, and she let us in. I told her what happened and why we did what we did."

"You two are crazy if you think I'm going to believe that story." Lisa picked up the phone. "All I know is that I saw you kill Jake. I'm calling the police."

Chez said, "I can't let you do that, Lisa. This is our chance to be free of that animal. Put the phone down, Lisa."

"Lisa, please, I'm not lying to you, it was an accident. Please put the phone down. Lisa don't do this."

She started to dial. "I'm not gonna ask you again, hang up that phone." Chez pulled out the gun and pointed it at Lisa. "Put the phone down."

When Lisa saw the gun she freaked out, she started screaming. "You're gonna kill me!" Then she ran at Chez. They fought for the gun.

"Stop it! Chez, stop!"

"The gun went off. I looked at Lisa. I could see it in her eyes. Chez dropped the gun and backed away from her. I watched Lisa fall to the floor."

"Don't tell me. It was an accident."

"Nick, you have to believe me. I'm telling you the truth.

That's exactly how it happened. We never meant to kill anybody. We never meant for any of this to happen."

"That's a pretty fantastic story, Mrs. Childers." I got up and looked around. I picked up my glass and walked slowly into the other room. I needed a drink. I poured a glass of Johnnie Black and drank it down. I poured another one. I could hear her crying. I didn't know what I was going to do. I thought about calling the police. But I didn't want to. She was in enough pain. She had killed her brother, and she was just as responsible for Lisa's death as Chesará. Maybe it was an accident, her story fit the facts. I couldn't be sure. She had been lying to me from the start. Everything she had told me was a lie. She was good at it. I poured her a shot of Henessey and took it to her. "Here, drink this, you look like you could use it."

Her hands were shaking. "Thank you." She drank hers straight down and let the empty glass fall out of her hand. She looked up at me with those eyes. They didn't look so pretty now. Her tears left a trail of black from her mascara. "What are you gonna do now? Are you gonna call the police?"

"No. Well, that depends."

"On what, Nick?"

"You have anything else you want to tell me about?"

"Like what?"

"Did you kill Pamela or LaShawn?"

"No."

"What about Rocky? You and Chesará kill him too?"

"No!"

"You sure?"

"No! I mean yes! I'm sure."

"Who shot Monika?"

"I don't know."

"What about Jett? Who killed Jett?"

251

"I don't know anything about either of them, Nick. Please you've got to believe me."

"Why should I believe you now?" I had to ask. "You've told me nothing but lies since page one. Why should I believe anything you tell me now, Mrs. Childers? I'm sorry, Gee. Tell me why should I?"

"I have no reason to lie to you now."

I finished my drink and stood up. "Okay." I picked up the phone and dialed.

"Who are you calling?"

"I'm not calling the police." Freeze answered on the first ring.

"Yo."

"I need you to back me up."

"When and where?"

"Now. I'll be there to pick you up in about an hour."

"I'll be here."

I hung up the phone and started for the door. Mrs. Childers got up and ran behind me. "Where are you going?"

"To a family reunion."

Chapter Twenty-four

I was tired.

I hadn't slept in two days.

And I needed a shower.

But I didn't care.

I drove as fast as I could to Cuisiné to pick up Freeze. As I drove, I couldn't help but think about the story I'd just heard.

"Wow."

That was about all I could say about it. "Wow."

I had to reconcile within myself that fact the Chilly hadn't killed Jake or Lisa. He probably didn't have anything to do with Rocky, Pamela, or LaShawn either. I pretty much figured that LaShawn's death was, like everything else, an accident. She more likely then not just got hold of the wrong package.

It was Mrs. Childers who dominated my thoughts. I couldn't turn her over to the police. She had been through enough in her lifetime. Her life to this point had been filled with nothing but betrayal and violence. For the rest of her life, she would have to deal with the site of Jake's dead body, staring at her. Hearing his last words, "Why, Gee?" over and over again. She would have to live knowing that Chesará killed Lisa so she could be free. And all this was the result of her association with Chilly.

That to me was punishment enough.

But now Chilly was dead.

I killed him.

He had caused so many people so much pain. In a way, he was responsible for all the deaths. Maybe he deserved to die, maybe not. It wasn't for me to judge. I understand now why it was so important for Mike to get out of the drug business and go legit. He had too much of a conscience too much love for life to continue with the legacy that André set out for us. The path Chilly followed. I respected and appreciated Black more now than I had at anytime in the last ten years. When all this was over, I had to call and thank him, not only for bailing me out, but for giving me so much to remind me of who I am and where I came from. Maybe I would even swallow my pride and make peace with Bobby. It was long overdue.

When I got to Cuisiné and went inside, I found Freeze sitting by the door, ready to go. "Took you so long?"

"Traffic."

"Well, let's go," he said practically jumping to his feet.

"You drive." We started out the door. "Wait! I need three clean weapons."

"Three 9's?"

"No, 45's."

"You? Packin' a 45? Why the chance?" he asked as we got in his truck.

"Kirk knows that a 9 is my weapon of choice. And I'm tired of talkin' to him."

"Oh by the way," Freeze said. "Wanda called looking for you."

"Did she really?"

"Yeah, she did. She said if I saw you, I should tell you not to do anything stupid."

"Okay, you told me. And I'm not goin' to do anything stupid. I'm goin' to kill somebody. And you're goin' to make sure that I don't do anything stupid."

"You startin' to sound like the Nick I used to know."

"I'm startin' to feel like him too."

"It's good to have you back, Nick. I don't want to sound soft or nothin' like that, but I missed you man."

"I missed all of you."

We stopped at Cynt's; one of the gambling houses we'd run for years. *"We."* I felt a part of all this again. Maybe this is what Wanda meant when she said I needed to recognize.

"Hey, Freeze. And who is this fine ass man you got with you?" Cynt said as she twisted her hips in our direction.

"How's it goin', Cynt?" She threw her arms around my neck and gave me a kiss that raised an eyebrow on Freeze. Like there was some past thing between us, that I never knew about.

"How are you, Nick? I heard you were back in the city. I was wondering, like everybody else, why you hadn't come around. But I see you picked back up with your old thug buddy here."

"Let's go to your office, Cynt. I need to get something out of your safe." Freeze said.

"You two, rollin' together, just like old times." Cynt said and turned toward the steps to her office.

I looked at Freeze. He looked at me. We both watched Cynt walk up the steps. We both smiled. "Just like old times."

Once we were in her office, Cynt opened the safe and stepped aside. She had a small arsenal in that safe. "Help yourself. They're all clean, acid on the serial numbers. Damn near impossible to trace."

I stepped up and picked out three 45's and two silencers. Freeze grabbed one too and an AK47, "Just in case things get thick out there."

"That should thin things out nicely." Cynt threw in.

"Got any gloves, Cynt?" I asked.

"What do I look like, Macy's?"

"Come on, Nick, I got some for you in the truck. Lets go."

"Good to see you again, Cynt," I said as I followed

Freeze out the office.

Cynt grabbed me by the arm.

"You make sure you come back and see me soon, Nick," she said and kissed me on the cheek.

"I'll do that."

As soon as we got in the truck, Freeze turned to me and shook his head. "What's up with you and Cynt?"

"I swear man, I don't know what was up with that."

"Nigga, when you gonna get enough of fuckin' with Bobby's women," Freeze laughed. "I'm just fuckin' with you kid."

"Bobby still fuckin' Cynt?"

"Naa, Pam got that nigga pussy whipped and on lock down since the day she met him."

"Pam, that his wife?"

"Yeah, she's a good girl. Real solid, you know. She's been good for Bobby. Mellowed him the fuck out."

"Maybe after this is over with we can roll by there."

"Time you and Bobby made peace and put that Camille shit behind y'all. Bitch been dead for ten fuckin' years and shit."

"I feel you."

"Where the fuck we goin', anyway?"

"Greenwich."

"Connecticut?"

"Yeah. Wake me up when we get there."

When we got to the house, there was gated entry and a guard posted. I told Freeze to roll by so we could get a look at the place. I sure missed Jett, he would have tapped into some satellite and had a birdseye view of the set up. But that wasn't the only reason I missed him. He was a good friend. I thought about Monika lying in that hospital bed, fighting for her life. I was here for them.

I didn't see any camera surveillance, but I knew there had to be some. Once I had satisfied myself with the layout of the grounds, I told Freeze to give me five minutes, and then drive to the gate and I would join him there. I made my way around to the gate. I put the silencers on the guns and waited in the brush for Freeze to pull up. As he approached the gate, the guard came out and stopped him.

"Good evening, sir. Can I help you?"

"No, but he can." Freeze pointed at me.

"What?"

He turned around and I put two shots in his head. I dragged him into the guard shack and opened the gate. Freeze drove through the gate, I got back in the truck, and we headed for the house. He stopped the truck around the side of the house. "Well what's the plan."

"Give me five minutes, then come in after me."

"You got it."

I moved toward the house, staying in the shadows. The lock was no problem. I moved quickly through the house, guns drawn, looking for my objective. Checking each room, before moving on to the next. The thought did occur to me that the bastard might not be there. If he wasn't, I'd burn the bitch down.

"Monika would like that," I said to myself.

I heard footsteps coming toward me. I got out of sight. Once he passed me, I put two in the back of his head. I dragged his body into the first room I came to. I recognized him. He was Lieutenant Commander Snow. He was in command of a different special ops unit, but he was a part of our little community. At that point, I knew I was in the right place. I had been through all the downstairs rooms and was making my way up the steps, when I heard more footsteps coming. I put my guns in their holsters and went over the rail. I would hold on until they passed.

I watched as they stopped at the top of the steps and talked. I hoped it wouldn't be a long conversation. My arms were starting to hurt. They started down the steps. I was in a bad stop if they saw my hands. I gave some thought to letting go if they did. I looked down. "Bad idea."

Fortunately, they passed me by. Once they were out of sight, I came back over the rail and continued up the stairs. I could have shot them too, but I figured it would give Freeze something to do. He always did like to compare body counts.

I walked down a long hallway until I saw a light coming from an open door. As I got closer, I heard voices. I heard his voice. My heart began racing, I moved faster. I came through the door and there he was, Uncle Felix, seated behind a marble desk. I should have blasted him on sight. But first I had to know why.

"Come on in, Nick, we've been expecting you," Felix said smiling. "Have a seat."

I took a step closer.

"Why don't you just put those guns down, nice and slow while you at it, Nick." I recognized that voice. Turned to see General Peterson seated on the couch with an M-16 pointed at me. He was my CO for our last tour of duty. It was all starting to come together. I took a deep breath and complied with his orders.

"That's a good soldier, Nick, but you always were." The general said, laughing. "Shit, I got half a dozen men in this house and one at the gate. But you walked right by them like it wasn't shit, didn't you, Nick?"

"Sit down, Nick. Take a load off." Felix said.

"I told you he was the best soldier I ever commanded, Felix. Made you a damn good operative, didn't he?"

"Yeah, he was good."

258

"Tell me about it, Felix, why'd you do it?"

"Do what, Nick? Oh, you mean Jett and Monika, don't you?"

"Yeah, Monika was too good to be taken by any of Chilly's boyz without gettin' off a shot. It had to be you."

"No, Nick, it was me," the general said. "Monika let me in, no problem. Perkins, that was the boy that Bronson cut up, well she made him while she was out on her little date with Chilly. Once he was compromised, it wouldn't take her long to put it all together just like you did. So Perkins had to kill her. Then Bronson showed up. Perkins covered while I left. His orders were to kill Bronson. But you see how that turned out."

"Then you brought in a cleaner to clean up after Jett. Who killed Jett?"

"Lieutenant Commander Snow had that honor, Nick. Bronson saw us when we were coming out of the house. So we let him follow us to Chilly's house. Your boy was careless, Nick. He let Snow walk right up on him and shoot him with a 22 in the ear. Very effective."

"I just want to know why?"

"Well, for that I got to take you back a ways," Felix said as he got up and poured himself a drink. "You see, Nick, the whole time you were in South America, you may have been under the General here's command, but you were working for me."

"Just what were we doin' down there, Felix?"

"You were conducting the war on drugs as a agent of the United States government, sort of." Felix and the General both laughed, but I wasn't amused. Maybe they would let me in on the joke.

"Well, not exactly," the General said.

"You and your unit were there, not to stop the flow of drugs into this country, but to stream line it. You see, Nick,

I have a friend down there. He came to me and asked for my help in eliminating some of his competition. In return we would be partners in his rather lucrative enterprise."

"Cocaine."

"Right. So I went to my friend the General here, and he was kind enough to donate the services of your unit. But he said to me that instead of just eliminating some of his competition, hell, let's get rid of all the bastards or at least do damage to their operations."

"So you sent us down there to assassinate key people and destroy drug labs. The whole time we're thinking it's for good old Uncle Sam, we were doin' it all for good old *Uncle* Felix. Good plan. What went wrong?"

"Who said anything went wrong. You and your unit were doing an excellent job. Especially your team, Nick. The entire campaign was a success."

"That's right. Your team was especially destructive. That Monika sure can blow some shit up." The general added. "How is she doin' anyway, Nick? I understand it doesn't look good for her."

"She's a fighter. She's gonna make it."

"No, she's not, Nick. If she makes it out of intensive care, she'll be dead before she gets to her room." Felix said.

"We'll see about that. But we'll pass that for now. So you brought us all back together to eliminate the eliminators, but we fucked it up when Monika broke her ankle. We were all supposed to die that day."

"I knew you were smart enough to figure that much out," the general said. "I was just gonna just line you all up and shoot you. But Felix said that he could use your team for some other jobs he had goin'. Said you three had a skill set that he would make excellent use of. So I got y'all out from down there. Handled the debriefing myself and turned you over to Felix."

"I figured that part out too. As long as Felix had his hand around our throats and we didn't know what was really goin' on down there anyway, we were non-threatening. What happened to change that?"

"My friend wasn't the only one with influential friends. There were stories in some circles of Americans service men participating in a drug eradication effort. If those stories ever made their way to Capital Hill there would be hell to pay," Felix said. "And all that hell would fall on me, Nick."

"You three were the only one's who lived, and like I said you were smart enough to figure it out," the general said.

"And I wasn't gonna take the chance of you bein' subpoenaed to testify before some fuckin' Senate sub-committee," Felix said.

"So you killed Jett and you tried to Monika."

"I didn't want to, Nick, but you can surely see where I didn't have a choice in the matter. You three were the best operatives I had. It's gonna be hard to replace you," Felix said.

"What about me? Why didn't you try to kill me?"

"You're a killer, Nick. You would be hard to kill. I thought about asking you to join us, but, as your presence here proves you're too damn loyal to your friends. Even if you said you would go along with it, there would always exist the possibility that you would flip and try to kill us all. Anyway, since you were making a fool of yourself playing private detective, I just figured that either that animal Chilly would kill you, or the cops would have you for murder. But if neither one of those options panned out, don't think I wouldn't send a team to kill you. And they would have to be good to get the job done."

"Thanks for the compliment."

"No problem."

"Well gentlemen, I've heard enough." I started to reach

for my third weapon.

"Good, so have I."

I turned around as Freeze came through the door and fired two shots to the general's head. Then he turned to Felix and fired two shots at him.

"What'd you do that for?" I screamed.

"What are you talkin' about? You said you had heard enough. I figured that meant it was time for them to die."

"Yeah, but I wanted to kill Felix."

"I tell you what, I'll let you kill the next one."

"It's not the same. Fuck it, nevermind. Let's just get the fuck outta here."

Freeze walked over and looked at Felix. "Why didn't you tell me he was the one you were lookin' for?"

"You know him?'

"Shit yeah. Didn't you hear him? He's partners with Estabon, who supplies Chilly."

"Why didn't you tell me?"

"You didn't ask me about him or Estabon. You just asked me about Chilly."

"Damn."

"Sorry, Nick, how was I supposed to know."

"Forget it, man. Thanks for havin' my back."

"Anyway, what were you gonna do with your guns on the floor?"

"I had three guns, remember."

"That's right. Yo, I was listening to them talk about you. You that bad a mutha fucka?"

"Yeah."

"Well, come on Shaft and I'll buy you a drink."

"Okay, but just a quick one. I got one more body to account for."

"You ain't thinking bout goin' to Peru to kill Estabon, are you?"

"No. Something a little closer to home."

Chapter Twenty-five

"Who is it?"

"Its, Nick."

Felicia opened the door and let me in. She threw her arms around my neck and kissed me. "I'm so glad to see you." Felicia kissed me again and again. I was glad to see her too.

"Surprised to see me?"

"Yes. I heard about Chilly. I thought you were in jail."

"Wanda got me out."

"Who is Wanda? Should I be jealous?"

"No. Wanda is not only family to me, but she's my lawyer."

"All right now. I just want to know who the players are in this game before I get in."

"Baby, this ain't no game."

"Oh, so you the real thing, huh?"

"Is there anything to drink?"

"Sure, I have a bottle of Zinfandel. You want some?"

"Is that a trick question?"

"What do you - - -" she looked confused. "Oooohh! You want some?" Felicia got up to get the wine. "Nick, you can have all of this you want."

She returned with two glasses and sat down next to me. "Here you go baby. You look tired."

"I really haven't slept in a couple of days." Felicia looked sad. "Smile Felicia. I ain't ever that tired." She smiled and sipped her wine.

"What happened with the police?"

"I'm out on bond. But Wanda thinks they'll be willing to accept that my killin' Chilly was self defense."

"That's good. What about the rest of them?"

"I think they'll probably drop the whole thing on Chilly

and call it day. He was responsible for all of it anyway." I finished my wine. "Felicia, do you mind if I take a shower?"

"Not at all." She popped up from the couch and held out her hand. "Come with me. Let me get you some towels,"

"Thank you. A nice hot shower is what I need," I said as Felicia turned on the light in the bathroom. "It will help me relax."

She turned on the shower and started to undress me. "Not too relaxed that you pass out on me."

I shook my head no.

"I could use a shower too. You want some company in there?" She asked as she removed the last of my clothes.

"Is that a trick question?" And I got in the shower.

Felicia bathed me, then we made love in the shower, and again once we made our way to the bed. I enjoyed making love to her. In spite of her tough cop exterior, Felicia was an extremely sensual and highly sexual woman. While we made love, I had to ask myself the question. Was I in love with her? And would it make things any different?

As advertised, I waited until after we made love to pass out. When I woke up, Felicia was gone. "Felicia!"

"I'm in the kitchen. Don't get up, I'm fixing you breakfast." She stuck her head in the room. "How does breakfast in bed sound to you?"

"Great. You're all right, you know that?"

"I'm more than all right, but I'm breakin' it on you slowly. I wouldn't want you to feel overwhelmed. I know how you brothers are."

Felicia went back to the kitchen while I got up and went to the bathroom. I took care of matters in the bathroom, got back in the bed and waited for Felicia. She came in carrying a tray with a flower in a vase. She made

Spanish omelets, hash browns with link sausages. "Toast, coffee, and a Mamosa."

"All this for me?" I said, trying my best to look surprised and honored all at once. "Will you be joining me?"

"Of course. I'll be right back." She came back with her food and got in bed next to me. She was a good breakfast cook. I'd be interested to see if that translated to being a good cook period. We ate and talked, sausages inspired sexual innuendo, mostly. I told her about Monika and Jett, she cried a few tears for me.

Man I was diggin' her.

When we finished eating, Felicia took the trays back to the kitchen. She came in the room and got back in bed and snuggled up close to me. Felicia told me she had an appointment with her professor the next day, to talk about her getting back into law school. "Now that it's over, I want to try to get my life back."

"That's good that you're gettin' your life back. But there's something that always has bothered me."

"What's that?"

"Why did you leave?"

"I told you, I was afraid."

"You know I don't believe that. But we'll pass that for now. If Chilly had Pamela killed because she knew what was goin' on, what did you have to be afraid of?"

"He might have thought that she told me." Felicia looked away from me.

I touched her shoulder. "Look at me Felicia. Why'd you come back?"

"I told you, I missed you."

"It's over Felicia, Chilly's dead. Jett's dead. Monika may die." I put my arm around her. "Please tell me the truth, Felicia."

"Nick." She kissed me on the cheek. "I told you the truth, I came back because I missed you. And you gave me the courage to face things. To finish what I started."

"What was that?"

"I told you why I left the force. Well, I didn't tell you the whole story. Once the shooting stopped, Morgan and I searched the house. I told you about the cocaine, well, there was a hundred and fifty thousand dollars in cash. Morgan said we could split it. He said he had an old friend who could get rid of the drugs for us. But I told him no, I didn't want anything to do with the drugs. Morgan said, fine. I could keep all the money. He could make twice that from selling the drugs."

"That's why you were so worried about the cops investigating you. You were afraid they would find out."

"Yes." Felicia looked away, but she turned back quickly. "So we robbed a bunch of dead drug dealers. Nobody would care about that, right?"

"You would think. What happened?"

"It was Rocky we robbed."

"When did you find that out?"

"I was looking at some of Pamela's pictures. I recognized two of them from pictures she took at Jake's party. Then Morgan called me and said that Rocky knew. He said he would kill both of us if we didn't give back the drugs and the money."

"How did he find out it was you two?"

"Morgan's source. He tried to sell the dope to one of Rocky's people. He told Rocky he got it from Morgan, before they killed him. Morgan called and said he wanted to see me. He had bought into his uncle's bar in Queens, he said to meet him there and we would figure out what to do. But he was dead when I got there. Police called it a robbery."

"What happened then?"

"Nothing."

"Nothing?"

"For the next couple of months, nothing happened. Then about a month ago, Rocky called me. He told me he wanted the money back. Or what happened to Morgan would happen to me. I was supposed to meet Rocky here the night Pamela died. I tried to call Pamela, to tell her to stay away from here. But I never did catch her. Pamela was dead when I got here."

"Is that why you killed Rocky?"

"Pamela died for something me and Morgan did. When I woke up and you were gone that morning, I called Rocky and told him I only had half of the money. He said to meet him at his club that night. I had the money, but I knew he would kill me anyway, whether I gave it to him or not."

"That much was obvious."

"I waited outside the club until I saw him pull up in the convertible. Two of his boyz were up front; Rocky was in the back seat. I walked up to the car and shot the three of them in the head. Then I swung around and put one each in their chests. I threw the gun on Rocky's lap a got away from there."

"Nobody would care if three piece of shit drug dealers got whacked in the street, right?"

"That was my plan, Nick. I made it look like it was just another drug related murder."

So there it is, I had actually solved the case. The big question now was, what was I going to do about it? I didn't know what I was gonna do. I knew one thing for sure, I knew then that I was finished trying to play private detective. Too much like being a cop for me. I looked over at Felicia, I put my arms around her, and she rested her head against my chest. Whether I was in love with her or not I couldn't turn her over to the police for what she'd done. She didn't do anything that I hadn't done. Felicia got revenge for her friend. I couldn't roll her over for that. Or Mrs. Childers, or Chesará for that matter. I just couldn't see myself helping the police. If they figured it out on their own, that would be different. But I knew they would make Chilly the fall guy.

    Case closed.

Order Great Fiction Novels & Non-fiction titles
directly from Brittney Press Publishing
Include $ 3.95 plus .95 per item for Shipping &
Handling

Private Deceptions
by roy glenn
From Brittney Press Publishing   ISBN: 1-893196-07-0
On Sale Now   List Price $14.95

Read the book that started it all!
Is It A Crime
a different type of love story
by roy glenn
From Brittney Press Publishing   ISBN: 1-893196-00-3
On Sale Now   List Price $12.95

The Paragons
By Cliff Chandler
Hard nosed detective Vic Morgan investigates the drug
related murder of an industrialist daughter
From Brittney Press Publishing   ISBN: 1-893196-03-8
On Sale Now   List Price $14.95

Ten Year Initiative For The
Empowerment Of Black America
From Brittney Press Publishing   ISBN: 1-893196-10-0
On Sale Now   List Price $12.95

ORDER FORM

TITLE		QUANTIT	PRICE
☐ 1-893196-00-3	Is It A Crime		$12.95
☐ 1-893196-03-8	The Paragons		$14.95
☐ 1-893196-10-0	Empowerment		$12.95
☐ 1-893196-07-0	Private Deceptions		$14.95

Subtotal: _____

Shipping: _____

Total: _____

Name _____

Address _____

_____

_____

Phone _____

Method of Payment

☐ Check

☐ Bill Me

☐ Visa

☐ MasterCard

☐ American Express

Credit Card # _____ Exp. date _____

Signature _____

Labor of Love

a
story
by
roy glenn

Labor of Love

a story by roy glenn

275

CLOSING ARGUMENTS

"Mr. Douglas, are you ready to proceed?"

Marcus stood up and glanced at the jury. "Yes, your Honor," he said and walked slowly over to the jury box. "Good morning, Ladies and Gentleman." Marcus paused briefly as his eyes scanned the jurors. "Well, here we are. It's been a long road we've traveled together."

Throughout the trial, Marcus had worked hard to develop a relationship with the jury. During his opening arguments he promised to act as their advocate. He assured them that he would ask the questions they wanted answers to. Whenever Marcus questioned a witness, he always stood in front of the jury box. When a prosecution witness said something he felt was damaging to his client, he would causally glance at the jury. Sometimes he would smile, other times he would just shake his head. This tactic proved most effective. So effective that when certain members of jury heard something they thought was questionable, they would look in Marcus' direction, seemingly seeking his approval as to whether they should believe it or not.

"When we first met, I told you that the prosecution would present you with a strong argument for finding Roland Ferguson guilty of the murder of his wife, Desireé Taylor Ferguson and Rasheed Damali. The prosecution promised that they would present to you, ladies and gentlemen, the facts in this case. And that once presented with those facts you will find Roland Ferguson guilty of these two brutal murders. However, I also made you a promise. I told each of you, ladies and gentleman, that their presentation would consist not only of the facts of this case, but it will be mixed with theory. A theory of how and why those events took place in order to lead you, ladies and gentleman, to believe that Roland Ferguson had the motive and the opportunity to commit this horrible crime. A theory, in which the facts of this case will be presented in such a manner that they support the prosecutions assertions. But a theory all the same. The American Heritage dictionary defines theory as an organized set of *assumptions* devised to explain a particular event or phenomenon. So let's talk about the facts in this case, and then we'll talk about theory. Okay?" he said, and each member of the jury acknowledged him. Marcus had them and he knew it.

"It is a fact that on Friday, December 2nd, at 6:30 pm, Mr. Damali checked into a cabin at Laurel Mountain Cabins in Hiawassee, GA. This fact is supported by records provide by Laurel Mountain Cabins. We know that Mrs. Ferguson arrived at the cabin occupied by Mr. Damali at approximately 8:00 pm. This fact is supported by testimony provided by William Anderson, who occupied the cabin next to the one occupied by Mr. Damali. He testified that he arrived at his cabin around 7:30 and there was a Black corvette, belonging to Mr. Damali, parked outside the cabin. However, at 8:15 when he returned to the car to get something he'd left, that the gold Mercedes Benz, belonging to Mrs. Ferguson was now parked next to the corvette. These are facts. The Coroner has established the time of death to have occurred somewhere between 1:15 and 1:45 that following morning. Now this is where the theory begins. It is the contention of the prosecution that Roland Ferguson entered the cabin and attacked Mr. Damali."

Marcus walked to the evidence table and picked up the murder weapon. "Hitting him repeatedly about the head and shoulders with this golf club," he said as he walked slowly back toward the jury, swinging the golf club in a cropping motion. "Nineteen times, until he was dead. After which, he turned to his wife, who was in the Jacuzzi, and hit her fifteen times, with this club. Theory! An assumption devised to fit the facts. The body of Mr. Damali was found on the floor approximately eight feet from the door. Mrs. Ferguson's body was indeed found beaten to death in the Jacuzzi. At the heart of the theory is Roland Ferguson's motive for these murders. According to this set of assumptions that the prosecution would like you, ladies and gentleman, to believe is that Roland Ferguson found out that his wife was having an affair with Mr. Damali. And once this was discovered, that he came to the cabin with this club in his hands and murdered the two of them. Adultery!" Marcus said loudly with one finger raised in the air to accentuate his point. Then he gave the jury an easy smile and said softly. "A pretty compelling motive for murder. But let's look at the motive as it relates to the facts, shall we?" Once again the jury acknowledged him, giving their consent to proceed.

"You, ladies and gentlemen, have heard testimony that on the night preceding the murders, that Roland Ferguson attended a reception hosted by the Atlanta business community. He arrived sometime around 9:00 pm and he remained there until sometime after 11:00 pm. He was seen by and spoke with countless people, most notably the mayor. Witnesses have offered, both in testimony offered in these proceedings and in sworn affidavits that Roland Ferguson was in good spirits throughout the evening. That he didn't appear to be distressed or anguished or apprehensive. When asked where Mrs. Ferguson was that evening, he replied on more than one occasion that Desireé was out with a business associate of theirs, a Rasheed Damali. So it is a fact that Roland Ferguson knew of his wife's association with Mr. Damali, but did not appear to be distressed by that knowledge. Now, after Roland Ferguson left the reception, he stopped for gas. Information from the store and his credit card company, supports that Roland Ferguson paid for his purchase at 11:22 pm. Mr. Ferguson said in his statement to the police at their first interview, which in fact, he volunteered to participate in without the benefit of counsel, that he arrived home at 11:40 pm. When the detectives asked him how he could be sure of the time, he responded that he was sure of the time because he noted that he was home before midnight, which is rare after attending one of these gatherings. After which he had a Brandy, and went to his study to call his assistant, Connie Talbert's voice mail to make some observations about the evening and to make recommendations as to several courses of action based on those observances. The tape of that conversation and the transcript has been entered into evidence and was heard by this panel. Telephone records support the fact that the call was placed at 11:54 pm. and concluded at 12:21 am. After which he went to bed. Now, according to the prosecutions *theory*, at some time immediately following this point, Roland Ferguson got in his car and made the 127 mile drive from his home to the cabin in Hiawassee to commit this crime of passion. Ladies and gentlemen, there are two questions that you must ask yourselves. One, how did he find out where they were? Did Mrs. Ferguson call and say hi, honey, I'm at Laurel Mountain Cabins in Hiawassee, GA with Rasheed Damali? Telephone records that have been entered into evidence prove that no calls, incoming, or outgoing were made or received at the Ferguson residence or the cabin. Cell phone, maybe? Maybe someone called his cell phone? But the phone records don't support that either. Maybe he checked his messages at home and one of those messages delivered the information about their whereabouts? No. The police obtained in their search of the premises, the answering machine tape, and found nothing to support that. But, the theory asks you to accept that he knew where they were and drove 127 miles to the cabin to commit murder. To make it to the cabin at the time the murders were committed, Mr. Ferguson would have to drive at speeds in excess of one hundred miles an hour. You heard the testimony of Officer Dunn, of the Towns County Sheriff Office that he was on duty, parked on Georgia State highway 76, the only road leading to the cabin. He offered, in his colorful testimony, that if any car came through there speeding that he would have given him a ticket. Which he didn't. So the second question is, once he had that knowledge, how did he get there so quickly? The logical answer is, he couldn't."

Marcus returned to the defense table to give the jury an opportunity to think about the questions he posed. He poured a glass of water and drank half, before returning to the jury box.

"Let's go to the murder scene. Mr. Damali and Mrs. Ferguson were in the cabin. Mrs. Ferguson was in the Jacuzzi and Mr. Damali had, at some point prior to the murder, removed his clothes. He was naked! It is the assertion of the prosecution that Roland Ferguson entered the cabin, killed Mr. Damali, and then his wife. How did he get in? There was no sign of forced entry. Did he have a key? No sign that a struggle occurred at the door. So how did he get in? Did Mr. Damali let him in? Now ask yourselves this question, if you're in a cabin in the mountains with somebody's spouse, I don't care how well you know him, are you going to let him in? I know that I'm not. And even if I were going to let him in, I would think that I would put some clothes on before opening the door.

But since the facts show no indication of forced entry, that's exactly what the prosecution would have you, ladies and gentleman, to believe. That a naked Mr. Damali let Mr. Ferguson in the cabin, while Mrs. Ferguson is naked in the hot tub. The Police report states that the body of Mr. Damali was found eight feet from the door and in clear view of the Jacuzzi. So I think that based on that fact, it is safe to assume that Mr. Damali unlocked the door, let Roland Ferguson in and took three or four steps before he was attacked."

Once again, Marcus picked up the murder weapon and walked back to the jury box. "While the attack is going on, Mrs. Ferguson is watching while her husband hits Mr. Damali nineteen times." He began swinging the golf club nineteen times.

Assistant District Attorney, Ms Izella Hawkins looked at Marcus in horror swinging the club wildly as he walked to the jury box. She looked at the jury's reaction. She sprung to her feet. "Objection your honor!"

"Sustained. Mr. Douglas there is no room in my court room for that type of theatrics."

"My apologies your Honor." Marcus looked at the jury and smiled, he accomplished his point. "And my apologies to you, ladies and gentlemen. However it was necessary to demonstrate how long it would take to beat somebody nineteen times. It took a little less then thirty seconds. And that is only if Mr. Damali's attacker didn't stop. Now, Mrs. Ferguson is watching this and is so petrified by what she is seeing to move. The attacker moves toward her and fifteen hits later, she is dead too. The attacker then drops the murder weapon and leaves the murder scene. The bodies are discovered that same morning about 11:00 am by housekeeping who testified that the door was locked, and she entered, after knocking of course, with her key.

So, after Roland Ferguson committed this crime of passion he is careful to lock the door on his way out, goes home, and gets in bed. End of theory, blended with fact. The murder weapon was left at the scene. Police inventory of the golf clubs found both in Roland Ferguson's home and at the country club where he is a member indicate that the murder weapon was not a part either of those sets." Marcus started to walk away from the jury but turned around quickly. "By the way, in case you were wondering, the police checked with the club staff and no one reported a missing nine iron."

Marcus turned away from the jury and was handed a piece of paper by Tiffany Powers. He stood before the prosecutions table. For the first time he addressed the jury from a different stop. He wanted the jury to be looking at the prosecution before he continued.

"Once the murder is discovered, Roland Ferguson is informed by police that his wife was murdered at seven o'clock that evening. Why the delay in notifying her next of kin? The detectives don't go into any detail about the crime. They don't tell him that she was found brutally murdered in a cabin with another man. Detective Benjamin testified that upon receiving the news of his wife's death, Roland Ferguson began to cry, and I quote from Detective Benjamin's testimony, 'he got weak in the knees and became somewhat hysterical'. Roland Ferguson comes in to identify the body his wife's body. He is asked to speak with the detectives assigned to the case. The murder occurred in the city of Hiawassee, in Towns County. Why are City of Atlanta police assigned to the case? You see, the prosecution had spoken with officials of Towns County and just that quick, had the case transferred to their jurisdiction. Before the investigation was complete the prosecution had already found their man. Roland

Ferguson was their only suspect. Roland Ferguson is the owner of Atlanta Life Insurance Company, among other things. He is a wealthy, well known and high profile member of the Atlanta business community. The press, after hearing of Roland Ferguson's arrest, had a field day. What a feather in their cap to bring down a man of his stature. States Attorney General, Justice Department, maybe even Attorney General of the United States. This city has a long history of unwarranted prosecution of high profile individuals like Roland Ferguson. This was a rush to judgement of the highest order. I submit to you, ladies and gentlemen that the prosecution looked no further than Roland Ferguson and created an organized set of assumptions devised to convict him of the murder of his wife, Desireé Taylor Ferguson and Rasheed Damali. Ladies and gentlemen, Roland Ferguson didn't commit these murders, he couldn't have. And the prosecution has not presented you with any evidence to support their theory of how this crime took place. I only ask that in your deliberations that you consider the facts of this case. That you then separate the facts from the organized set of assumptions. Once you do, I am confident that you will return a verdict of not guilty. I thank you, ladies and gentlemen for your attention."